HEARTS IN FLIGHT

This Large Print Book carries the
Seal of Approval of N.A.V.H.

HEARTS IN FLIGHT

PATTY SMITH HALL

THORNDIKE PRESS

A part of Gale, Cengage Learning

GALE
CENGAGE Learning®

Farmington Hills, Mich • San Francisco • New York • Waterville, Maine
Meriden, Conn • Mason, Ohio • Chicago

GALE
CENGAGE Learning®

LIBRARY OF CONGRESS CATALOGING-IN-PUBLICATION DATA

Hall, Patty Smith.
    Hearts in flight / by Patty Smith Hall. — Large print edition.
        pages cm. — (Thorndike Press large print gentle romance)
    ISBN 978-1-4104-8211-2 (hardcover) — ISBN 1-4104-8211-1 (hardcover)
    1. Women air pilots—Fiction. 2. World War, 1939–1945—Fiction. 3. Large
type books. I. Title.
PS3608.A54783H427 2015
813'.6—dc23   2015015585

Published in 2015 by arrangement with Harlequin Books S. A.

Printed in Mexico
1 2 3 4 5 6 7 19 18 17 16 15

But they that wait upon the Lord shall renew their strength; they shall mount up with wings of eagles; they shall run, and not be weary; and they shall walk, and not be faint.

— *Isaiah* 40:31

To my husband, Dan,
for giving my dreams wings

CHAPTER ONE

Georgia
1943
"You'll never catch a husband if you keep messing with that plane."

Maggie Daniels bumped her head against the instrument panel, the memory of her mother's words at the breakfast table faintly ringing in her ears. She leaned against the weathered pilot's seat, her fingers lifting to the knot forming at her hairline. Well, someone had to get her plane, Old Blue, up and running or Daniels's Crop Dusting would be permanently grounded.

"Ms. Daniels?"

The deep timbre of a man's voice rumbled against the worn-pine hangar like her two-seater right before takeoff. Hidden from the intruder's view, Maggie peeked over the cockpit. Less than a wingspan away, an unfamiliar man stood with his back to her. A field of khaki cotton stretched across his broad back, his olive suit coat flung over his shoulder like a kite's tail.

What's a flyboy doing in my hangar?

"There's no telling where the woman is at." The plane shifted slightly as he leaned against its nose. "I've got other things to do than stand around here."

Heat crept up Maggie's neck and into her cheeks. Why was it that men, at least the ones she knew, didn't seem to have a patient bone in their bodies? Always assuming that a girl was more interested in what she put on her head rather than what she put in it? She poked a stray curl into the wool binding of her snood. Well, this war had changed all that, and if she could put her two cents in, she would say it's about time.

She grabbed the leather handrail and pulled herself upright. "Lookin' for me, mister?"

The man turned. Steel-blue eyes stared over darkened lenses, sending her midsection into a tailspin. Taking a deep breath, Maggie climbed out of the cockpit and shimmied off the wing.

"So, you're my new pilot?"

The question irked her. "That depends." Maggie leaned back against Old Blue. "Who are you?"

The man stepped closer and extended his

10

hand. "Captain Wesley Hicks."

First rule of war — trust no one. Maggie stared at his outstretched hand. "Could I see some ID, please?"

He reached into his jacket, his mouth a grim line as he pulled out a worn leather wallet. He extracted a blue card and handed it to her.

Maggie skimmed over the typewritten information before settling on the black-and-white photo. The grainy photograph couldn't blur the determined set of the man's jaw or the sharp intelligence lighting his eyes. Something told her she'd have to watch out for this one. She handed it back to him. "So what brings you all the way out here, Captain Hicks?"

He pocketed his wallet. "Major Evans thought it would be a good idea if I met you before you continue your training on the B-29."

"No disrespect, but I'm home on family business." She patted the run-down crop duster, the feel of warm metal beneath her fingertips more steady than her life had been in the last few months.

"My condolences on your uncle."

"Thank you." Maggie stared out the hangar door toward the house, a gold star hung proudly in the front window. It still didn't seem real that she would never see Jackson again, at least not this side of heaven. She gave the antiquated plane one last pat before dropping her hand to her side. Blue had been Jackson's responsibility before he'd joined the air force to fly bombing raids over occupied Europe.

"I have to be honest with you." The captain cleared his throat, jarring her away from her somber thoughts. "You're not quite what I expected."

The gruffness in his voice put Maggie on alert. "What exactly were you expecting, Captain?"

"When I was given the assignment to train Air Transport Command pilots for the B-29, I didn't know I'd have a woman in the ranks."

Maggie stretched to her full height and looked up. He towered over her like a hundred-year-old pine. She pressed her lips together. "Is that a problem, Captain?"

A muscle in his throat jerked as he glanced at her. "Not unless you make it one."

"Why would I?" She balled up her hands to keep from shaking her fist at him. "I'm only trying to serve my country the best way I know how, transporting planes to airfields all over the country so that able-bodied men can be assigned to squadrons on the front."

"I hope that's true, because we're not talking crop dusters here, Ace." Flinging his coat on the wing of the plane, the captain tugged at his tie as if it were a noose around his neck. "This is the big leagues."

Maggie opened her mouth then clamped it shut. She refused to lose her temper with this man, not when she wanted the chance to pilot one of the first B-29's to roll off the Bell Bomber Plant's assembly line. She had to be in that jump seat if only to prove to her family that she could.

Maggie took in a deep breath. "I've been briefed on the importance of the B-29 to our boys in the Pacific."

"Then you're aware of the problems we've been having."

She ground her back teeth together. What did this guy think, that she woke up one morning and figured she'd fly planes on a lark? "I've spent the better part of the winter working with the guys on the problems with the safe seal tank. It took us a while, but we think we got the fuel leak problem licked."

"Sounds like you're up to speed." The captain turned, glancing toward the house. "How about your folks? What do they think about all of this?"

If I were a man, Wesley Hicks wouldn't even think of asking me such a question! She

13

marched over to the workbench. Momma and Daddy had never kept it a secret that they wished she was settled with a family of her own. But they also understood her desire to use her abilities in a time when qualified male pilots were needed on the front. When she told them of her decision to sign on with the Women Air Force Service Pilots, a civilian group of women pilots known as the WASP, they had wholeheartedly supported her. Yes, Maggie had heard the concern in her father's voice as he prayed over her at the train station the morning she left for Sweetwater. But she also felt she had earned her parents' respect for the first time in her life.

If only the rest of her family and friends had as much faith in her calling.

Maggie grabbed a wrench from the table. "Momma and Daddy don't have a problem with it."

"Are you sure?"

She closed her eyes. *Lord, this man makes my blood boil.* Drawing in a breath through her nostrils, she opened her eyes, a flutter coming to life at the pit of her stomach. "Captain, if my parents were worried, they would've never let me near a plane in the first place."

"What about a boyfriend?" The captain

14

grinned, as if the thought of her having someone special in her life was a novel idea. "Got some Joe over there in the trenches, counting the days before he comes back to your welcoming arms?"

The nerve of this man. "Since when did my private life become any of your business?"

"Since the brass assigned you to my class." He crossed his arms over a massive chest that reminded her of the green fields where she often landed. "The last thing I need is some weepy-eyed female disrupting our training."

Finally, an issue they could agree on. Flying the B-29 as they rolled off the Bell assembly line would be an uphill battle as it was. But it still irked her that he asked. "No, sir. I don't have a boyfriend."

"Good."

His sigh of relief sent her temper over the top. "How about you? Got a girl waiting back home?"

The captain's eyes widened before darkening to a shade of midnight blue, as if he'd been caught in an ambush. After several long seconds, he shook his head. "No attachments on this end."

"Good." Maggie slapped the wrench against the palm of her hand, the weight of the metal a comfort in her awkwardness. "We wouldn't want you moping over some Dear John letter."

The air rumbled with his laughter, surprising Maggie with its warmth. "You know, Director Cochran only picks the best and the brightest gals for her program."

A compliment? Maggie swallowed past the lump of disbelief lodged in her throat. "Thank you."

"You're welcome, even though you might change your mind come Monday morning."

"Why?"

The captain walked the length of the hangar, his boots squeaking softly against the packed red clay. "You've got a lot to prove."

She'd lived with that fact her entire life. Grabbing a nearby towel, Maggie rubbed at the grease that had pooled at the tips of her short fingernails. "How so?"

"The Air Transport Command squadron isn't too keen about having a hen in their hangar."

"Is that all? Then I guess they'll just have to get used to it."

"Ms. Daniels, please try to understand."

"Why?" she asked.

"These men are fighting for a position, an opportunity to fly the first B-29 out of the plant. They're not used to going up against a woman." His mouth narrowed into a fine line. "For most of these guys, it's the only way they're going to be able to serve in the war effort."

She threw the dirty towel on the nearby worktable. "And I suppose I should just go down to the Red Cross and volunteer to roll bandages rather than use my abilities in the cockpit."

"These are men, Ms. Daniels."

"And we're in a war, Captain Hicks." She shrugged. "Why are they afraid of one woman? It's not like this kind of thing isn't going on everywhere. Women have been working in factories all over this country for the past two years."

"Maybe so, but that doesn't mean the guys left behind are taking it too well." The captain hesitated before continuing. "There have been reports of abuse."

Maggie glared up at him. "Captain Hicks, are you trying to scare me out of doing my duty?"

"No." He shook his head. "But if you're bound and determined to do this, I have a few suggestions."

His ominous tone didn't bode well, but Maggie was positive that once she showed the captain and his men what she was

17

capable of doing in the air, their opinion would change. "I'm all ears."

"Both Major Evans and I feel that it would be in the best interest of everyone involved if we eased you into the squadron's routine. At first, you'll be inspecting repairs and going through some additional training. That way, you won't be crossing paths with the guys too much."

"And later?"

"We'll see how things go. But for now, stay close and follow my lead."

Maggie bit the inside of her lip. Last time she'd blindly followed a male into the unknown, Jackson and her cousins had shaved her hair within an inch of her scalp. She wouldn't be making that mistake again, not without some answers. "How much do you know about planes, Captain?"

"You want a résumé?"

"Maybe." She smiled at his quick comeback. "If you're going to lead me in this situation, I need to know I can trust your abilities."

"Fair enough." His chest expanded against the confines of his service-regulation shirt as he drew in a deep breath. "I majored in aeronautical engineering at Georgia Tech, with an emphasis on aeronautic design. I was in the middle of an internship when the blitz started over in England so I joined the Royal Air Force."

That piece of information threw Maggie for a second. "You were in the dogfights over London?"

His eyes hooded, the man gave her a sharp nod.

"How did you end up at the plant?"

"I interned at Bell before I left for England." He gave his wristwatch a quick glance. "Look, I hate to cut this interview short, but I have to catch my bus back to the plant. Could you be in my office at 0700 hours Monday?"

Maggie studied him for a moment. In his guarded expression, she found bits and pieces of memories better left untouched. *He's running from something. But what?* She gave herself a mental shake. Didn't she have enough problems of her own? Why should she borrow more from this man?

Maggie nodded. "I'll be there."

Wesley pulled a small notepad from his jacket pocket. "The plant bus stops in downtown Hiram at five-thirty."

"I won't be taking the bus."

He looked up. "I don't understand."

Maggie smiled, mildly satisfied she had gotten the best of the captain. "My Aunt Merrilee owns a boardinghouse about a mile down the road from the plant, and she's offered me a room."

Wesley's focused glare peered at her over his wire-rimmed frames. "Merrilee Davenport is your aunt?"

"You know her?" Not that that fact surprised Maggie. Her aunt thrived on taking care of others, whether treating neighborhood kids to the occasional sweet or workers at the bomber plant.

No, it was the way the captain had said her aunt's name, as if he found the very thought of Maggie living in the house unacceptable. But there was no reason for him to feel that way, not unless . . .

The very idea made her midsection tumble in a nervous dive. Sure, housing near the bomber plant was at a shortage, but Aunt Merrilee wouldn't rent a room to the man who wasn't keen on having a woman in his training class. There had to be places in town, a room available where Captain Hicks could live until his mission was completed.

But any reprieves Maggie might have hoped for died when she stared at him. Storm clouds had gathered in his eyes, and she swore she heard thunder rumble when he finally spoke.

"Well, Ace," the captain said, annoyance

in his voice. "Looks like we're going to share a landlady."

The antebellum plantation house stood in its regal splendor in front of Wesley, the screen door unable to contain the mouth-watering aromas of fresh green beans and seasoned pork that drifted on the breeze. He glanced down at his wristwatch. Ms. Merrilee must be setting the table about now, giving them a chance to talk before the rest of her boarders gathered. Taking the stairs two at a time, he rushed through the front door.

"Is that you, Wes dear?"

Wesley couldn't contain the smile he felt curving his lips as he walked down the paneled foyer toward the dining area. Nobody but his mother had ever called him Wes until his landlady. *Mom.* Just the thought of her kind eyes, her strong yet feminine hands grasped in prayer, caused a lump to form in his throat. If only he could talk to her, take her for a stroll down to Henderson's Drugs and have an ice-cream soda. A familiar heaviness pushed against his chest as it always did whenever he thought of the mother he had lost his first year at Tech. His grandfather was the only family he had left now, and Wesley couldn't face him, not

21

after breaking his promise.

A failure that had cost Beth her life.

Pushing the memory aside, he stood at the entrance of the dining hall, his mouth watering at the tantalizing aromas coming from the room. He leaned against the door frame, considering the woman scattering crocheted potholders across the oblong hardwood table. He should have seen the similarities between Maggie and her aunt — the same high cheekbones and creamy complexion, the same shade of pale green eyes. The two could have passed for sisters. "Something sure smells good."

Merrilee Davenport gave him a welcoming smile as she continued to work. "We're putting everything out now so it'll be just a few minutes. How was work today?"

"It was a day." He leaned forward, grabbing a cherry tomato from a plate of fresh vegetables and popping it in his mouth. "I met my new pilot this afternoon."

Merrilee fussed with the tablecloth, straightening one corner then another. "How is Maggie?"

She's stubborn and insubordinate and . . . interesting. "Why didn't you tell me she was your niece?"

A slight movement at the door drew Wesley's attention. Balancing a ceramic pot in

22

one hand and looking very uncomfortable, Edie Michaels stood just inside the doorway. "Am I interrupting something?"

"No, dear. Wes and I are just flapping our gums." Merrilee bustled around the table, anxious eyes watching Wesley. A dense cloud of steam rose like a smoke signal as she lifted the pot's lid. "What have we got here?"

"Black-eyed peas."

"Why don't you put them right here?" Merrilee pushed a pitcher of tea aside and pointed to a doily near the end of the table.

Wesley quietly observed the latest addition to the Bell Plant as the women fussed over the dinner spread. While Abner Eller-bee, the plant manager, spoke highly of his new secretary, something about Edie Michaels just didn't add up. True, she kept to herself most of the time so he didn't know her very well. But she carried herself with a dignity more befitting a debutante at a cotillion than a girl in the typing pool at a bomber plant.

"Edie, could you check on the corn bread for me?" Merrilee walked with the young woman to the doorway. "I'll be just a minute."

"Yes, ma'am."

Edie's footsteps faded out of earshot, and Wesley's landlady piled the cloth napkins on the edge of the table. She faced him. "I know I should have told you about Maggie, but I'd hoped you might be able to talk some sense into her."

So Maggie's family wasn't completely sold on this whole flying business like she'd led him to believe. Wesley grabbed for one of the napkins and worked it into a neat fold. "Ms. Merrilee, F.D.R. himself couldn't talk that woman out of this assignment."

"Maggie's always had a stubborn streak a mile wide." Pride shone from Merrilee's green eyes as she chuckled. "Guess it runs in the family."

"Thanks for the warning." He lifted another napkin from the pile. "That's just the kind of attitude that'll get her in trouble."

"Oh, Wes, I hope not. Her momma and daddy have already dealt with so much, losing Jackson."

"Wasn't Jackson Mrs. Daniels's kid brother?"

Merrilee nodded. "But they took him in after his momma died in childbirth. Mr. Clark couldn't handle a baby, and Maggie's parents, Mae Belle and Jeb, had given up hope of ever having one of their own. Then Maggie came along. I don't know if they could take it if something happened to . . ."

The tone of her voice rose a step, as if twisted in pain. "I normally wouldn't ask this, you not being family and all."

"Ms. Merrilee, you know I'd do anything to help you out."

The woman rested her hand on his forearm, much as his mother did whenever she needed to ask something of him. "Then watch out for our girl, Wesley. Keep her safe."

Wesley swallowed hard. Anyone who had ever climbed into the cockpit of a plane, ever felt the rumble of the engine as they catapulted down the runway, knew that death was an occupational hazard. Maggie had faced the realities of this truth in her uncle's death and accepted them anyway. Wesley had dealt with it, too, the memory of dove-gray eyes inherited from their mother whispering through his thoughts.

Beth.

He shook the memory away. How had he found himself in this situation again? War wasn't the time for the piecrust-promises Pops had warned him against making. Easily made, easily broken. Wesley glanced at his landlady, the worry lining her face giving him pause. It wasn't as if the girl would be flying into a firefight. If he had anything to do with it, she wouldn't be flying at all.

Regret rifled through him even as the words formed on his lips. "I'll make sure nothing happens to your niece, Merrilee. I promise."

CHAPTER TWO

Maggie's eyelids fluttered open as the old buckboard jerked to a halt. She rolled onto her back and stretched, the fresh-cut hay crunching beneath her, its unique scent filling the air with memories of playing hide-and-seek with Jackson in the barn. Above her, tufts of white formed abstract images on a canvas of blue sky.

As a child, she'd spent hours looking to the heavens, thinking that death meant sitting on a cloud with the Lord. She extended her hand toward heaven, her fingers tracing the imaginary lines of God's masterpiece. If that were the case, Jackson must certainly be enjoying the view.

Maggie dropped her arm to her side. Was that why she always loved being in the air, so that she could feel the mist of God's handiwork against her face and hands, breathe in the fresh scent of His presence? Soaring high above the clouds, she felt closer to Him there than she ever did here on earth.

"We're almost there, Magpie."

The wagon lurched forward as Maggie struggled to stand up. Wrapping her arms around her father's lanky form, she hugged him close. "Don't you think I'm just a bit too old for the nicknames, Dad?"

He shook his head, a smile playing along the corners of his mouth. "Nope."

She pressed her head against her daddy's back, the steady rhythm of his heart in stark contrast to her own. In a few more minutes, she'd start living her dreams.

"Worried, baby girl?"

Daddy knew her so well. Lifting her head, she looked at him. "Do you think I can do this?"

"I think you can do anything you put your mind to doing."

"Really?"

Her father's Adam's apple bobbed up and down the tan line of his throat. "Keep your eyes on the Lord, and all things are possible." He gave her a halfhearted smile before turning his attention back to the road.

The air squeezed out of Maggie's lungs. Jackson's death had affected them all, but no one as much as her father. The lines around his eyes and across his forehead had deepened, as if a sharp blade had plowed through the steadiness of his world and broken his spirit. Maggie closed her eyes.

Lord, use me as You will, but please keep me safe for my parents' sakes.

The steady beat of horse hoofs against the red clay ignited a crimson fog around them that left Maggie sticky and hot. The smell of yesterday's turned soil hung in the air, the fields quiet. Even with the war going into its second year, no God-fearing farmer would be caught working his spread on a Sunday. As they entered a lush parasol of water oaks, a gentle breeze rippled through the leaves, cooling Maggie's face.

"She's here!"

Maggie broke into a smile as she caught sight of her aunt stepping out onto the whitewashed porch. With a grace that would have put Scarlett O'Hara to shame, Aunt Merrilee hurried down the steps, her lace handkerchief waving like a flag on the Fourth of July. Her dad's low "whoa" brought the buckboard to a fitful halt at the foot of the staircase.

Maggie scrambled to the edge of the wagon. "Hi, Merrilee!"

Before her saddle shoes could touch mortar, she was surrounded by Merrilee's warm embrace, the scent of magnolias and yeast bread engulfing her in a homey welcome. She relaxed into her aunt's arms, already homesick for the feel of her momma's velvet cheek against her own.

"Don't coddle the girl." Maggie looked over her aunt's shoulder to see Uncle James descending the stairs. "After all, she wants to fly in this war like a man."

"All the more reason to show her how much we love her." Merrilee loosened her hold, draping one arm around Maggie's waist. "So if I want to spoil my only niece, I don't need any comments from an old stubborn-headed coot like you, big brother."

"All I can say is that if she were my daughter, we wouldn't be talking such nonsense." James crossed his arms in front of his chest. "I'd have her married off with a house full of youngins."

"But she's not your daughter, now, is she?" The buckboard creaked as her father jumped down beside her. "As far as I'm concerned, anyone who says a thing against her is as bad as those fellows we're fighting over there in Europe and in the Pacific."

"Well done, Jeb." Merrilee's mouth spread into a victorious smile and for one moment, Maggie wondered if she would stick her tongue out at her elder brother. There had always been bad blood between the two for as long as Maggie could remember, but things had taken a turn for the worse in the year since Granddaddy Daniels had died and left the family homestead to Merrilee. Uncle James hadn't taken too kindly to being a squatter in the home he believed rightfully belonged to him.

"So how are you doing, brother?"

Tiny plumes of dust rose as Maggie's father slapped his old straw hat against his dingy overalls. "Fine."

"Where's Mae Belle? I thought she'd be coming with you." Merrilee searched the area behind him.

"She's keeping close to home right now."

Uncle James leaned against the handrail, clicking his tongue against the roof of his mouth. "Mae Belle would be a sight better if her daughter stayed at home, minding the house where she belonged."

Guilt tightened its fingers around Maggie's heart at her father's attempt to withhold the truth. Since news of Jackson's death, Momma hadn't left the house, not even for Sunday morning services. But this afternoon, she had stood on their front porch, waving her encouragement until her petite figure disappeared from Maggie's view.

"Ignore him," Merrilee whispered loud enough for everyone to hear. "James barely made it to Europe before President Wilson declared victory."

Jeb bowed his head, his soft chuckle causing a smile to tug at Maggie's lips.

"You are going to stay for supper, aren't you, Jeb?" Merrilee smiled, effectively changing the subject. "I made your favorite, peach cobbler."

"I need to get goin' if I want to make it home by dark." He shook his head, his eyes skirting the perimeter of the yard. "But I could do with a piece of that cobbler."

"How about some tea?" In two shakes of a pig's tail, Merrilee was up the steps, pulling Maggie along with her. As she opened the screen door, Merrilee turned and called out to Uncle James. "I'd appreciate it if you'd take Maggie's things up to her room."

"No," he answered, spraying black-brown tobacco juice onto the ground. "If she's goin' act like a man, she can get her own bags."

"I'd be happy to get that for you, Ms. Merrilee."

Maggie glanced down the length of the porch. Wesley Hicks, his shirt sleeves neatly rolled up over tan forearms, sat in the far corner just within Maggie's view. He rose, sending the rocking chair into a frenzied dance that matched the sudden beating of her heart.

She cringed. How long had he been sitting there, listening to her uncle belittle her? Too long, if the tight pull of his mouth and furrowed brow was anything to go by. Well, this just wouldn't do.

Maggie bounded down the stairs. "I appreciate the offer, Captain, but I can manage on my own."

She leaned against the dilapidated wagon, silently praying that her one good dress would survive its brush with the splintered wood siding. The split leather cracked beneath her touch as she grabbed it and gave it a tug.

"Around here, the name's Wesley." The captain's voice tickled her ear as his hand closed over hers. A slight shiver traveled up her arm in a pleasant sort of way. Maggie slipped her hand out of his grip.

He gave the suitcase a tug. "What did you pack in here? A bag of rocks?"

"Betcha diamonds to donuts my girl brought her books with her." The pride she heard from her father tempered her frustration. "You see, Margaret Rose wants to go to college."

"Margaret Rose?" The captain's eyes —

33

Wesley's — danced with laughter. "Like the little English princess?"

"Yes, but Maggie had it first." Merrilee smiled from the top of the stairs. "We like to think King George borrowed it from her."

Uncle James snorted. "She don't look like no princess to me."

Heat shimmied up Maggie's neck and across her cheeks. No, *regal* wasn't exactly the word she'd use to describe herself at this moment. She itched from the sprigs of hay that clung to the faded cloth of her dress, and her hair swirled around her face as if she'd flown through a windstorm. A pig in mud looked a sight better than she did. Why hadn't she followed Momma's suggestion and sat up front with her father?

Too late for that now. Why should she care how she looked to Wesley Hicks, or any other man for that matter? She had a job to do, and she intended to do it to the best of her ability.

"You're the new squadron leader over at the airfield, Captain Hicks?" Daddy leaned against the porch railing.

She didn't think her cheeks could grow any hotter. "I'm sorry, Daddy. Captain Hicks, this is my father, Jebediah Daniels. Daddy, this is Captain Wesley Hicks."

Wesley extended his hand. "Pleased to

meet you, sir."

"The pleasure is all mine." Jeb shook his hand. "I hear you saw some action over in England. Where abouts?"

"Around London mainly, though I did get into some skirmishes over the Channel."

Her father nodded, his stance straightening. He had always had a deep respect for the soldiers of the armed forces, but it had grown even more in the time since Jackson's death. "We need a few good men, both here and overseas, if we intend to win this war."

"And a few good women, too, sir." Wesley glanced over at Maggie.

Another compliment? Heat flushed across her chest. She almost opened her mouth to thank him, but caught herself as he moved away. Had there been a hint of sorrow in his expression? Maybe his statement wasn't necessarily meant for her. Did the captain have someone in mind? Could it be that he hadn't been honest with her about a girlfriend back home?

Or maybe he had. Maggie grasped hold of an idea. No man would ever admit that their girl was serving overseas while he waited at home. She glanced at him. It made sense. She could respect the position he was in, but he should have been upfront with her.

"Which room should I put her bags in,

Ms. Merrilee?" Wesley asked.

Her aunt waved a hand in the air like an airman guiding a plane in for a perfect three-point landing. "The one down the hall from yours."

"It ain't proper, Merrilee!" Uncle James decreed. "What will people around town think?"

"It can't be helped. Major Evans came around last week and asked if I could make every room available for all the folks coming into town to work at the Bell." Merrilee winked at Maggie. "I'm just glad I still had enough room for Maggie."

"All the same. People are goin' to talk. Unmarried folks living in the same house might be all right in the big city, but this is Marietta." James's eyes bored into her. "We're God-fearing people."

"Then maybe you need to start spending some time with Him, James." Jeb made his way down the brick steps. "If Mae Belle and I trust our daughter's judgment, I don't see where this is any of your business."

"That's where you're wrong, little brother. As the eldest son of Jacob Daniels, it's my responsibility to see that our father's will is followed to the letter of the law." Uncle James hardened his jaw so tight, Maggie thought it might snap. "And we all know that Daddy held very high standards. Cohabitation is not an immorality that he would have taken lightly."

"James, I'm raising Claire in this house. I wouldn't think to offer anything less than a respectable and decent place for my daughter as well as my boarders," Merrilee answered. "Stop talking such foolishness."

"Me?" Her uncle pointed an accusing finger at Maggie. "Why, she's the one making a fool out of herself with this flying nonsense."

Everything went suddenly quiet around Maggie. Is that what her family thought, that her dreams were nonsense? She didn't dare look at any of them, couldn't bear the thought of seeing the answer in their faces. A heavy weight settled over Maggie's shoulders. Would she ever be able to prove to the people she loved the most in the world that flying was God's plan for her life?

"I'd think you would be proud of her, Mr. Daniels." Wesley pulled even with Uncle James on the stairs. "It's not just anyone who gets issued an invitation to join the WASP."

Maggie swallowed hard. What was Wesley Hicks doing?

Jeb glanced at him. "What do you mean?"

Wesley shifted her suitcase from one hand

to the other. "It's my understanding that only eleven hundred women were accepted to serve in this civilian program."

Uncle James smirked. "So what?"

"Your niece was picked out of more than ten thousand women who applied, and of them, only eleven hundred got their wings." Wesley nodded toward Maggie. "If anything, her selection should make your family proud."

Maggie lowered her chin to her chest, her heart hammering against her breast. Wesley Hicks had stood up for her. But why?

He took the brick stairs two at a time, the suitcase in his hand as if it weighed nothing. One day, he brow-beat her with questions about her flying abilities; the next, he defended her against her uncle's outdated views on women. If she didn't watch it, she might grow to like the captain. That wouldn't do, not when she was on the verge of realizing her dreams. So many questions regarding the man, but one thing she knew for certain: serving under Wesley Hicks's command would be like running full-throttle into the stratosphere.

Wesley chanced a glance over his shoulder at the woman coming up the stairs behind him. Maggie had been deathly quiet since her uncle's outburst. So much so, he had held the faint hope she might turn tail and run. But she hadn't. With a look of the resolve he'd caught a glimpse of yesterday at her place, Maggie had snapped to attention and climbed the stairs to her temporary home.

At the landing, he turned and headed for a freshly painted white door on the far end of the hall. He turned the knob, pushed open the door and stepped back. "Here you go, Ace."

She stepped past him into the room, the scent of sunshine and freshly cut hay trailing after her. Wesley checked the hall before following her inside, leaving the door wide open. No sense giving people something to talk about, especially after the way James Daniels had voiced his concerns to anyone who would listen.

Oddly enough, Wesley understood his meaning. If any man had so much as looked at Beth the wrong way, he would have taken a punch at them in a heartbeat. But Maggie's uncle seemed more worried about the family's reputation than his niece's well-being.

Was that why he had jumped to Maggie's defense? Or the way her delicate jaw had lifted in defiance in the face of her uncle's insults? Well, she'd better get used to it. Though he would do his level best to temper the men's comments, he couldn't rescue her every time someone made a crack about her. Talk about setting tongues to wagging.

Wesley stood at the doorway and scanned the room. Merrilee had a talent of making any place a home, and this room was no exception. A thick, homemade quilt draped the bed while sunlight danced through matching lace curtains.

Maggie stood next to the nightstand, her fingertips caressing a single rosebud surrounded by a handful of dandelions in a mason jar. A silky curtain of reddish-gold hair fell across her face as she bent toward the white blossom. Her eyes closed, she took a deep breath, trying to engrave this moment in her memory.

She turned, her gaze meeting his. "I've always loved roses."

His heart tightened for some reason he didn't understand. "Ms. Merrilee sent me out to cut that bud right after church this morning. She said something about white roses being your favorite."

"They are."

Wesley took a step closer. "And the dandelions?"

"It depends." Her lips rounded into a smile. "Who picked them?"

"Your cousin Claire," Wesley answered. "She said she wanted to give you a handful to make a wish on until Merrilee reminded her that those wishes turned into weeds."

"Then I'll have to make a point of thanking her." She took another deep breath before straightening. "These are perfect. Thank you, Captain."

He didn't like that her comment pleased him so much. "We're at home here. Call me Wesley."

"Okay." A faint shade of pink colored her cheeks. "Wesley."

Wesley nodded toward her suitcase. "Where do you want me to put your things?"

"On the bed would be fine."

He walked across the rug-laden floor and tossed the case onto the corn-husk mattress. The suitcase settled, carving out a large dent. "What kind of books did you pack?"

"Jackson's engineering books." Maggie opened the closet and gathered several hangers. "I figure they'll give me a head start when I apply to Georgia Tech after the war."

He'd never seen a woman on campus the entire time he was a student unless he

41

counted Ms. Wise, and no Tech man had ever discounted the tough professor. Wesley frowned. Another battle for Maggie to wage. "Your uncle must have started right after I left school to work at Bell."

"Probably." Maggie opened the lid of her case. "He was a junior when he joined the air corps last year."

"What was he majoring in?"

"Look." Maggie turned from her packed case to glare at him. "It was nice of you to jump to my defense with my uncle downstairs, but I really don't need your help."

Wesley shook his head. "It didn't look that way to me."

"Some people in my family have got this old-fashioned idea that women shouldn't have a life outside of marriage and kids." She grabbed a pair of overalls from her case and shook them out. "I've got to prove myself to them."

"Why?"

She shrugged one shoulder as she picked up a hanger. "I just have to, that's all."

"And if you don't?"

Maggie's chin rose in that obstinate determination he had gotten a glimpse of at their first meeting. "Thank you for carrying my suitcase up. I appreciate it."

He'd been dismissed! The muscles in Wesley's jaw tightened as he walked out of the room. Maggie may think she'd had some rough skies with her family, but that was nothing.

The real battle would start tomorrow.

CHAPTER THREE

A fine sheen of moisture plastered Maggie's pajamas to her body. She rolled over on her side for the millionth time, her limbs crying out for the escape sleep would provide.

The day had left her alert, her brain firing on all cylinders. Not one to waste time, she had cleaned out her suitcase by the time her daddy had come up to her room to say goodbye. A dull ache bundled in her chest. Her father had always been so strong, almost invincible, but this afternoon in his arms, she had felt the slump in his shoulders, recognized the sorrow in each new line that creased his face. Her once-vibrant parent had aged terribly since Jackson's death, and she couldn't help but mourn yet another loss.

Thank heavens for Merrilee! The dust had barely settled in the yard before her aunt hustled her into the sitting room to meet the other occupants of the house. As introductions were made, Maggie couldn't help noticing Captain Hicks's obvious absence.

He asked me to call him Wesley. Untangling the sheets from around her legs, she tossed back the covers and sat up, skimming her fingers across the nightstand for matches. Within seconds, eerie shadows from the kerosene lamp danced untamed against the wall. Maggie quickly glanced toward the windows. Good, at least she'd remembered to close the blackout curtains.

She grabbed her robe, the scent of Momma's lavender soap cradling her in memories of home. For one split second, she wished she was stretched out on her bed, the sounds of her parents stirring in the next room a comfort. In those moments, in the peaceful conversations between her mother and father, Maggie longed for something more. A home. A family of her own. But most important, a man who loved her, flying and all.

No, it was best if she traveled this unconventional path alone.

Picking up her watch from the nightstand, Maggie glanced at the time and grimaced. Three in the morning. Maybe some warm milk would lull her to sleep. She grasped the base of the lantern. Balancing the light in one hand, she slipped out of her room.

The lamp cast shadows down the hallway, guiding her around bits and pieces of furniture. The night air nipped at her bare legs. The hardwood floor moaned its soft protest beneath her feet as she tiptoed down the stairs. At the hall landing, she stopped. A ray of pale light shone from under the sitting room door.

Who else would be up at this hour?

Setting down the lantern, she plastered herself against the wall. At training camp, she had been prepared for everything, including possible intruders, but never in a million years could she imagine it could happen here, in Merrliee's home.

But the country was at war and anything was possible. She scoured the corridor for a weapon. Claire's jump rope dangled from the banister. Maggie frowned. Hopalong Cassidy might know how to hog-tie a bad guy, but lassos were out of her league.

A low whimper from behind the partially closed door caught Maggie off guard. She peeked inside. Twin Queen Anne chairs in faded sapphire sat in front of the fireplace, which remained unused except for on cool nights like tonight. One of Merrilee's handmade rugs graced the hardwood floor beneath the chairs, giving the room a cozy feel.

Her imagination must be playing tricks on her. There it was. A sniffle, as if someone were crying. She walked deeper into the room, her tongue sticking to the roof of her mouth like a cotton dress in mid July. The wooden planks beneath her let out a soft groan.

A woman leaned over the side of the chair. Maggie took a deep breath. It was one of the people she'd met this afternoon. She grasped for a name. Edie something or other.

Good thing You called me to fly planes, Lord, 'cause I'd make a rotten spy. Combing her fingers through her wild hair, Maggie stopped by the chair. "I didn't mean to intrude on you."

"I was just catching up on the news from home." Edie shoved a folded paper into an envelope. A hint of tears glistened on her cheeks in the firelight.

"Where's home?" Maggie slipped into the chair beside her and stretched her legs out toward the warmth of the fire.

"Detroit."

"That must be hard, being so far away from everyone you know."

"It is, but it's the only way I can move up

47

in the company." Edie fiddled with a piece of yellow ribbon tangled in the end of her braid.

Was that a note of frustration in Edie's voice? "What do you do?"

"I'm secretary to Mr. Ellerbee."

"Abner Ellerbee?"

Edie nodded. "Does everyone know everybody else in this town?"

Maggie chuckled softly, snuggling into the cushions of the chair. "I guess it seems that way. It was that way before the war, but with all the new folks moving in, I don't think I know everyone anymore."

Edie cocked her head to the side and studied her. "So how do you know Mr. Ellerbee?"

"He and my uncle James have been in cahoots since their days at the old agricultural school in Powder Springs. When Bell announced plans for building the bomber plant here in Marietta, Uncle James went before the executive committee and recommended Mr. Ellerbee for the plant manager's job."

"Oh."

Edie lowered her gaze, but not before Maggie caught the guarded look in her eyes. Maggie reached out and covered one of the woman's hands with her own. "I've got no use for Abner Ellerbee myself, not since I happen to know he has the same opinion of women as my uncle does."

"You mean, outdated and insulting."

"Exactly." Maggie smiled, happy to see Edie relax. She moved her hands down the length of the armrest and stretched. "Still, you've got to be a brave woman to take on your job. It's a huge responsibility."

"It is." Edie raised one of Merrilee's teacups to her lips and took a sip. "But it's a great opportunity, and if I hope to get a position in the drafting department one day, I couldn't pass it up."

Poor thing. Abner Ellerbee would rather die than promote a woman to a man's job. But there were some who once thought a woman would never pilot a plane, either. "I felt the same way about joining the WASP. Like, if I didn't do it, I'd be missing something wonderful."

"Merrilee mentioned your first day is tomorrow. Are you excited?"

"Yes." Maggie covered her mouth as she yawned. "And nervous. Which is why I'm prowling around in the middle of the night."

Edie lifted her cup in a slight toast. "Care to join me?"

"I'm thinking a glass of milk might do the trick." Maggie stood and walked to the mahogany table pushed up against the wall. Because the kitchen was detached from the main house, her aunt always left a pitcher full of milk in a large bowl of chipped ice every night. Grabbing a tumbler, she filled her glass until it was almost full.

"I can't get used to fresh milk, especially when it's still warm." Edie wrinkled her nose.

"Just one of the pleasures of country life." Cupping her hands around the glass, Maggie took a sip. "So how long have you been living here with Aunt Merrilee?"

"Almost three months. I roomed with some girls down in Little Five Points, but with my hours, it didn't work out." Edie stretched her neck to the side. "When I put out the word I was looking for a place to stay, Wesley recommended Ms. Merrilee."

"You know the captain?" She wasn't sure why, but the thought of this woman and Captain Hicks together caused an uncomfortable knot to form in her chest.

"We talk when he comes in to visit with Mr. Ellerbee."

Sure, the captain was nice to Edie. She wasn't honing in on the man's job. "It was good of him to help you out."

"Mr. Ellerbee thinks a lot of him." Edie set her cup down on the table beside her.

"Wesley turned down a job in the aeronautical division at the Buffalo plant so he could serve in the Royal Air Force." She leaned back. "He'd be considered necessary personnel, but Mr. Ellerbee couldn't talk him out of it. He has a lot of respect for what Wesley did."

Sitting down beside Edie, Maggie took another sip of her milk, her thoughts tangled. She'd read about the pilots of the Royal Air Force and watched their stories play out on the movie screen at the Strand before the matinee began. These admirable men had fought the enemy with nothing more than a dilapidated piece of machinery and sheer guts, had put their lives on the line to save their country.

And Wesley Hicks had once been one of them.

But his visits with Abner Ellerbee bothered her. If Wesley was the a-okay guy everyone made him out to be, why would he associated with a man whose beliefs were as antiquated as Abner's?

A thunderous boom from the direction of the front hall shook the house. With a quick glance at Edie, Maggie bolted from her chair. Looking back to see her new friend grab the matches and a lantern, she hurried to the door and peeked down the hallway.

Moonlight streamed in through the front door, transforming the delicate figurines decorating Merrilee's tables into playful ghosts. Maggie inhaled a steadying breath. Maybe the wind had blown open the door.

A lump on the floor moaned.

Her eyes followed the path of the carpet. Her heart kicked into high alert at the sight of a body slumped inside the doorway.

"Who is it?" Edie whispered behind her.

"I don't know. Wait here."

With as much courage as she could muster, Maggie started down the hall. The pane-glass windows from the front door rattled softly, in sync with the jittery beat coursing through her nerve endings. The doorknob banged against the wall, muted by the billowy pillow of the cotton curtains.

The mass on the floor rolled over onto his back. Shadows and light revealed sunken cheeks, a broad forehead, and a gaping hole for a mouth. Maggie went down on her knees beside him, the sickening odor of sweat and corn liquor clogging her throat.

"Is he dead?" Edie asked from the doorway.

"Dead drunk."

Maggie lifted her head at the familiar male voice. There on the stairwell stood Wesley Hicks, his hair mussed as if he also had been having a hard time drifting off to sleep. One side of his bibbed overalls hung loosely, barely covering the muscular expansion of his chest.

Her eyes locked with his and for a spilt second, she was lost in his gaze. Maggie's stomach dipped and swayed, as if she had hit an air pocket that had lifted her higher into the atmosphere. She finally found her voice. "Do you know this guy?"

"Let me introduce you. This is Jimbo Hayes, another one of Merrilee's renters." Wesley took the last two steps and joined her by the door. "And my best test pilot."

Wesley stretched his hand over his mouth in an unsuccessful attempt to stifle another yawn. Everyone at the Bell knew Major Evans could be longwinded when he got started, but this welcoming speech for Maggie took the cake.

How was the guest of honor holding up? Wesley stole a look at her and grimaced. For someone who'd had only a couple of hours of sleep, the woman positively glowed.

"Ms. Daniels, I can't tell you what a pleasure it is to have you here. General Arnold speaks highly of Jackie Cochran's pilots. Personally, I can't wait to see you in action," the major said, turning to Wesley.

"Isn't that right, Captain?"

"Yes, sir."

But Wesley had already seen the feisty redhead at work. The major continued to talk as Wesley sifted through the moments after he'd found Maggie leaning over his inebriated pilot. She had been stunned, but no more than he when he had knelt down beside her and filled his lungs with the fresh lavender scent that clung to the air around her.

Maggie had moved first. While he dragged Jimbo into the front parlor, she'd shuffled Edie up the stairs. He'd barely had time to get the man situated on the long sofa when the aroma of fresh coffee penetrated the room. Quietly, Maggie carried a tray of steaming brew and thick pieces of homemade bread. For the next hour, she coaxed Jimbo into small sips. The first light of dawn pushed against the edges of the blackout blinds before Maggie retired.

Wesley clenched his teeth together to hold back a yawn. Why didn't she hightail it back home and make life easier for the both of them? But she didn't strike him as someone who would back down. Maggie Daniels would face whatever dangers came her way, even if it killed her.

As it had his sister.

He'd have to find another way to keep the woman grounded, which might be hard to do if the major's reaction was anything to go by. Wesley studied the major. The man had never seemed so delighted, leaning his beefy body back in his chair to get a better look at Maggie. Evans was enchanted by the woman.

Not that Wesley could fault the man. Wesley glanced over at his new squadron member. She did have a certain charm. A cream-colored snood held back a knot of thick hair, save a single curl that burned a trail down her pale throat. No powder or rouge covered the light dusting of freckles sprinkled across her nose and cheeks. Though not like the glamorous girl pilots he'd met in England, Maggie had a small-town innocence that he found irritatingly refreshing.

"Your family has done a great service to this country." Major Evans leaned on his forearms. "I'm sure you'll do the same."

"I hope so, sir," Maggie answered with a smile.

"Now all we've got to do is get you a bird to fly." The major looked over at Wesley. "Have you given Ms. Daniels a tour of the plant?"

"Not yet, sir," he replied. He recalled the

awestruck excitement on Maggie's face as they entered the plant that morning. "But I think Ms. Daniels is already impressed with what she's seen."

Tilting his chair back, Evans peered out of a window to his side. "Beautiful, isn't it?"

"The old ball field never looked so good, sir."

"You know this area?" The major glanced at her.

"I believe you know her aunt," Wesley offered. "Merrilee Davenport?"

"Merrilee?" The major's question was filled with interest, as if saying the woman's name brought him great pleasure. "She's such a gracious soul, loaning her home out to our staff."

"That's just my aunt's way. She's always thinking up ways to help other people."

Maggie must have picked up the major's interest in her aunt, judging from the smile tugging at the corners of her mouth. Good grief! Last thing Captain Hicks needed right now was a female with romance on her mind. "Ms. Daniels spent a great deal of time at her aunt's while she was growing up."

"It was my grandfather's house then, but I practically lived there."

The major smiled. "It must be wonderful

to serve your country right here where you grew up."

Maggie's simple nod surprised him. Was his new pilot not excited by her hometown assignment? The woman had a great family: her father, Merrilee, Claire. They were all fine people. As good as gold. Granted, her uncle James left something to be desired, but there was always one problem in every family.

Or was that Maggie?

"I take it she hasn't met her squadron yet?" Major Evans asked.

Filing away his thoughts for later, Wesley sat at attention. "No, sir."

Evan's expression grew grim. "Watch out for her, Captain. Make sure those scalawags treat her with respect." He focused on Maggie. "Once again, it was a pleasure to meet you, Ms. Daniels. Dismissed."

Pushing back from his chair, Wesley stood ramrod straight. Maggie mimicked him in a quick salute before turning to leave. He walked to the door and held it open for her. What was he doing here, stuck babysitting a bunch of test pilots and a girl flyer? *I've always trusted You, Lord, but I don't understand. First, You take Beth, then You stick me stateside. What is it You want from me?*

Much like Wesley's radio during a bombing run, God appeared to be maintaining His silence on the subject. Wesley walked down the hall leading to the outside breezeway, Maggie quiet beside him. He had barely stepped out into the sunshine when sweat beaded up on his forehead like big drops of rain.

"Boy, this place sure has changed." The chain-link fence clanged out a little tune as Maggie clenched her hands in the metal webbing. "We used to play baseball right here."

Wesley stared out over the tarmac. He could almost see her as she was then, a little bit of a girl, her red curls bouncing as she rounded second in a close game with the neighborhood kids. He wasn't sure why, but he liked that image.

She pointed to the building that housed the paint shop. "Right over there was some of the tallest water oaks you ever could imagine. Whenever we came to visit Granddaddy, Jackson and I would sneak over here and climb up as high as we could." Color flooded her cheeks. "We used to pretend we were flying into battle."

Wesley leaned against the fence. "Sounds like you caught the flying bug early."

"Not really." She rested her shoulder

against a metal post. "Daddy used to tell us all his war stories of shooting it out with the Germans in the skies right outside of Paris." She chuckled. "But I wasn't all that impressed."

Her candor startled him. "Really?"

A lone curl along her neck bobbed up and down as she nodded. "Then Daddy bought his own two-seater. I'll never forget the first time he took me up." She lifted her face to the heavens, her mouth forming a peaceful smile. "The minute the air lifted Old Blue's wings and the wheels left the ground, I understood what all the fuss was about."

"So you goaded your old man into teaching you how to fly?"

Her throaty chuckle caused a pleasant warmth to spread across his chest. "Daddy thought it would be a good idea to have a few more pilots in the family business. Jack and I applied for the Civilian Pilot Training class at Georgia Tech and got our licenses there."

"Why'd you join the WASP?"

"If you haven't noticed, everyone in my family has served in the military." Her stubborn chin raised a notch before she gave a feminine snort. "Okay, so all the guys in the family have served, but being the only girl, I don't have the opportunities they do. Even

59

though the WASP is a civilian unit, we're contributing to the war effort." Her eyes shined, full of girlish dreams. "I've waited my whole life to make a difference. God finally provided the way."

Wesley shifted his gaze to the building directly behind her. His sister had thought much the same way, that flying to protect England was her moral obligation. He'd tried to talk her out of it, tried to convince her that she didn't fully understand the situation, but Beth wouldn't hear of it. In the end, he had agreed with her.

Never considering she could die.

"Come on. We're going to be late." Wesley took Maggie's arm. He nudged her toward the entrance tunnel, away from the relics of the past and toward the realities of the present.

A cloud of smoke circled the small group of women as one after another took a drag from their cigarettes outside the main entrance. Wesley opened the door, then stood to the side as Maggie slipped by him. The morning shift had arrived and divided its masses into two orderly lines, as if Noah himself had orchestrated the move.

Maggie tugged at her collar and checked her ID badge for what seemed like the fifteenth time.

Wesley leaned toward her as they waited. "Nervous, Ace?"

A set of pale green eyes seemed to bore holes through him. If he'd hoped to get a read on the woman, he was sadly disappointed. Maggie shook her head. "More excited than anything."

He glanced down the line. Maggie needed a healthy dose of fear. Heck, every person going into battle did, and, whether she believed it or not, she was about to face her biggest enemy of all — the men in her own squadron.

"Nothing wrong with being a little nervous, Maggie. Keeps a pilot sharp."

"And are you sharp today, sir?"

Touché. Wesley bit the inside of his mouth to keep from chuckling. This woman just might be able to handle the rough leathernecks under his command. But until he knew that fact for sure, he'd have to watch her like a hawk.

He drew in a deep breath. "I'd rather be a little nervous than dead."

The light in her eyes dimmed slightly, replaced by an emotion he couldn't name. Maggie fell into silence beside him as the line moved quickly. If he hurt her feelings, well — better to bruise her ego than allow her to get herself injured or killed.

61

Wesley waited to the side, mentally going over his checklist for the day while the inspector verified Maggie's ID against his list. Once she was given the okay, she headed for the side door. Wesley followed her into the yard and around a small outbuilding.

A crowd of people walked with them as they made their way toward the largest building on the lot. Four and a half stories high, the gleaming steel walls disappeared into the pale blue Georgia sky. On one side, crews stood atop scaffolds, the railing lined up along long tubes of welded metal moving down the assembly line until it reached the open-air fourth wall. Across the room, row upon row of tables sat, sparks flying as men and women behind protective masks soldered the small bolts and seams necessary to put the B-29 into action.

"Holy cow!" Maggie exclaimed, her eyes wide with excitement.

"Impressive, isn't it?"

Maggie's simple nod caused Wesley to smile. The thought of so many people coming together for the common good, the trust placed in them to build these planes and transport them to our troops all over the world was never lost on him. Nor did it seem lost on this woman.

A sense of humility and awe rose up inside him. "I come in here sometimes after I get off duty to watch these guys. Now, every time I climb into the cockpit, I think about the sweat and determination these folks put into every part of their work."

"It reminds me how important each and every one of us are in this battle." She glanced at him. "I imagine that's how you felt flying with the RAF."

Wesley grimaced at the wonder in her voice. Duty hadn't driven him into enlisting in the Royal Air Force. Flying for His Majesty had been the only way to keep the peace in his family.

"Captain?"

Something in the way she spoke, with a gentleness that threatened to put a dent in the steely armor encasing his heart, caught him off guard. She almost sounded as if she cared. She didn't know him. But if she did, once she learned of the mess he'd made in England, she'd never speak to him again. Just like his grandfather. He'd have to keep his distance. But, how? After he'd already promised Merrilee to keep Maggie safe.

"Ms. Daniels, it would be best if you remember our mission and avoid personal chitchat. Here, these men consider you the

63

enemy," he snapped, his voice harsher than he intended. "Welcome to the war."

CHAPTER FOUR

"At ease."

Only Maggie couldn't release her stance, not with a dozen sets of eyes bearing down on her as if she had a bull's-eye on her back. Granted, their reaction wasn't anything new. She'd dealt with this kind of response at every airfield she'd been assigned.

But this time felt different. Some of these men were her neighbors, childhood friends of her cousins. Why, she had sprayed Ernest Cunningham's fields for free when he fell and broke his ankle a couple of years ago. And Matthew Cobb had asked her to the homecoming dance her sophomore year. But you wouldn't know it now, not from the stony look of disgust on their faces.

"As I'm sure you've noticed by now, we have a new crew member joining us today." Wesley walked the length of the tarmac, then turned. "I'd like to introduce Ms. Maggie Daniels, one of the ladies in the Women

Air Force Service Pilots."

A low whistle hissed behind her. Heat rose in her throat, the rapid sound of her heartbeat banging in her ears. She curled her hands into tight fists. One thing her cousins had taught her was a good right hook. If this guy behind her thought she wouldn't lay him out flat on his backside, he had another thing coming.

"She will be working with me over the next few weeks in preparation for our maiden flight."

"I'd love for such a doll to work with me," a man to her right whispered. A low chuckle rose up from the men around her.

"Anyone, and I mean anyone, who is less than respectful to Ms. Daniels will answer to me." Wesley's voice sharpened into a hard edge. "Is that clear?"

"Yes, sir!"

"Reconvene at 0900 hours for our hike to Kennesaw Mountain."

Kennesaw Mountain. Sadness welled up in her chest, knotting into a lump in her throat. The last time she'd been to the mountain, Jackson had challenged her to a race. It had been fun, darting in and out of the trees, forgetting that in less than twenty-four hours her favorite uncle would be on a train that would take him halfway around the world to the front. He had told her that God had a big dream for her. His words had propelled her forward in those first days after his death and during basic training at Sweetwater. The knot in her throat loosened.

I'm shooting for the sky, Jackson!

"Dismissed!" Wesley ordered.

The men broke rank around her. A few glanced at her, but most chose to ignore her as they dispersed to the locker room.

Maggie picked up her duffel bag and swung it onto her shoulder. Was there a ladies' locker room?

"I told you they can be kind of rough." Wesley came up alongside her.

That was supposed to be rough? She had to bite her lip to keep from laughing out loud. "Trust me, Captain. I've seen worse."

"I bet."

He didn't believe her. Most folks didn't unless they'd grown up around boys. Maggie shifted her belongings higher on her shoulder. "You don't have brothers, do you?"

"No, a sister."

The shadow that passed over his face disturbed her slightly, but she pushed the feeling away. "Well, I grew up with five boys. And every single one of them had their own unique way of giving me a hard time."

"That's family." He crossed his arms over the pale green fabric that spread over his chest. "I'm sure Jackson and the rest of your cousins didn't allow any nonsense from other men."

"No, but you know men." The weight of her duffle bag pulled on her collar, the only release from the tight band of sweat forming around her neck. "I'm sure your sister would understand what I mean."

"I doubt it. We were very protective of Beth even after she joined the service."

So that's what he'd meant with his comment about needing a few good women. He had a sister, and in the service of all things. Probably joined up in an effort to serve her country and get away from her overbearing brother at the same time. At least his remark had been aimed at his sister rather than a girlfriend, as she had thought. The truth was oddly comforting.

"But you couldn't be there all the time," Maggie replied, ambushed by her slight feeling of relief. "That's when the other guys swoop down on you."

"I'm sure Jackson and your cousins knew a lot more than they let on."

She scoffed. "Don't bet on it."

Wesley laughed. "If he was anything like

me, he probably saw more hand-to-hand combat in the woods behind Merrilee's house than he ever did in training."

If that comment was meant to make her feel protected, it had fallen on deaf ears. Her whole life she'd been looking through the window, never allowed inside while the boys came and went as they pleased. It was one of the reasons she had waited to enlist with the WASP until all of her cousins were safely overseas. She wouldn't have to listen to their bellyaching.

Maggie tried to straighten to her full height, but her bag weighed down her shoulder. "Don't kid yourself, Captain. I'm quite capable of taking care of myself."

"That's what you keep telling me." The humor dancing in his eyes irritated her to no end.

"Then I guess I'll just have show you," she answered, shifting her bag to the other shoulder. This conversation was finished. It was time to prove her point. She headed across the tarmac. Maybe she'd find a ladies' restroom where she could change.

"Where are you going?"

She stopped and turned back to him. "To find a place to change. You can't expect me to go on a five-mile run in this getup, now can you?"

Maggie had barely turned toward the main building when Wesley was there, blocking everything in her view. Steel blue eyes glared down at her from over the top of his sunglasses. "What makes you think you've been invited on this run?"

She stared straight ahead, hoping to steady herself. Instead her view of his muscular chest, a rainbow of ribbons pinned to his breast pocket, threw her off balance. Maggie swallowed. She'd never make it five miles on her wobbly legs. "I've been given an order."

"No, you weren't."

Blast the man! Heat settled in the pit of her stomach. Her family's protectiveness she had to deal with, but Wesley Hicks? Thanks, but no thanks. Maggie drew in a deep breath. "Did you order your squadron to prepare for a run, sir?"

"Yes."

His answer gave Maggie just the ammo she needed. "And am I not a part of that squad?"

His mouth flatlined. "Yes, but . . ."

"But what? How will your men ever trust me in the cockpit if you excuse me from something as simple as a five-mile run?"

His eyes narrowed. "Five miles is simple?"

She had about had it with the man. "The

Women Army Service Pilots are trained the same way as any man in the Army Air Corp." She nodded toward the men's barracks. "Just like those guys, we worked out every day, starting with a five-mile run."

Wesley hesitated for a moment, as if waging an internal battle of his own. "So you're bound and determined to do this."

She may hurt like the devil in the morning, but nothing was going to stop her from following her squadron up that mountain of granite. Maggie gave him a brief nod.

The hairs on the back of her neck stood at attention as he studied her from the top of her head to the tips of her spit-shined boots. What was it about this man that sent her in a tailspin?

"Your foot locker is in the women's restroom, just inside the door to your left," he finally said. "Report back here in ten minutes."

Maggie couldn't help but smile. "Yes, sir!"

"And make no mistake about it, Ms. Daniels. If you're one second late, I'll leave you behind. Is that clear?" He made a sharp turn toward the barracks.

"Thank you, sir!" Maggie called out as he marched away.

Hurrying as fast as she could, Maggie hardly made it into the confines of the ladies' room before slumping against the wall, her legs wobbling beneath her. The first battle was over. She had faced down her squadron's opposition and managed to come out unscathed. Maggie closed her eyes for a brief celebration. But she would have to remain strong if she had any intention of winning this particular war.

Turning on the spigot, Maggie splashed cold water on her heated face, not sure if the warmth came from the insults her squad had thrown at her or the brief exchange with Wesley Hicks. She reached for a towel. What had the man been thinking, excusing her from orders? Didn't he understand that the success of her assignment depended on these men? General Arnold's words whispered through her memory. *Show these boys that this plane is so easy to fly, even a woman can do it. The only way this war can be won is with the Super Fortress.*

Maggie blotted her face with the soft cloth. By the end of the day, she was going to need a hot bath and a dose of Aunt Merrilee's home cooking. Bending down, Maggie lifted the lid of her foot locker. A piece of folded paper fluttered in the air before landing on the cement floor. Picking it up, she unfolded it. The edges crumpled under her tightening fingertips as she read it once, then over again.

"The only good WASP is a dead one."

Raindrops splattered against Wesley's T-shirt and fanned out over his shoulders and down his back, offering some relief to his heated skin. A light breeze rustled through the thatch of hardwoods, green blossoms shimmying in the air like fields of new heather that had danced below as he flew toward London to meet the enemy.

Wesley drew in a measured breath. A perfect day for a run if he hadn't sensed a shift in Maggie.

He glanced over his shoulder at his girl pilot. She was keeping up with the squad step for step, a fact that didn't surprise him, knowing Jackie Cochran. The woman was bent on teaching her fly girls "the Army way," and from the looks of things, succeeding. No, the physical aspect of the job wasn't a concern.

"How are you doing back there, Ms. Daniels?" Wesley waited for her response. Only the rain lightly thumping against the new leaves answered him. "Ms. Daniels?"

"Yes, sir?"

At least, she'd heard him this time. "How are you holding up?"

"Never better, sir."

"Good." But Wesley wasn't buying it. Something had clouded Maggie's thinking between the time he had directed her to the ladies' changing room and when she had rejoined the squad. But what? His mind wrestled with the possibilities but came up empty.

Wesley sucked in a breath through pursed lips. The air blazed a fiery path down his windpipe before bursting into flames throughout his chest. He concentrated on the cadence of heavy footsteps echoing against the beaten dirt road between Marietta Square and Kennesaw Mountain.

The tree line thinned, giving way to a field. The velvety stems of dandelions stung his shins like nests of angry yellow jackets. Off in the distance, over the next grove of towering treetops, sat Kennesaw Mountain. If he closed his eyes, he could almost smell the gunpowder from eighty years before, hear the sickening thuds as the mini balls hit their blue or gray target.

"Look, Mama! Soldiers!"

Wesley searched amongst the foliage for the source of the childish voice. There, beside a pink dogwood, stood a young boy, no more than nine or ten. Towheaded and skinny, his mud-caked knees peeked out from holes in his threadbare denims.

Merrilee had told him how tent cities had sprung up in the outlying areas where the Civilian Conservation Corps had set up camps five years ago. Folks must still be desperate for work if this patchwork of tents with strings of wet clothes connecting each canvas like telephone wires was anything to go by.

"Tent trash," a man behind him whispered.

Wesley's gut tightened with anger. The boy flinched as if he'd been slapped before retreating back into the woods. These folks weren't trash, simply in need. He'd have to make things right, find the boy and his family then figure out if there was any way he could help. Merrilee had a heart for these people. He would talk to her, maybe offer to buy some of the vegetables from Merrilee's victory garden to share with them.

Cresting the mud-walled trench near the base of the mountain, Wesley picked up the pace, sprinting for the open field like a runner pushing toward the finish line. The tall grass swished softly against him, the muscles in his calves and thighs screaming in protest.

"Company, halt!"

Men fell out around him, some dropping to their knees while a few landed flat on their backs. Wesley did a quick search before focusing in on Maggie. Bent forward with her hands resting on her knees, Maggie blew great puffs of air through puckered lips. She pressed her chin to her chest, stretching out the tight muscles in her neck.

Wesley jogged toward her. "Keep moving, Maggie. You'll be glad you did this evening."

"I don't think anything is going to help my poor muscles later on, sir." Maggie glanced up and smiled.

He studied her for a moment. Rain-soaked strands of hair curled in waves against her forehead and along her flushed cheeks, giving her a girl-next-door look that any red-blooded man would find hard to resist. Her oversized sweatshirt grazed the hemline of her shorts, hiding whatever curves the woman possessed. Only her mud-spattered legs, long and shapely, gave a hint to Maggie's feminine form.

Wesley gulped in a lungful of air. Okay, so there was an attraction, but he wouldn't allow himself to be swayed from his objectives. Not by some girl pilot who had no business behind the controls of a flying coffin like the B-29.

"Just keep moving," Wesley ordered, his voice gruffer than he would have liked.

Maggie's smile faded. "Yes, sir."

Wesley broke into a walk, and the scent of fresh earth slowly replaced the fierce burning in his lungs. He stopped and flexed, first to one side then the other. Through the mist of moisture clouding his vision, he could still see a colorful burst of dogwoods, azaleas and bluebells blooming on the mountain. Beth always loved this time of the season. Every year, he'd goad her into a springtime run around the village where their grandfather had lived. And every year, she'd followed him.

But not this year. Never again.

Wesley snapped into a rigid stance. Time to get back to the business of winning a war. "Attention!"

The squad wobbled to their places, their backs ramrod straight, though Wesley noted some were struggling to breathe. Well, too bad. Someone should have thought of that before mouthing off about the tent camp. "I would have thought that a five-mile run through the backwoods would silence any further comments from the peanut gallery." He weaved his way in and out of the straight lines until he stood in front of Maggie. "Obviously one of you thinks you can still flap your gums and get away with it."

The woman tensed. So she had heard the comment about the tent camp. Good. At least she knew the kind of men she was up against.

Wesley marched over to Bob Meldrum, a good pilot, though a gust of wind could probably blow the man over. "So who was it, Meldrum? Who made that crack back there about the tent camp?"

The man's silence sent a chill down his spine. Time seemed to slow down as he waited for an answer.

But there wasn't one.

So that's how things were going to go. "See you at the top, Lieutenant."

The man's face blanched and, for a minute, Wesley thought he might break. With one deep breath, he slowly jogged to the tree line along the mountain's rim, then faded into the landscape.

Over the next few minutes, Wesley called out one name, and then another, giving them the same opportunity to come forward with the information he sought, but to no avail.

Finally, it was down to Maggie and Jimbo. Wesley paced back and forth, wearing down the new growth of weeds. He didn't care if he had to send every last one of his squadron up that mountain. No one under his command would treat others with so little respect.

Maybe Maggie would give him his answer. Wesley shrugged. He knew what he had to do, but it didn't mean he liked it.

Wesley stopped directly in front of her and leaned toward her, close enough for her to hear him. "Maybe the little princess will be more accommodating."

She jerked her head up, her gaze tangling with his as if daring him to take Merrilee's story about her name and use it against her. Disappointment pressed her mouth into a taut line.

Shame knotted in his throat. She had thought him a better man. Well, so had he. "Maggie?"

"What, sir?"

The woman answered as sweetly as if she were pouring tea to a group of housewives rather than mucking through the woods with a squadron of men! Why couldn't she simply tell him who the offending officer was and be done with it?

Whether they like it or not, they're my brothers in arms.

Her silent words drifted over him. The last thing he wanted to do was send her up that mountain, but he would if forced.

But not before giving her one last chance. "You and I both know Jimbo made that comment."

The words came out in a whisper, more like words of love than an accusation. Maggie didn't flinch, continuing to stare straight ahead. If Jimbo had made that hateful comment, then Maggie refused to play judge and jury.

"Ms. Daniels?"

She responded by lifting her chin and, for the first time since he'd met her, held her tongue.

Wesley edged closer. Blast, the woman was stubborn! But he couldn't deny the respect he also felt for her decision. He drew in a breath, the words at the tip of his tongue.

But the woman beat him to it. Jogging past him, Maggie gave him a quick salute. "See you at the top, sir."

CHAPTER FIVE

"When are you going to put me on the flight schedule, Captain?" Maggie asked as she walked beside Wesley down the corridor.

He glanced down at his clipboard. Two weeks of avoiding her question had been difficult, especially when the flight assignment appeared to be the only thing on her mind. What would she say if he told her the truth, that he had no intentions of putting her in the cockpit until he had been given a direct order? He decided against it. Better to leave the woman in the dark.

"I believe this is our stop, Ms. Daniels," he replied, opening the door, then stood aside to let her pass.

He almost ran into her when she ground to a halt just inside the door. "What are we doing here?"

He smiled to himself. Moving up her testing in the Bell's pressure laboratory had been a brilliant idea. A steel box the size of a crypt stood in the corner, and an occasional hiss disturbed the silence of the room. Oxygen cylinders lined the wall behind the man he recognized as Wib Hubbard sitting at the controls. Wib had been a sophomore the year Wesley had arrived at Georgia Tech, an aeronautical engineering major just like himself, and a good one.

"Wib."

The man glanced up from the instrument panel and gave him a brief nod. "Wesley. How are you doing?"

But when his gaze shifted to Maggie, he blinked as if witnessing a mirage. The stool he was sitting on fell as he stood and hurried to a desk in the opposite corner.

"You haven't answered my question, Captain Hicks," Maggie said, a hint of aggravation lacing her voice. Her pale green eyes bore straight through him like a drill bit through cadmium-plated steel. "What are we doing in the pressure lab?"

At least, he'd gotten her off the subject of flight schedules for the moment. "I can't assign you to the schedule until I'm convinced you're capable of handling the stratospheric temperature changes and pressure conditions at the altitudes the B-29 flies."

"Don't you think the boys in Washington thought of that before even considering me for this mission, Captain?" Maggie crossed her arms and stared at him as if he didn't have a lick of sense. "I've done this before and passed."

"I haven't seen those results yet." Wesley glanced back down at his clipboard. No, he hadn't read those results. Hadn't even examined her file like he should have, but he had heard plenty. If only half the stories were true, it was no wonder the brass had picked Maggie for this mission. She was most likely the best pilot in his squadron.

"Sir, with all due respect, I don't understand," she stammered, her hands balled into tight knots beside her. He really shouldn't get this much enjoyment out of keeping Maggie off balance, but he did. "I've trained the exact same way that all your men have, and I've passed all the tests." She paused for a moment. "Why am I the only one in the squadron being retested?"

Because I made a promise to keep you safe, he thought. A twinge of guilt raced through him. Why should he feel dishonest about keeping his word? He glared at her. "Are you questioning my orders?"

"No, sir. Simply inquiring." Her gaze met his, never wavering, never retreating. She must have realized there would be no more discussion because she snapped out a quick salute then headed for a row of flight suits hanging along the wall.

Wesley stared at her. If only the rest of his squad had an ounce of the spunk and loyalty she'd demonstrated over the past several days. He'd seen it when she'd chosen Kennesaw Mountain over ratting out Jimbo, though the truth had eventually come out, and the man had been punished. While he didn't agree with her decision, he respected her sense of duty.

She rejoined him, a leather and fleece jumpsuit slung over her arm, a pair of boots dangling from her hand. "I hope this one fits better than the last monkey suit I had to wear. It was so large I had to fold up the sleeves and pant legs to reach the controls."

Wesley hadn't thought about that. Standard army-issue wasn't made to fit the female form. Looked like the army was no more prepared for women flyers than he was.

"Where's the ladies' restroom?"

Wib joined them. "Down the hall to the left, ma'am."

"Thank you." Maggie gave the man a grateful smile then turned to Wesley. "I'll be ready in a few minutes."

After the door clicked shut behind her,

Wib turned to Wesley. "You're not seriously thinking about putting that girl through the pressure chamber, are you?"

Wesley didn't have to ask the engineer's opinion of a female in his laboratory. His wide eyes and slack jaw were proof enough. He clapped a hand on Wib's shoulder. "Don't worry about it. She's done this before."

"But I haven't," the man answered. "And there's nothing in the manual about testing a woman. What if she gets sick or passes out in the middle of the test? What am I supposed to do then?"

The image of Maggie prostrate on the floor of the pressure chamber bothered him. But he had a job to do. "Look, she's got to be tested. Major Evans is considering her for a copilot position on the B-29."

"The War Department's going to put a woman at the helm of the flying coffin?" Wib shook his head. "They're having enough trouble getting the boys into the cockpit as it is."

"Yeah, I know, that is why General Arnold decided to let the WASP give it a try," Wesley replied with a sigh. "He figures that if a girl can fly the fort, then the guys will see that it's not that dangerous."

Wib didn't look convinced. "I don't know,

Wesley. It's one thing to ration food and gas and stuff, but putting our women in danger? I don't feel right about it."

Neither did he, but it didn't matter what he thought. Maggie would eventually get her flight assignment and off she'd go, in harm's way.

Away from his protection.

Uncomfortable with that thought, Wesley scratched the back of his head. "Look, just do the test. If anything happens to her, I'll take full responsibility."

"Thank you, Wesley, but you don't have to do that. We've all got a job to do." Wib walked back toward the steel chamber. "Even when we don't like it."

"I appreciate that, Wib." Wesley jammed his pencil into his pocket. *Lord, why am I fighting this battle for Maggie? I don't even want her in one of my planes.*

"Are we ready to get started?" Maggie asked from the doorway.

Wesley turned to look at her. The leather flight suit hung off her petite frame as if she were a little girl playing in her mother's closet. Rolls of thick leather pooled over the sides of her loose boots. The hard soles clunked heavily against the tile floor when she started toward him.

Wesley met her halfway, working hard not

to notice how dainty she appeared, even though the oversized jacket and pants erased all signs of her feminine curves. White fleece from her flight cap rimmed her face, making her cheeks appear even rosier than usual.

How could a woman who looked so lovely voluntarily climb behind the controls of an untested plane?

Wesley reached for her elbow. "Here, let me help you."

Through the soft leather, her arm stiffened beneath his touch. "Do you help the rest of your men like this?"

"No," he replied, holding on to her just a bit tighter as they took a couple of steps. "But they're not about to slip out of their boots."

Maggie surprised him by laughing. "I guess you've got a point there."

It took several more seconds to finally reach the steel double doors of the chamber. She leaned against him as she slowly lifted first one foot, then the other over the metal railing.

Wib joined them at the door. "Good afternoon, Ms. Daniels. I'm Wib Anderson, lead engineer in the pressure lab. I'll be conducting your test today."

Maggie pushed up her sleeves in an attempt to free her hand, then extended it to the man. "Nice to meet you, Wib."

"Good to meet you, too." Wib held her hand just a second longer than Wesley thought necessary before letting go. "I have to be honest with you, ma'am. I've never tested a woman in the chamber before."

"I understand. Just remember that I'm going to be flying at the same altitudes as the guys are, so I need to be tested exactly like them." Maggie tugged on the straps of her flight cap, using her hand to push clouds of fiery curls beneath the leathery binding.

"But what if you pass out?" He looked back at Wesley as if for assurance. "It has happened with the men a couple of times, you know."

Her lips curved into a playful smile that sent warmth racing down Wesley's spine. "Better here than at thirty thousand feet."

A chuckle rose from deep down, but Wesley caught it before it had the chance to escape. That was another thing he realized he liked about Maggie. Her cheeky sense of humor.

Wib must have liked her joke, too, because he laughed. "Okay then. But please tell me if you feel sick or get too cold, won't you?"

"I will."

"Then let's get started." Wib walked back

to the instrument panel and sat down.

Wesley had never noticed how thick the hatch was until he closed one panel of doors. He leaned inside. Maggie had already slipped the oxygen mask over her nose and mouth, then pulled the straps tight.

"You remember how this works?"

One perfectly arched eyebrow lifted. "I'm pretty sure I can handle it, Captain."

"I'm ready," Wib called out from behind him.

Wesley stepped back. With a quick salute, Maggie grabbed the door handle. The clang of the solid steel and the click of the lock had never bothered him, but, today, the sounds echoed in his ears.

He walked around to where Wib sat, holding a microphone. "Okay, Ms. Daniels. I'm going to take it through the standard procedures and see how you do."

"Roger." Maggie's voice cracked over the speakers.

For the next few minutes, Wib put Maggie through the paces, first at lower altitudes where the P-47 and P-51 were flown, then at the B-29's levels. "How are you doing in there?"

"It's a bit cold, probably because this monkey suit doesn't fit right." Her voice was strong in a sea of cracks and pops.

"Other than that, I'm great."

"She's holding up a lot better than I would have thought." Wib adjusted a gauge. "She's a natural at this."

It figures. Wesley nodded. "Great."

But it wasn't great, wasn't even close to being good, not if he wanted to keep his word to Merrilee and keep Maggie safe, at least for a while. Maybe he should give her an assignment ferrying repaired planes back to their bases. Anything to keep her out of the Super Fortress.

Grief crashed through his veins. No, he'd broken one promise, and his sister had paid for it with her life. His landlady was counting on him, and nothing on this earth was going to stop him from keeping his word.

"Ms. Daniels, we've completed our testing. I need to get you readjusted to room pressure. Then you'll be good to go," Wib said into the microphone.

A few moments later, the double doors swung open, and Maggie stepped out. If she wobbled a bit, it was more from the oversized boots than any ill effects of the test. The thick leather soles clunked against the floor as she walked over to him. She pulled off her cap, shaking out a stream of auburn curls that flowed over her shoulders and midway down her back.

"Not bad for a girl, huh?" Her smile taunted him.

Wesley glanced at her. None of his pilots had ever looked as rosy or as appealing as Maggie after being put through the drill. It felt as if he were being tested, not her.

He cleared his throat. "You'd better get changed. We've got some preflight checks to do before the day is gone."

The spark went out of her expression. "Yes, sir."

She was barely halfway across the room when Major Evans entered. His hand raised in a salute, Wesley snapped to attention. Whatever salute Maggie had given the major had been covered by her sleeve.

"At ease." Evans walked over to Maggie. "I heard you were in the pressure chamber, Ms. Daniels. How'd it go?"

"It went very well, sir, but Captain Hicks can give you more information." She gathered her pants' legs into her fists. "If you'll excuse me, I need to get changed."

"Oh, yes." The major stood to the side as Maggie headed out the door. He walked toward Wesley, a wide smile across his face. "How did our girl pilot do?"

Our girl? What was he doing, sharing Maggie now? Wesley held out Maggie's test results. "Very well, sir. She didn't have any problems with the atmospheric temperatures and pressure conditions. Wib feels that she's a natural."

The major nabbed the papers out of his hand and gave them the once-over. "Good! Then it's time we talk about putting her on the flight schedule."

Wesley drew in a deep breath. "I'm not sure if she's ready for that yet, sir."

"You know Jackie Cochran, Captain. She trains those girls just like they're men." A smile slowly spread across the officer's face. "And Ms. Daniels isn't some greenhorn. I've done some snooping around. Did you know she was the top trainer at the flight school in South Carolina?"

He really needed to read her files. "I didn't know that, sir."

Evans gave him a stern look. "Let's take a walk."

He was in trouble. It wasn't a big secret that the major liked to use his walks to correct his officers. Wesley followed the man out of the room. He didn't have to guess where he'd made his mistake. This was about Maggie.

"I learned a bit of information about you today too." They turned the first corner before the major glanced at him. "My condolences on your sister."

Wesley flinched. The phrase still had the power to punch him in the gut. "Thank you, sir."

"Why didn't you tell me your sister died in a ferrying accident for the Royal Air Force?"

What had he been thinking, keeping the details about Beth's death a secret? Maybe it was his way of denying the truth; if he had been a better brother, given Beth a little more guidance after their mother died, she might still be alive. Maybe even settled down with a husband and a houseful of kids. Instead, Beth was gone.

And he was responsible for that fact. Turning his head, Wesley looked the man straight in the eyes. "I didn't think it was relative to my job here. I'm sorry, sir."

"It has to be tough working with a girl pilot." The major gave Wesley a look of compassion before his voice went stern. "But Maggie Daniels has been trained to do a job, and she needs to be doing it. Is that understood?"

"Yes, sir."

"Good. I expect to see her name on the next flight assignment." Major Evans slapped him on his shoulder.

Loud and clear. Wesley nodded. "Yes, sir."

As the major walked away, Wesley took a

deep breath. So he hadn't been able to dodge a bullet. Whether he liked it or not, Maggie Daniels was about to get her wish.

"Aunt Merrilee?"

Maggie burst through the kitchen door, the succulent aroma of roasted chicken mingled with fresh bread making her mouth water. Lunchtime had passed with her up to her elbows in grease, making valve adjustments on a Thunderbolt. With supper still a good hour away, Maggie was hoping for one of Merrilee's applesauce cookies to tide her over.

The warmth from the stove radiated throughout the stone-walled room, wrapping Maggie in a cocoon of homey comfort. Scouring the countertop, she spied the half-filled cookie jar. She'd been looking forward to one of these cookies since she'd left Merrilee baking them this morning. With sugar in short supply, she hated the thought of missing out on the treat.

After laying out a couple of cookies on a paper towel, Maggie made a beeline for the ice box for the milk. She retrieved a glass from the cabinet and settled herself at the table.

It had been another long day. She closed her eyes and took a deep breath, twisting her head from side to side. Not that her time in the pressure chamber or checking out engine belts had been difficult. Compared to the routine she kept before reporting to Bell, the past few days had been a walk in the park. She frowned. Bored was more like it. She'd been at the Bell for over two weeks now, and the closest she'd come to touching the sky was on Claire's tree swing.

Good thing she hadn't told anyone about the note.

Opening her eyes, Maggie reached for the pitcher and tilted it toward her waiting glass, her mind on the scrap of paper she'd stuck back down in her foot locker. She'd been shocked at first, and if she was honest with herself, just a bit scared. But once she settled down and thought about it for a while, she realized the note was no different from the threats they had dealt with at Sweetwater, and those hadn't kept Commander Cochran from getting them trained.

But Wesley Hicks wasn't Jackie Cochran.

Maggie broke off a piece of cookie and dunked it in her milk. No, Wesley Hicks was a different piece of work altogether, but Maggie couldn't fault him on his abilities. More than once over the last fourteen days, she had witnessed the way his squadron relied on his leadership, his fairness in conflicting issues that had arose among the men. She had even begun to wonder if the slight shift in their attitude toward her was due to the captain's influence more than her hard work.

Tossing the bite in her mouth, Maggie sucked milk out of the cookie until it disintegrated into a million pieces. Had she been going about earning the men's respect the wrong way? Maybe you have to catch the lead dog to get the pack to follow.

The screen door of the kitchen slammed shut. "Margaret Rose Daniels! I baked those cookies for dessert this evening!"

"I missed lunch today." Maggie gulped down the last of her milk. "You wouldn't want a girl who is serving her country to starve to death, would you?"

Merrilee huffed as she pulled her flowered apron from a nearby drawer and tugged it over her head. "What made you forget to eat this time?"

"A blown engine on a Thunderbolt."

Her aunt eyed her for a moment, then smiled as she tied the apron around her waist. "Well, I can't take food out of the mouth of one of our service people, now can I?" She walked over to the cookie jar and extracted another one. "Here," she said, handing it to Maggie. "I always make a few extra if I've got the sugar."

"Thanks." Maggie broke off a piece and popped it in her mouth. "How did your day go?"

"Busy." Merrilee pumped water into a kettle and set it on the stove. "I heard Mr. Jarvis got in a shipment late yesterday afternoon, so I was over at his grocery store before he even unlocked this morning." She opened the door to the stove, checked the pilot light, then quickly shut it. "I swear you don't know what a fight it is just to get a good piece of meat these days. Once I made it home, I spent the rest of the afternoon weeding out the garden. I was hoping tonight after dinner you could help me pick the tomatoes. That is, if you don't have anything planned."

"Just a quiet evening at home." Maggie leaned back and stretched her legs out beneath the table. Mercy, it felt good to relax.

Merrilee gave her a disapproving look as she walked to the ice box. "That's not very ladylike, sweetheart."

"No disrespect, but I seriously doubt very many 'ladies' have been hunched over the engine of a P-47 all day."

"More than there were three years ago.

Anyway, that doesn't give you permission to slouch."

Gracious gravy! Maggie didn't care what she looked like but she wouldn't do anything to upset her sweet aunt. Planting her feet on the floor, Maggie pushed herself upright in her chair.

"There. Don't you feel better?"

"Not really." Maggie brushed the crumbs into a delicious hill in front of her. "I haven't flown once since I got here."

"That doesn't surprise me," Merrilee answered, retrieving two jars of canned green beans from the pantry. "Wesley warned you he was going to break you in to the squad's routine slowly."

"Yeah, but snails move faster than he does." Maggie crossed her arms on the kitchen table. "At this rate, the war will be over before I get my first flight assignment."

"Be patient, sweetheart. Rome wasn't built in a day." A whispered hiss exploded from each lid as Merrilee opened the jars. "Why don't you talk to him about it?"

"I have." Maggie rested her chin in the palm of her hand. "But he keeps stalling. I have a hard enough time with the guys without whining about the schedule."

A motherly warmth enveloped her as Merrilee slid her arms around Maggie's shoulders, her cheek nestled on top of her head. "What are you going to do if those men never accept you as a pilot?"

Maggie leaned back into her aunt's embrace. She'd heard the question before, listened as the girls argued over it in the barracks during WASP training. She wasn't sure how she'd handle it if the guys never accepted her as an equal. They had to know that this country needed women who could take the burden of ferrying and training from the men who were sorely needed at the front. The knowledge that God had opened this door for her meant it would be wrong not to go through it, even if she was ridiculed.

Maggie opened her eyes and glanced at her aunt. "Then at least I can stand before the Lord and know I've tried my best."

"That's all any of us can do, dear." Merrilee pressed a kiss to her forehead then moved away.

Maggie stood up and followed her to the sink. "Well, with no flights, I'll be around here a lot more. Doing what, I don't have a clue."

"I'm sure we can find some projects to keep you occupied."

The expression on her aunt's face led Maggie to believe she already had something in mind. "Like what?"

Instead of answering, Merrilee went to the kitchen door, looking around outside as if she thought there were spies in Grandma Daniels's rose bush. She finally shut the door.

"Merrilee?"

Her aunt extracted a handkerchief from the pocket of her dress and patted her lips. "I'm sorry for being so secretive, but if your uncle James heard what I'm doing, he'd pitch another one of his fits and start up that talk about taking the house away again."

"What are you up to, Aunt Merrilee?"

Merrilee leaned back against the door. "A few days ago, I had a visit from Preacher Williams and his wife, and they told me about a tent camp they had been ministering to."

"Are you talking about the one next to Kennesaw Mountain?"

"That's the one. Anyway, it's crowded and a few of the families would like to find a place closer to the plant."

Maggie could vouch for the crush of tents in that small field. "What has that got to do with you?"

Merrliee smiled. "I gave Preacher Williams permission to use a clearing at the back of my property to house some of those folks."

Merrilee was right. Uncle James would have a stroke if he knew. "How many families are we talking about?"

"Four, maybe five. But it's near the back corner of the spread where nobody ever goes." Merrilee lowered her voice. "This has to be just between me and you."

Maggie nodded. The biggest problem she saw was keeping this information off the community's radar range. "I wouldn't dream of spilling the beans. What would you like me to do?"

"I knew you would help." Merrilee beamed at her. "I'm going to try and get out there a couple of days a week. You know, to take their mail to them or carry whatever extras I get out of the garden to barter." A serious line replaced her smile. "I don't think those people have enough to eat."

"You've already met them?"

"Yesterday afternoon. They had some beans and a cake of cornbread, but not much else."

"Why not just give them the extras?"

Merrilee shook her head. "I've tried, but these people have their pride. They believe if a man doesn't work, he doesn't eat."

Maggie didn't understand. Why wouldn't a person accept food if their family was hungry? She popped the last piece of cookie in her mouth. "I can probably go out there once or twice a week."

"I know that's a lot to ask, but I just hate the thought of them going hungry."

The idea of people going without food a stone's throw from their home bothered Maggie as well. She stood and joined her aunt at the kitchen door. "I'd be happy to."

"You don't know how much I appreciate you helping me like this." Merrilee wrapped her arms around her and gave her a gentle hug. "You've grown into such a sweet woman."

Maggie linked her arms around her aunt's trim waist. "At least it gives me something to do while I wait for Wesley Hicks to put me on the schedule."

Stepping back, Merrilee cupped Maggie's face between her hands. "Be patient, darling girl. Remember, God's in control."

Maggie nodded. But she was tired of waiting. When did her life begin?

"Dinner's almost ready." Merrilee pulled the apron strings loose and tugged it over her head. "I've got some ripe tomatoes in the garden that will go nicely with dinner. Be right back."

Maggie watched through the window as her aunt cut across the yard and around the corner of the house. Momma, Aunt

Merrilee, Grandma Daniels. All of them had taken care of their families, working the fields in the summer, storing vegetables for the winter, always with a ready smile and a set of patient hands. God had blessed her with such wonderful role models. If she could be half as good as either of the three, she'd consider herself a blessed woman.

A movement from outside caught her eye. She rose and walked over to the sink. At the edge of the woods bordering Merrilee's yard, Jimbo stood, looking over his shoulder as if he were up to no good before slipping into the trees.

You can give me a hard time, Jimbo Hayes, but not my aunt! Quickly folding a handful of cookies into a dish towel, Maggie hurried toward the kitchen door.

CHAPTER SIX

Wesley ambled down the stairs, his muscles relaxed after a hot shower. Nothing beat the feel of clean clothes after a grueling workout. His five-mile run to Kennesaw Mountain had been murder today with the sky-high humidity and an electric storm threatening to burst overhead.

He'd enjoyed his visit to the tent camp. Playing stickball with Bobby and the other kids had taken his mind off the new flight schedule sitting on his desk, at least for a while. As he waved goodbye to the boys, he'd agreed to another game in the future, the weight of other promises he had broken, showered down on his soul.

Wesley stood on the bottom step. The only way he could even begin to make amends was to prove that the B-29 was flight-ready and train his squad to do the job his sister had believed in enough to die for. One that Maggie Daniels had dreamed of all her life.

At least Maggie will be getting her wish.

He'd spent the better part of his day in Major Evans's office, going over next week's schedule. His goal was to keep Maggie's hours in the air to a minimum. In the end, Major Evans had given him his orders.

Put Maggie in the cockpit. Now.

The door opened. Edie Michaels, her arms loaded down with wrapped parcels, surged through the doorway.

Wesley moved toward her. "Let me help you with those."

"Thank you, Wesley. You can just leave them right here for now." She deposited her packages on the nearby loveseat. "How was your day today?"

"The usual." He stacked up her papered boxes so that they wouldn't tumble across the foyer's floor. "And you?"

"Any day off is a good day." Edie tugged her gloves off and laid them with her purse on the front table.

"Looks like you've cleaned out the local merchants."

"Not quite. Some of those packages are for Maggie."

"Why didn't she go with you?"

"I suppose if I'd held the keys to her airplane hostage, she would have." Edie smiled, a teasing hint to her lipstick-enhanced mouth that might have appealed to him in the past. But now, it left him with the vague yearning for something more. "Anyway, she said she had to go do her daily calisthenics."

He didn't know why that news surprised him. From what he'd seen of her, when she wasn't dwarfed by her flight suit, Maggie Daniels had the shapely femininity of an all-American girl. "Why would she do that?"

"I'm not sure." Edie removed her hat pin. "But I think it has something to do with growing up with all boys."

"Maggie mentioned something about it."

Edie lifted her hat from her head and set it down. "Merrilee told me that the competition between Maggie and her cousins was horrible. She spent most of her time worrying those boys would goad Maggie into something and Maggie, being Maggie, was always bound and determined to come in first."

Wesley nodded. It was the same determined resolve he saw in the feisty redhead when she worked through a tough problem at work. "Do you know if she ever bested the boys?"

"I asked Merrilee about that, and I have to be honest, her answer struck me as strange."

"What did she say?"

Edie turned to him, her nose wrinkled in awkwardness. "Of course not. Maggie's a girl!"

Wesley blinked. No wonder his girl pilot was out to prove herself. The members of her own family didn't even believe in her abilities. For some unknown reason, he sympathized with her. How would the news of her new flight status be received by her relatives? "Do you know where I might happen to find her?"

Edie shook her head. "She's probably out in the kitchen, helping Merrilee with dinner."

"Thanks."

Wesley walked down the hall toward the back of the house. He could appreciate the pressure Maggie was under with her family. He'd had some experience with that kind of situation himself. This assignment wasn't another game to use in her competition with her cousins, not when her life depended on it.

Opening the back door, Wesley stepped out onto the screened porch and glanced toward the stone-walled building on the southern corner of the yard. A mist of smoke signaled that Merrilee was in her kitchen, busy preparing the evening's meal.

His hand on the doorknob, Wesley stopped short as Maggie came quietly out of the kitchen and headed toward the tree line at the edge of the property.

What is that woman up to now?

Behind the mesh of metal, Wesley studied her. Her exercise program seemed to agree with her, judging from the natural glow in her cheeks. Her starched short-sleeved shirt tucked neatly into the trim waist of a blue jumper, the feathery ruffles at the shoulders reminding Wesley of wings.

But this was no celestial being. His breath hitched as Maggie nervously pushed a strand of auburn hair behind her ear. This was a very real, extremely attractive woman.

Who, at the moment, was ducking into the woods.

Wesley pushed open the screen door and hurried down the staircase. At the edge of the yard, he found the beginnings of a trail. He peeked through the tree limbs, watching Maggie as she moved deeper into the woods. When she had barely slipped out of his sight, he started down the trail.

Twenty minutes later, Wesley sat crouched beneath a hickory tree. He peered over a trench like a marine ready to storm the beachhead. In the clearing below sat a group of tents like the ones he'd visited today. A team of boys played in the distance while a handful of girls grouped together near the center of the camp. A painfully thin woman worked over a fired pot, the sounds of bubbling water cascading through the green leaves. Whoever these people were, Wesley figured they hadn't been here more than a few days.

A twig broke behind him. Without thinking, he swept his leg out and felled whoever had snuck up on him. A fist flew at him, and he grabbed it, rolling over to pin the squirming creature beneath him. Only when he had subdued his prisoner did he notice the pair of pale green eyes shooting bullets at him.

He had found Maggie.

Maggie froze, her limbs tangled with Wesley's masculine arms and legs. Growing up with a pack of boys, she'd had her fill of wrestling matches, even beaten a neighborhood boy a time or two. But nothing in her twenty-one years had ever prepared her for the warmth of Wesley's breath against her cheek or the feel of his hard angles crushed against her soft curves. Like a magnet, she lifted her eyes to meet his, the silvery sparks framed against the steel blue irises like firecrackers against a night sky. He seemed startled, then intrigued. Was he feeling the same emotions she was? Or was this attraction hers alone?

Her breath caught in her lungs when his gaze slid down to her mouth and settled there. She had never been truly kissed, not with five male cousins guarding her as if she were as valuable as Fort Knox. Instinct told her that if Wesley ever took the chance and kissed her, life would never be the same.

This is almost like flying. Whatever curiosity she might have about kissing Wesley Hicks was dashed by the thought. What was she thinking, when she had a job to do? She pushed at his shoulder. "Do you usually go around knocking people over?"

"I'm sorry." Wesley rolled off to the side and sat up. "I didn't know it was you."

Maggie struggled to get to her feet. "Who'd you think it was? Mussolini?"

Was that a ghost of a smile haunting his face? "Blame it on being in the war."

She'd never thought of that, but he had a point. Being near the front lines, watching the battle unfold would change a person's perspective. Maggie brushed leaves from the seat of her pants. Her backside felt damp from the recent storm. "What are you doing out here in the first place?"

"Maybe I should be asking you that." He

stood and wiped his hand against his thighs. "What are you doing sneaking back here?"

"I'm not sneaking. I saw Jimbo slip into the woods and decided to follow him." Maggie glanced down at her hands. Red clay stained her fingertips. "I had to make sure he didn't get drunk and show up on Merrilee's door later tonight."

"And you thought you were going to stop him?" Wesley scoffed, sweeping his hand against the mud spackling the knees of his pants. "Are you nuts?"

Maybe she was crazy, but Merrilee had enough problems to handle without the test pilot adding to them. "I didn't do such a bad job of handling Jimbo the other night."

"I was there, remember?"

Yes, she remembered. How could she forget how handsome he looked with his hair ruffled? Her fingers had itched to smooth a stray strand from his forehead. She'd had to move to keep from acting on her impulse. What stayed with her the most was the way Wesley had fed Jimbo sips of coffee with no reprimands. It was a kindness she hadn't expected.

Maggie glared at him. "I can't have Jimbo causing problems at Merrilee's."

"You know how mean that man is." His hands grasped her shoulders, causing goose

111

bumps up and down her arms. "He's twice as bad when he's been drinking."

She shook his hands away. "You're telling me he's shown up at my aunt's drunk before, and you didn't do anything about it?"

"What was I supposed to do? Not let him out of the house?" Wesley stretched out to his full height, those eyes that had just moments ago made her shiver now glaring at her in anger. "As much as I hate it, Jimbo isn't breaking any laws."

"You could have had him arrested for disturbing the peace."

Wesley was quiet for a moment before he spoke. "Merrilee wouldn't let me."

She should have known that her aunt wasn't in the dark about this. Merrilee had to know Uncle James would have a field day if he found out. "My aunt thinks too much with her heart sometimes."

"One of the qualities I like about her."

She glanced at Wesley. "Me, too. It just gets her in trouble at times."

"And there's nothing that you do that worries her?"

Maggie sighed. She refused to let him bait her, not when he held all of her hopes and dreams in his hands. "Look. Why don't we find Jimbo and make sure he's okay?"

"Sounds like a good idea." He pointed to an area beyond the ridge. "There's a group of tents like the ones at Kennesaw Mountain right over that hill. A couple of women were out doing the wash. Maybe they saw him."

So much for keeping Aunt Merrilee's secret. "Let's go ask them."

"Are they supposed to be there?"

She looked at him. His face was a mask of such genuine concern, she couldn't find it in her to be annoyed. But then, his protectiveness was aimed at her aunt, not her, and she found that quite touching. With Wesley, Merrilee's covert operation would remain a secret.

She nodded. "A few of the families wanted to be closer to the plant, so Merrilee told them they could set up their tents here."

"That was good of her." His mouth lifted in a soft smile. A pang of envy shot through Maggie.

"Yes, well, Merrilee's a nice person," she stammered. Of course, her aunt was a good woman, a great woman. No doubt in her mind about that.

She stole a glance at Wesley. What would it feel like to be on the receiving end of one of his smiles? Have this man look at her with such respect and admiration? Her stomach fluttered, and she grimaced. Those kinds of thoughts had no place floating around in her head. God had a plan for her, and that would have to be enough.

Maggie took off toward the camp. "We're burning daylight."

"Now, wait a minute." His fingers wrapped around her elbow and pulled her to a stop. "Do you think it's such a good idea to stroll in there unannounced?"

"Why not? Merrilee met them yesterday. She thought they were nice."

Wesley seemed to struggle for words. "And loose lips sink ships."

In all the fuss, she hadn't looked at it from that point of view. There were people in this world who wouldn't think twice about taking advantage of her aunt's kind heart. Invading the woods close to the bomber plant would serve their own ill purposes.

Stars and stripes! Why hadn't she asked more questions about the people Merrilee had already met? She stared off in the direction of the camp, the canvas tops barely in view. "I didn't even think about the possibilities."

"Don't be too hard on yourself. It's not something I would have thought of a few years ago."

"So you'd rather err on the side of caution?" She glanced at him as they walked toward the campsite.

His soft chuckle caused most of her concerns to melt away. "Come on. If Merrilee has met them, they can't be too dangerous."

When they reached the rim of the ravine, Wesley slid down to the outskirts of the campsite, then turned. He held his hand to her. "Here."

Maggie stared at his outstretched hand. Wesley wanted to help her. All the boys she had ever known had left her to slide down hills on her backside, leaving such courtesies at the movie house with Cary Grant or Jimmy Stewart. It seemed so perfectly romantic, there within the velvet-laden walls of the theater.

But to have an attractive man — no, she corrected, *this* attractive man — holding out his hand to her, ready to help her, was better than anything Hollywood could cook up. She slipped her hand into his, threading her fingers between his. A pleasant warmth spread through her as his other arm went around her waist.

"Take it easy. It's slippery here," he warned her.

Maggie took a careful step, her hand firmly in his. She let him lead her, though she knew every root and rock in this particular hill, indulging in a bit of make-believe. Like the fizz of a soda squirting out of the soda fountain, she felt all bubbly inside.

Her foot slipped, the magic replaced by reality. She had an assignment to complete and so much to prove to her family and her friends. For some reason she couldn't fathom, she added Wesley's name to the list.

The minute her feet were planted on level ground, Maggie tugged her hand free. "Thank you."

"Anytime, Ace." Wesley released his grasp on her waist. "Anytime."

Maggie didn't have time to think about the tenderness she'd detected in his voice when she heard a loud greeting. "Hello!"

A band of girls not much younger than herself tripped up a recently marked path toward them, chattering like little magpies. She couldn't make out what they were chirping about, but one look at their threadbare dresses and scrawny arms and legs told her that Merrilee had been right. These people were starving and in desperate need.

"One at a time, ladies," Wesley called out over the roar of girlish voices. "One at a time."

The cackling stopped, replaced by the tit-

116

ter of youthful giggles. Wesley shot her a look of pure male satisfaction and smiled. So he could turn the heads of some naive teenagers. Good for him, though the hot coal in the pit of her stomach reminded her that she didn't like it one bit. She glanced back at the girls. "Now, tell us. What is going on?"

"Someone broke into our camp this afternoon and stole most of our food," the short brunette, who was the obvious spokesperson for the group, answered. "Our flour and meal, and all of the sugar."

"Did anyone contact the police?" Wesley asked.

Maggie worried her lower lip. If Chief Hartley was called in about the robbery, how long would it be before Merrilee's secret was out, and the whole town knew about this tent camp? "If it just happened, they probably haven't had time to contact the chief yet."

"The police don't have much to do with us anyway." A tall blonde treated Wesley to a shy smile that Maggie found altogether too forward for a young girl of her age.

But Wesley didn't seem to notice. Instead, he turned to Maggie. "Has Merrilee got enough supplies to give these people until I can talk to Major Evans?"

Maggie nodded. Why did this man's thoughtfulness move her more than anyone else's? Maybe it was because he had seen the horrors of war and managed to hang on to his faith. Whatever it was, it had a strange effect on her.

"Girls!" Maggie looked up to see a tired-looking woman, her pale gray dress faded from what Maggie was sure was once a vivid blue. "Get on back to your chores. Now go on." As the girls ran back into the heart of the camp, the woman faced Maggie and Wesley. "I don't know what they've been telling you, but there ain't nothing wrong."

"But they said you'd been robbed," Wesley said.

The woman shook her head. "Them girls are just making up stuff. We shared our supplies with one of our kinfolk who was running a little low."

"Who is this person?" Wesley asked.

"My brother-in-law. He's been having a hard time since he lost my sister and their baby a few months ago," the woman answered. The shroud of sadness that cloaked her caused a shiver to run through Maggie. "But he's doing better now."

Could this woman's brother-in-law be Jimbo? He had been heading this way when she'd been ambushed. She'd have to run

118

the idea by Wesley later.

"I'm so sorry." Maggie reached out and touched the young woman's hand. "Is there anything we can do?"

"No." A nervous expression crossed the woman's face, as if she regretted speaking her piece. "Nothing's been taken that wasn't given freely."

"We were just concerned, that's all." Maggie looked around. "You've fixed up a nice place here . . . um . . ."

"Eliza Beth Cox."

"Are you related to the Coxes from Bremen?"

"That's my aunt and uncle." She gave them a wary smile. "How do you know them?"

She exchanged a look with Wesley. Thank goodness, his suspicions hadn't been founded. "We went to church with them before they moved. I'm Maggie Daniels, Jeb and Mae Belle's daughter."

"Merrilee's niece?" Her eyes sparkled, as if the mention of the Daniels name had lightened her burden. "It's so kind of your aunt to allow us to pitch our camp out here. This is better than we could have hoped for."

"She'll be so pleased." Maggie nodded to Wesley. "This is Captain Wesley Hicks."

The woman gave him a slight nod. "Sir."

"The pleasure is mine."

Maggie pointed to a white bit of cloth in her hand. "What's that?"

Eliza Beth stretched out a snowy handkerchief, a braided vine of pink peonies and sunny daisies making a neat trail along the corners. "I like to stitch."

"That's lovely. So detailed."

The woman blushed. "Thank you."

"I've never been very good with a needle." Maggie almost touched the threads before remembering her dirty hands. "I don't have enough patience for it."

"You've been working on your flying, Ace."

Maggie lowered her gaze. The way Wesley said it, as though having her head in the clouds was a good thing, filled her being with a lightheartedness she'd never experienced.

She couldn't think about that now, not with these people hungry and in need of food. "You know, Momma's birthday is coming up soon. She'd appreciate needlework like this." She looked up at Eliza Beth. "Would you be interested in a trade?"

"What are you offering?"

A quick look around the camp proved that these people were in dreadful need of food

120

and necessities. She had to be careful not to offer too much, or Eliza Beth might turn it down. Shoving her hands into her pockets, her fingers closed over Merrilee's cloth-covered cookies. They had survived the tumble she had taken!

"I've got a down payment right here." She pulled the cookies out of her pocket and showed them to her. "My aunt's applesauce cookies."

Eliza Beth's thin lips broke into a wary smile. "I don't know. Ms. Merrilee has done so much for my kinfolk, I should just give this to you."

"Then Maggie would be beholden to her aunt, and that wouldn't be good." Wesley threw her a private smile. "So tell us, Eliza Beth, what's a fair price?"

The woman glanced at her, then at Wesley. "We don't have any sugar right now. But I'll take whatever you consider is fair."

"How about ten pounds of sugar? Would that be a fair price?"

Eliza Beth's eyes brightened at Wesley's offer. "That's more than fair."

"We'll bring it back after supper tonight if that's okay with you."

The man knew how to charm the ladies. First, the girls they met as they entered the camp, now Eliza Beth Cox. Though the deal was between Eliza Beth and herself, it was Wesley's hand she shook.

"That gives me plenty of time to finish it up and set an iron to the wrinkles." Eliza Beth stretched up on tiptoes and pressed her lips against Wesley's cheek. "Thank you."

An uncomfortable knot formed in the pit of Maggie's stomach. She chalked it up to the unexpectedness of the woman's display of affection. It couldn't be anything more.

CHAPTER SEVEN

They left the camp an hour later. Most of their time had been spent talking with Eliza Beth, assessing her family's needs and making arrangements to barter for goods the group could use to sustain them.

Wesley walked in silence, a prisoner to the thoughts tumbling around in his head. On some level, he'd always known that there were people who did without, but never to the magnitude he had seen today. The threadbare clothes, the bare feet, the hungry faces on the kids had stuck a knife through his heart. He had to intercede for these people, and the only way he could do that was with Maggie's help.

He stole a glimpse at the woman walking beside him. Maggie had been an interesting surprise. Sure, he'd known she was intelligent; she had to be to get the kind of scores she put up in ground school, and she was handy with a lug wrench. The jury was still out on whether she could take care of herself or not.

But, for a moment this afternoon, he'd glimpsed another side to her, a compassionate woman with a heart for the needy who found a way to allow them their dignity. He may have been planning to help, but she had acted on it. Her offer of Merrilee's cookies for the handkerchief for her mother's birthday had been genuine. Something about her simple gesture had touched him deep down inside.

"You're unusually quiet." Maggie plucked a leaf from a low-hanging limb.

"Just thinking. Do you know anything about Eliza Beth's brother-in-law?"

She shook her head. "No, but if I remember correctly, Daddy always said the Coxes were closemouthed."

Picking up an oak switch, Wesley swatted it lightly at passing tree trunks. "I'm surprised. If anyone knew what was happening in this county, I figured it would be Merrilee."

"Not anymore," she answered. "There are so many families moving in to work at the Bell, it's hard to keep track of all the new people."

Wesley drew in a deep breath, the scent of earth, new blooms and Maggie doing nothing to slow the continuous thoughts alive in his head. "Do you think Jimbo is Eliza Beth's brother-in-law?"

"I trailed him in that direction before you . . ."

Had dropped her to the ground like he'd come face-to-face with the enemy. He swallowed. But he hadn't treated her like any enemy he had ever known. Not when she'd looked so beautiful pressed into the earth, her hair spread out in a fiery tangle, her lips soft and full. Keeping Maggie off-kilter may have become his favorite pastime, but she had won that battle.

Wesley walked away. "But we can't be certain."

"If Jimbo did take those supplies, what could he possibly need with that stuff?"

Another reason he was beginning to like her. Her refreshing innocence. He hated to tell her the possibilities. "Maybe he sold them on the black market."

"Here, in Marietta?" The incredulous expression on her face told him she hadn't fathomed that particular idea.

He smiled slightly. "I hate to tell you, but yes, there's probably a black market even here."

"I can't think of why anyone would be doing that here in Marietta," she answered, the thought dulling the light in her eyes. "As if it weren't bad enough that Jimbo drinks himself silly most nights, now he's doing this." Maggie turned to him. "Why hasn't he been kicked out of the Air Transport Command?"

Wesley shrugged. He had asked the same question more than once, and he'd always been given the same answer. "The Air Transport Command is a civilian organization, just like the WASP. On top of that, he's a hometown war hero. Management says his dismissal will cause a dip in community morale."

"What if he crashes a plane? Or buys supplies on the black market?"

He knew what she was asking. How would such a revelation affect the plant's morale? But he knew she was bright enough to figure out the answer. "I don't think that's what Jimbo is up to. If he was, he'd be sporting a lot of cash."

Maggie looked back in the direction of the camp. "He's not giving it to them."

Wesley shook his head. "Why take their food and leave them hungry, then give them the cash? No, something else is going on here."

"He must have hit rock bottom to steal from his family like that," she whispered.

"Yeah, well." Wesley took a savage swing at a pine sapling. "Grief does strange things to a person."

"You speak like someone who knows."

Wesley ignored her. He didn't want to talk about Beth, wasn't sure he ever would in this lifetime. But his gut told him that if he ever needed to confide in someone, Maggie would be a willing listener. The thought offered him a bit of comfort. "And you don't?"

She mashed her lips together, but not before he caught the slight quiver in the corner of her mouth. Her eyelids fanned down across her cheeks, and he wouldn't have been surprised to see tears track down her suddenly pale cheeks.

You're a jerk, Hicks, a real jerk. Just because he couldn't stomach talking about Beth didn't mean he couldn't give Maggie a shoulder to cry on.

Wesley touched her shoulder, and she lifted her head, her chin quivering slightly, her eyes sparkling with unshed tears.

Yeah, he was a jerk all right. "I'm sorry. If you don't want to talk, that's okay."

"I can talk about Jackson." Maggie stared off into the forest, unfocused, as if conjuring her uncle up from somewhere deep in her memories. "It's just, sometimes, I think that he's still around, you know, over in a

127

trench or locked up in a prison camp or something. Then I remember."

"I understand." Wesley dropped his hand from her shoulder. It was exactly like that for him, as if the thought of Beth being alive and somewhere on this earth made everything all right.

Except he always knew the truth — that she wasn't. The world had gone mad, and nothing in his life would ever be the same again.

Stepping over a dead log Maggie stole a quick glance at Wesley, concern for him coursing through her. That he'd lost someone important was evident in the slouch of his shoulders, the sober line of his mouth, the kinship of sadness reflecting in his eyes. But the emptiness in his gaze told her that he had lost a great deal more, as if death had seeped into every corner of his world.

Help him open up about this, Lord. Maggie lifted up a quick prayer as they reached the trail. *Doesn't he know he'd feel a lot better if he did?*

Or would he? Had something happened to make the loss that much worse?

"That was nice, what you did back there — giving them those cookies," Wesley said, effectively changing the subject. "I'm sure they appreciated it."

Great, now he's closed up tighter than a clam. Maggie shrugged. "Pastor Williams says you can't expect people to understand God's love when their stomachs are growling or they're shivering in the cold."

"He's got a point." He gave her a soft smile, the first one since they'd left the camp. "I got the impression you were prepared for something like this."

"Not really. Mama and I used to visit the sick boys over at the Civilian Conservation Corps when they were camped over at Kennesaw Mountain. But I was a little girl then."

"So you are an old pro at this," he replied. "Maybe I could help you out on the days you have some free time."

"You mean like every day?"

"Not tomorrow," he said, dropping the limb in the bushes.

She shook her head. What was the man saying? "I don't understand."

"Well, tomorrow, you're flying to Greenville to deliver a Mustang."

"I'm on the flight schedule?"

Wesley nodded slowly. "Yeah, as of this afternoon."

They stepped out of the woods. Was it the

afternoon sunshine or the possibilities that had suddenly been opened to her that ignited a flame in her very soul? She giggled, unable to contain the happiness bubbling up inside. She looked into Wesley's handsome face, took in the genuine smile he gave her and, without thinking, looped her arms around his neck, hugging him close. "Thank you, thank you, thank you!"

He seemed startled at first, his arms hanging by his sides. Then he relaxed, nestling his cheek against her head, his breath gently ruffling the hair around her ear, causing her to tighten her hold on him. When his arms came around and held her close, she felt as if she had been searching for a safe place to land and had finally found it in his embrace.

The sharp click of metal against metal interrupted Maggie's thoughts. She had barely turned her head when the coal black of a double barrel entered her sights. She put her hand on Wesley's chest and pushed, but his arm around her waist held her against him.

"What are you doing, Mr. Daniels?" Wesley's words vibrated beneath Maggie's hand.

"Defending what's left of the girl's honor, though with her, there's probably not much to save." Uncle James pushed the flush end of the rifle into Wesley's face.

Maggie twisted around, though Wesley kept his arm around her waist. "Put that gun down before you kill someone, Uncle James."

"What were you doing out in the woods with this man?"

Her face burned hot. Why did her uncle have to make it sound as if she and Wesley were doing something wrong? "If you'll move that gun out of the captain's face, I'll explain."

The older man glared at them for a moment before lowering the barrel of his weapon. "I'm listening."

Wesley loosened his hold on her, and Maggie took a step back, the early evening chill raising goose bumps along her exposed arms. Or was it the loss of Wesley's arms? She pushed away the thought. Whatever happened here, Uncle James couldn't find out about the tent camp. She'd made a promise.

"We were discussing the new flight schedule," she finally answered.

Her uncle eyed her suspiciously. "Didn't look like you were doing much talking a minute ago."

No, they hadn't been talking. She'd been thrilled by the feel of Wesley's arms around her, enjoyed the feel of his breath against her ear.

Wesley glanced at her for a long second. Was he thinking about their embrace? "Maggie got a little excited about her first assignment, that's all."

An odd twinge of disappointment settled in her chest. Of course, Wesley was right. It was just a bit of excitement. Like flying straight for the stars.

"Then what were the two of you doing in the woods?" Uncle James asked, bringing the barrel up once again.

Time to stop daydreaming and answer his question. "Flight schedules are a matter of national security, Uncle, especially anything coming out of the Bell. You know, loose lips sink ships."

James scoffed. "I don't believe that for a minute."

"Believe what you want, but I needed to brief Maggie, as she is due to fly out first thing tomorrow morning," Wesley answered, giving her a questioning glance.

James's gaze flicked over one, then the other before settling on her. He pointed his finger in her face like the barrel of his shotgun. "You know what kind of talk gets started when a girl goes off by herself with a man. You'd best think twice about that next time."

Maggie swallowed past the lump of embarrassment lodged in her throat. "Yes, sir."

"Any more of your secret talks needs to be done at the plant, Captain. Is that understood?"

"Completely," Wesley replied.

"Good." Easing back on the trigger, Uncle James lowered his weapon and headed off in the direction of the house.

Closing her eyes, Maggie fought back the anger that threatened to go unleashed. She was completely mortified. How could things get any worse than having to turn and face Wesley after her uncle's outrageous performance?

"Why didn't you tell your uncle about the tent camp?"

And there's your answer! Shifting around, Maggie raised her gaze to face him. "Because Uncle James would use it against my aunt."

"How could helping a group of people in need be used against Merrilee?"

Maggie drew in a breath. "You've heard my uncle talk about taking her to court?"

His brows drew together for second. "Yes. Why is that?"

An ugly piece of family business she'd

rather not go into. "My grandfather left the homestead to Merrilee rather than my uncle, and he's been determined to snatch it away from her ever since."

"But your grandfather left it to Merrilee fair and square. How does your uncle think he's going to take it away?"

The fact that Wesley stood soundly on her aunt's side made Maggie's stomach flutter. She pressed a hand to her midsection to calm the butterflies. "It hasn't been that long since women were given the right to own property. Granddaddy being Granddaddy, he decided that if he left the house to Merrilee, she'd have to live up to his standards."

"His will has a moral clause?"

No wonder the man was considered an engineering whiz if he could figure out the workings of Granddaddy Daniels's mind. Maggie nodded. "James has already complained about Merrilee boarding men and women in the same house. But if he knew she had okayed that camp on family property, he'd take her to court for sure."

"You don't think the judge would see that Merilee is doing her patriotic duty?"

Maggie didn't reply. Wesley was like no one she'd ever met in her life, believing that the law would see the good in Merrilee's work. For a moment, she believed it, too.

But she'd seen the "good ole boys" in action, and they wouldn't stand by and allow Merrilee to keep her home if James gave them any reason to think it was rightfully his.

"Don't worry, Maggie." His voice held her in a comforting embrace. "I'll keep quiet about the camp for now. But if your uncle makes any more noise about taking this property away from Merrilee, the major may get involved. She supplies quite a few rooms to some of Bell's necessary employees."

Maggie clasped her hands together, fighting the urge to hug him again. Wesley was more decent and kind than she'd given him credit for. Maybe with him in the know, everything would work out all right. A sudden burst of happiness sliced through her as she remembered what tomorrow held.

She was finally going to fly!

CHAPTER EIGHT

"I heard through the grapevine that you're some sort of hot shot in a Mustang, Daniels," Jimbo called out from under the wing of a P-51. "Aren't you afraid you might break a nail on the bomb switches?"

The sound of muffled laughter trailed after Maggie as she walked through the maze of recently repaired aircraft. Three weeks had passed since she had been included on the flight schedule, and the cat calls and offensive remarks had only escalated. She had thought that, over time, the men in the Flying 83rd would have grown tired of the childish behavior; but if this morning's comments were any indication, some had obviously not.

Well, if they wouldn't back down, neither would she. Maggie turned, checklist in hand. "Why, Jimbo? You afraid I'll aim my gun sights at you?"

Heat climbed up the man's face as his

buddies snickered around him. "I wouldn't be acting all high and mighty, little miss. You never know what might happen around here."

Her fingers tightened around the clipboard, her lungs refusing to breath. No, Jimbo Hayes couldn't have just threatened her, not in front of the entire squadron. He was just mad she'd bested him in front of his buddies and needed to blow off a little steam. The men retreated back to their work.

"I wouldn't put you on report if you took a shot at him." Wesley came up alongside of her, his voice barely a whisper. "It might scare some sense into that thick skull of his."

"I doubt it." She struggled to breathe, though from fear or from the man standing beside her, she wasn't sure.

"It was just a suggestion." He flashed her a smile that she had grown quite fond of in the past few weeks. "I'm on my way to the major's office for a short meeting. Anything you need?"

He's giving me the chance to report Jimbo.

But she wouldn't, not if she had any hopes of earning the respect of the squadron as a whole.

"I could go for a three-day pass," she teased, enjoying the flash of humor that ignited the silver sparks in his eyes.

He laughed. "You wouldn't take a break even if the president himself signed the order."

The man had gotten to know her well. Maggie caught herself from smiling back. *Maybe too well.*

"I got flight clearance to deliver this Mustang back to Augusta this afternoon."

"What time?"

"Thirteen hundred hours." She noticed the look of concern on his face. "Why? Is there a problem?"

He shook his head. "Just a front coming through. Supposed to bring in some pretty big storms."

"Should I put in a request to move my departure time up?"

"Let's just wait and see what happens," Wesley replied. "If a downpour does come, you can hold off delivery until tomorrow."

Dropping her arm to her side, Maggie came to attention, then snapped off a sharp salute. "Yes, sir."

With a ghost of a smile, Wesley saluted her. "Later, Ace."

Maggie clutched her checklist tight against her chest as she watched Wesley weave in and out of repaired aircraft before slipping out the hangar door. She'd spent a lot of off-duty hours with Wesley, visiting the tent camp, sitting on Merrilee's front porch talking planes and movies and anything else that popped into their heads. He'd even shared a pew with her during Sunday service, though Merrilee told her later that Wesley had been a regular since his arrival.

Best if I keep busy.

Then she wouldn't have time to wonder about the ominous memory that would flash across Wesley's face from time to time, marring his handsome features with a pain unlike anything she'd ever seen. And just as fast as a bogey on the radar screen, it would disappear.

"Leave it to you to get a dreamboat for a commanding officer."

Maggie spun around at the familiar voice. Leaning against the nose of her plane was her friend and fellow WASP, Donna Lane. In three short steps, she wrapped her in a welcoming hug. "What on earth are you doing here?"

"Bringing in a bucket of bolts for repairs. What about you?" Donna glanced toward the hangar door and gave her a knowing smile. "Met any interesting people?"

She'd forgotten. Donna always played matchmaker during the girls' leave at Sweetwater. "A few. How are the boys in Savannah treating you?"

"Like a queen." She dropped her gear to the floor as she stretched her shoulders. "I've only found a dead mouse under my pillow once this week."

"At least it was dead. You remember those Texas rattlers we used to fish out of our barracks constantly?"

"That's what we get for wanting to soar through the skies," Donna said, drawing her hand along the contoured edge of the fuselage. "But it can only get better from here."

Would it? Maggie couldn't help but wonder if she was grasping at straws. "I don't know."

"Hey, there's a lot of guys in the Army Air Corp who are already coming to realize what valuable assets we are," Donna said.

Crossing her arms in front of her, Maggie leaned back against the body of the plane. "Wait a minute. Last time I heard, you had convinced some navigator out of South Carolina you were the greatest thing since sliced bread. How's that going for you?"

"Very well." The soft smile Donna gave Maggie turned dreamy, her eyes luminous. She lowered her gaze, her sooty lashes resting against the pink glow of her cheeks. "In fact, Bill asked me to marry him."

"You're engaged?"

Donna pressed her finger against her lips. "You don't have to act so surprised."

"I can't believe you're getting married," Maggie whispered, glancing around as if Donna's announcement were a breach of national security. "I never figured you for the type to give up on your dreams."

"Who said anything about giving up?" Donna sounded slightly hurt.

"Isn't that what a girl usually does when she gets married?"

"Is that what you think, that marriage is a war where a woman has to surrender her hopes and dreams?"

Maggie ducked under the belly of the plane, feigning interest in the wheels of the landing gear. That's exactly what she thought. Maybe at some point in the future, she could think about including a husband in her plans; someone like Wesley who shared her love for aviation and her faith in God. But not now. Not until she'd reached her goal. A sadness she hadn't expected nipped at her heart.

"Have you ever been in love, Maggie?" Donna asked, leaning down to watch Maggie.

Maggie shook her head. "No."

"Well, when you are," Donna started,

brushing her bangs out of her eyes, "you'll find out that those dreams you've been having aren't enough anymore. They grow to include the person you love."

Maggie stared down at her checklist. Maybe that was true for Donna, but Maggie had grown up around men; she knew how their protective nature would interfere with her goals. No, the dreams that God had given her were big enough already.

"Then how are you going to get the flight time you'll need to fly commercial jets if you get married?" Maggie marked the landing gear off her list.

Donna joined Maggie under the plane. "We thought about that. Bill and I both agreed we should wait until after the war's over so I can continue to get in my hours."

Maggie studied the metal seams along the underbelly of the plane, trying to think through gaps in Donna's logic and finding none. "Whose idea was that?"

"Mine, but Bill agrees with me," Donna answered. "Look, he's known from the first that I want a career, and he's behind me 100 percent."

"Your Bill sounds like a peach of a guy."

"He is!" Happiness radiated from every pore in her being. "Hey, I've got an idea. I'm meeting Bill downtown at the USO tonight. Why don't you come with me, get to know the man for yourself?"

"As much as I'd love to be a third wheel, I'm flying out in a couple of hours."

Donna shook her head. "I doubt it. There's a storm front just west of here, a real gully washer. I barely made it in myself."

Handing Donna her clipboard, Maggie marched to the hangar door and flung it open. The scent of rain hung like a thick velvet curtain in the air, the wind cool against her heated cheeks.

"It'll be pouring within the next hour," Donna called out from behind her. "You can trust me on that, Georgia."

Maggie smiled at the nickname the other recruits had given her within hours of arriving for basic training. She'd felt like a duck out of water those first few days until one by one, each of them shared their hope of being part of something bigger than themselves.

What part did love play in those dreams?

Rain slowly began to fall. Maggie couldn't afford love right now, not in a world still struggling to change, not when she still had so much she wanted to do. But the truth didn't stop her from asking herself what kind of man she would want for herself.

The storm grew fierce, chewing up the tarmac inch by inch until a heavy dampness could be felt in the air. A door to her left slammed against the metal siding like a clap of thunder, and she turned her head. Through the gray soup, Maggie made out the figure of a man, his hand cupped over his hat, his body pushing against the driving wind. He put his head down, his wide shoulders pummeled by the torrent of rain. Only a determined man would not cower in the face of such a storm.

That would be a man worth knowing.

Maggie stepped back as Wesley came to stand next to her. He pulled his hat from his head, droplets of water hugging his blond hair as if for dear life. "You folks have showers like this often?"

The smell of rain and Wesley's soap invaded her senses like mustard gas, killing her dreams. She clutched her jacket around her and nodded. "They're pretty common for this time of year."

He slapped his hat against his thigh, sending a spray of water in a circle around him. "Would you please remind me to bring my rain gear and stow it in the office?"

"Yes, sir." Maggie glanced out as puddles began to form on the tarmac. "I guess I won't be flying out today."

Wesley shook his head, tiny droplets raining down like diamonds on his shoulders. "We're supposed to be socked in for most of the afternoon."

Maggie swallowed hard against the knot of emotions cluttering her throat, her fingers itching to smooth the rivulets of water sliding down Wesley's face. Maybe a night on the town, meeting new people was just what she needed to put these silly notions she was having about Wesley in perspective.

"Captain Hicks?"

He turned to her, his expression gentle as if the rain had washed away all the worries he normally carried, leaving in its wake a face she liked altogether too much. "Yes, Ms. Daniels?"

"I'd like to request the rest of the afternoon off, sir."

"Any particular reason?"

Maggie had to keep herself from squirming under his appraisal. Yes, a night on the town was just what she needed. "A friend of mine from flight school flew in right before the storm hit. I'd like to catch up."

"Another WASP?" Wesley glanced around her before focusing on the only other woman in the room. "Wow, this place is getting to be a regular hive of activity."

Maggie pressed her lips together. The man

was no Bob Hope, but knew how to make her laugh.

Her amusement died, however, when Wesley leaned close, his voice dropping off to a whisper. "You've flown more flights in the last three weeks than most of these guys have in months. You need some rest after that many hours in the air. So go. Take the afternoon off." He stared at her for a long moment. "That's an order."

Her heart revved up like a P-51 on takeoff. Maggie raised her hand in a perfect salute. "Thank you."

"And Ace?"

"Yes, sir?"

"Have a good time."

"Captain?"

Wesley turned around, his thoughts still focused on Maggie. He wasn't sure how long he'd been standing there, watching her dancing between the fat raindrops. His insides warmed when the soft lull of her laughter drifted back to him. He didn't much care for the weather, but, today, it had provided a good excuse to give Maggie a much deserved afternoon off.

"Captain Hicks?"

Wesley blinked. Lieutenant Mike Hogan, Major Evans's assistant, stood before him waiting for some response, his hand raised to the brim of his cap. Wesley returned the salutation. "At ease. What can I do for you, Mike?"

"Major Evans would like to see you in his office as soon as possible."

Wesley gave the soldier a brief nod. Had he forgotten a scheduled meeting with the major? He walked the short distance to his desk where his appointment book sat and flipped to today's date. Nothing was marked. He glanced up at Lieutenant Hogan. "We don't have a meeting scheduled."

"I know, sir, but the major is anxious to speak to you." The lieutenant lowered his voice. "On a very urgent matter."

"Give me five minutes."

"Thank you. I'll let him know you're on your way." With a salute, the lieutenant turned and headed across the hangar floor.

Something was up, but what? He looked down at Maggie's paperwork to see what assignments still needed to be completed, but he found that everything, save the cancelled flight, had been finished. No surprises there. The woman was meticulous to a fault.

Tossing the clipboard on the desk, Wesley turned and took a shortcut to the administration building across the tarmac.

The rain had started up again, though not as heavy. Hopefully Maggie had made it home before she got soaked, not that she would have minded. No, the girl he knew wouldn't melt in a little sprinkle. It was just that attitude that might land her the lead-pilot position of her own crew.

Stepping up to the door of the administration building, he pulled up short. When had his attitude toward Maggie changed? She'd worked hard for the chance at her own crew. She was a natural in the air and undoubtedly the best pilot in his squadron. But it wasn't just those qualities. Maggie had spunk and wasn't the least bit put off by a little hard work.

Truth be told, she was the kind of woman a guy could depend on in rough skies.

Wesley grasped the door handle and pulled it open. Best be getting that nonsense out of his head. He had a squadron to prepare. Love was not on his radar. Wesley picked up his pace.

Rounding the corner to the major's office, Wesley hit a somber nest of suited engineers and uniformed high-ranking officials. So he wasn't the only one summoned. Wesley noticed Wib Hubbard along one wall and stopped alongside him. "What's going on?"

"I'm not sure," Wib answered, nodding

toward the end of the hall. Coming toward them was Abner Ellerbee. "But it must be something big to get Mr. Ellerbee off the plant floor."

Wesley nodded. Ellerbee wasn't one to leave his post. Why, just a couple of months before, Evans had ordered the man to his office where Margaret Mitchell sat waiting.

"Do you think the war might be over?" Wib asked.

Before Wesley had a chance to answer, the door to Major Evans's office opened. Lieutenant Hogan stepped out and to the side. "Gentlemen, the major will see you now."

It took several minutes for the group to crowd into the small space. Wesley hung back, leaning against the wall near the door. A couple of the engineers he knew from the Buffalo plant were seated beside Major Evans. Odd that no one had mentioned their visit to him, but he had been busy training the men.

And one certain woman.

Major Evans stood. A hush fell over the crowd. Ramrod straight, he was the picture of the perfect soldier. But there was a strained look around his eyes, a tightness in the line of his mouth that twisted Wesley's gut.

"Gentlemen, I'm not going to waste your time but simply cut to the chase. Another Super Fortress has gone down in a cornfield outside our base in Kansas." Evans cleared his throat. "There were no survivors."

CHAPTER NINE

Maggie took one look in the mirror and smiled. Petite polka dots danced like bright stars on a sky of navy blue across the bodice and skirt of the dress. Black gabardine pumps graced her feet, making her slender legs look even longer. Reaching up to straighten the sailor collar, she noticed how her hair glimmered red-gold against the white background. "What do you think, Merrilee?"

"You look lovely, dear," her aunt answered, holding up another outfit for Maggie. "But then, you are one of the prettiest girls in Cobb County when you're not covered in engine oil."

Maggie laughed, taking the dress. "But I like working on engines."

"So I've noticed." Merrilee sat down, glancing over the selection of gloves and handbags the saleslady had chosen for them. "It was very nice of Wesley to give you the afternoon off."

"I'd only wished I'd known that Donna was meeting up with Bill to get her ring sized." She hung the dress on the peg then turned to shut the door. "Then I wouldn't have asked him for the time off."

"But we wouldn't be having such a lovely afternoon." Her aunt's voice was muffled by the dressing room door. "Though I have to admit, I was a bit surprised you actually wanted to go shopping."

"I don't mind shopping every once in a while," Maggie said, glancing at her flushed cheeks in the mirror, giving her appearance a patriotic theme of red, white and blue.

The truth was she didn't have anything to wear except overalls and jumpers, and that wouldn't do, not for her night out at the U.S.O. The fact that Wesley might see her in something other than an oil-stained bib played a tiny part in her sudden desire to go shopping. She was a woman after all, and she wanted to look her best.

Maggie undid the cloth buttons and shucked the dress off. This was a silly notion, trying to get Wesley to notice her. The only thing he needed to be aware of was her ability in the air.

But it didn't mean she couldn't ask questions. Her aunt was sure to know something about the man. Maggie collected the dress off the floor and hung it on the hanger. "Merrilee?"

"Yes, dear?"

"Has Wesley ever told you anything about his family?" Maggie stepped into a green seersucker and slipped one arm then another into the long sleeves.

"Not much really," Merrilee started, then stopped. The dressing room grew quiet, as if her aunt was thinking through the question before answering. "I know he's got a grandfather that he stayed with awhile after his mother died. He lived somewhere in England before moving to Washington, D.C."

No mention of his sister. Maggie laid her forearms across the top of the dressing room door and peeked over. "What about his dad?"

"He told me once that his father was a doughboy during the Great War. That's how his parents met; he was stationed near the village where she lived. Once they married, she moved to the States to stay with his family. Wesley's father died in the influenza outbreak a few months before Wesley turned two."

A great sadness fell over Maggie. What had it been like for him, growing up without his parents' love and encouragement? She couldn't begin to imagine it. "Does he talk about his grandfather much?"

"No, but when he does, it's about when he was still just a boy. I get the feeling something's going on there, but he's never given me a clue as to what it is," Merrilee said, digging into her purse and pulling out a roll of Life Savers. She tore into the paper and extracted a cherry-red candy. "I don't think he's seen him in a long time."

"But Washington isn't that far away."

Merrilee glanced up at her. "It can feel like forever when something is standing in the way."

So Wesley was all alone. Maggie sighed.

"I know," Merrilee said. "Families can be a pain sometimes."

Maggie turned her head to stare at Merrilee. Her aunt's good nature didn't allow her to say such a negative thing about any of her kinfolk. Well, maybe one. "Uncle James giving you fits again?"

Merrilee's lips pursed, as if the candy in her mouth had suddenly turned sour. "He's been watching that tree line alongside the kitchen ever since he caught you and Wesley coming out of the woods. It's like he's a soldier guarding his post or something."

"So why not tell him about the tent camp?

No judge in the county is going to break Granddaddy's will because you've gone out on a limb to help people."

"I don't know about that. James has always had his eye on the homestead." Merrilee stared off, her usually lively eyes shadowed in doubts. "He was as surprised as I was that Daddy left it to me, especially after John left me."

Merrilee never talked about John Davenport, at least not that Maggie could ever remember. "What was he like? Uncle John, I mean."

"I don't know." She shrugged her shoulders slightly. "That was a long time ago."

"Claire's only ten, Merrilee."

A rosy hue stained her aunt's cheeks and she ducked her head. "Okay, so it hasn't been that long."

Maggie plunged ahead. "Did you love him?"

A faraway smile touched Merrilee's lips, as if reaching back in her memories to a time and place when she was young, when dreams still had a chance to come true. Before her heart had been broken. "Very much."

"How did you know?"

"I'm not sure," Merrilee said. "I had

skipped school that day, and John was working a field on the outer edges of our homestead. He looked so tall and strong out there, chopping cotton. My heart almost beat out of my chest that day." Merrilee blushed a deeper shade of pink. "But he wasn't just nice to look at. He was good and decent and caring. It didn't take much to lose my heart to him."

"What happened?"

"You remember how your granddaddy was. I didn't even tell him that I was married until he had John arrested for kidnapping me."

"Aunt Merrilee!"

"I know. It was foolish of me," Merrilee answered, looking quite ashamed of herself. "But I was very young, barely seventeen, and I had never gone against Daddy before."

"Granddaddy didn't like him?"

"He liked John good enough as long as he turned a good crop and was making money for him. But Daddy thought I should have married someone in his social circle, like a doctor or a lawyer. He even pushed Abner Ellerbee at me as suitable husband material." Merrilee shook her head. "Daddy thought I had settled for a farmer."

Maggie didn't understand the problem, seeing how her grandfather was a farmer himself. But then she'd only known him as the kindly old man who always had a quarter for her to spend at Woolworths. "What did you do?"

"What do you mean, what did I do?" Merrilee asked, pulling on a pair of gloves with a bit more force than necessary. "I moved out to the small parcel of land John was sharecropping for Daddy and tended the fields with my husband." She studied the stretched fingers of her left hand as if imagining the ring her husband had once given her — for better or for worse. "Our house wasn't much, just a couple of rooms. But it was home."

She's still in love with him.

Maggie wasn't sure how she knew that, but there was no doubt in her mind. Merrilee still harbored strong emotions for John Davenport, even after he'd left her to fend for herself all those long years ago. "How did you end up back at Granddaddy's?"

"The crops got washed away. Daddy called in his loan on us, and John refused to ask Daddy for an extension."

Maggie scoffed. "Stubborn men."

Merrilee gave her a sad little nod. "John decided the best way to pay Daddy back was to enlist in the Civilian Conservation

Corps. As he told me, it was honest work with a steady check. We decided I would stay in our place, giving Daddy as much of John's paycheck as I could while I held down the farm."

The expression in her eyes softened. "But then I found out I was expecting. Daddy couldn't bear the thought of his grandchild being born in a sharecropper's house. So he offered me a deal — I could come home and take care of the main house, and he'd make sure that me and my child would always have a place to live." Merrilee snorted. "Of course, that was before I had Claire."

Maggie smiled. "Granddaddy figured you'd have a boy."

"You know me." Merrilee chuckled. "I had to be ornery."

"What happened with Uncle John?"

"I sent him dozens of letters, but I never heard anything back." Merrilee looked at her, her expression begging for understanding. "Not that I expected anything, mind you. He traveled all over the place, and I was never sure where he'd be from one day to the next." She dropped her gaze to her lap, her fingers busily picking at some unseen lint on her dress. "Then right before Claire was born, a lawyer from Atlanta showed up with some papers. John had filed for a divorce."

Merrilee let out a sad little sigh. "I guess marriage was just too hard for him."

Maggie flinched. It must have been difficult for John, to know what his wife had given up, to realize he couldn't give her the life she had once known. But he couldn't have been much of a man, abandoning Merrilee when she was pregnant with his child. What would drive a man to miss out on knowing his own child? Did he have any idea the opportunity he had given up by not being a part of Claire's life, part of the joy she brought to everyone in her world?

Something didn't feel right here, not when Maggie weighed the character of the man Merrilee had described against his actions.

Did John Davenport even know he had a child with Merrilee?

The idea bothered her. Maggie took a breath, the question poised at her lips, then paused to study her aunt. Yes, Merrilee wore her usual smile, but the glow that generally lit her features was gone, dimmed by a sorrow that Maggie had never recognized before today. If Maggie had questions, they would have to be answered by someone else.

But who? She'd never heard anyone in the family ever talk about John Davenport. A divorce would have been a horrific scandal to live down for a family as widely known as the Daniels; especially to a man stuck in a bygone era, as her grandfather was. In his mind, Merrilee would be a fallen woman, what with a broken marriage and raising Claire on her own.

If Merrilee couldn't make a marriage work, what makes me think — with all my dreams of flying — I could manage any better?

No, Maggie had to guard her feelings, at least until she was firmly settled into her career. But what if her heart didn't listen? What if she fell in love like her aunt had with John Davenport?

Her aunt's failed marriage was still fresh on Maggie's mind as she stared into the oval mirror hanging over her makeshift makeup table a few hours later. She took a tissue from the box and wiped off the patriotic red staining her cousin's face from nose to chin. "It's like drawing with crayons, Claire Bear. You've got to color between the lines."

"Good advice, Georgia." Donna handed her a tissue in return. Maggie glanced in the mirror and noticed her own feeble attempts at lipstick weren't much better.

"I'll have to remember that when I am old enough to go to dances." Claire loaded up a brush with baby-blue eye shadow.

"Well, little lady, you'll be there before you know it." Maggie laughed, gently pulling on Claire's unruly pigtail. "Enjoy being a kid while you can."

Claire's gaze dropped to the lace doily draped across her aunt's vanity, her mouth quirked into a sad little smirk. "I guess."

Maggie exchanged a worried look with Donna. Something was troubling her little cousin. Maggie tugged Claire onto her lap, cuddling her small body against hers, breathing in the fresh scent of Ivory soap. "What's wrong, squirt?"

Claire burrowed deeper into Maggie's neck. "Nothing."

Maggie dropped a kiss into her soft hair. "You can tell me, Claire Bear."

A sob racked Claire's body. A lump formed in Maggie's throat as she spent the next few minutes rocking her younger cousin, holding her close. Whatever the problem was, it was too big for Claire's small shoulders.

"You feel like telling me about it now?" Maggie asked once her cousin had cried herself out.

With a hiccup, the little girl lifted her head. "At school, Ms. Phillips —" Claire glanced at Donna "— she's my teacher. Well, she asked what our families are doing

161

to help out in the war, and I told everyone how Momma takes care of a lot of people who work at the bomber plant."

Maggie nodded, not sure why that would upset her cousin. "And that's a good thing for your mother to do."

"Yes, it is." Claire sniffed. "But then Bradley Tucker said Momma wouldn't be doing it much longer 'cause Uncle James was going to kick us out of our house."

Now the kids were talking about Uncle James's nonsense! Maggie hugged Claire close. "You know that's not going to happen, don't you?"

"But Uncle James told Momma that he would take away our house right after he caught you sneaking out of the woods with Captain Wesley."

Maggie refused to meet Donna's gaze studying her in the mirror. Instead, she put her hands on Claire's shoulders and gently pushed her back so that she could get a good look at her. "You know better than to listen in on other people's conversations."

"I'm sorry. Momma was crying and I got scared."

Claire's contrite expression pulled at her heart. The poor little thing, worrying about her momma like that. Uncle James should be ashamed of himself, upsetting Merrilee

162

and Claire so.

"You don't worry about it anymore, you hear me?" Maggie cradled Claire close. "Let the grown-ups deal with this."

Baby-fine hair brushed across Maggie's bare arm as her cousin's head fell back. "So we're staying here?"

"Yes." Maggie kissed the tip of Claire's nose, then shooed her off her lap. "Now scoot, or we'll never make the train to Atlanta."

Claire headed for the door, then spun around. "Thanks, Maggie."

Maggie smiled. Boy, how she loved the little runt. "Close the door behind you, squirt!"

Once the door clicked shut, Donna twisted around to face Maggie. "You were hugging the captain?"

"It's not what it sounds like." Leaning into the mirror, Maggie uncapped her mascara. "I was excited about getting my first flight assignment and ended up hugging Wesley. See, nothing to it."

"I don't recall you ever giving Captain Harper a hug when he passed out flight assignments," Donna said, chuckling softly. "But then you never were on a first-name basis with him, either."

"Look." Turning to Donna, she pointed

the mascara wand at her. "Wesley and I are friends. That's all. Nothing else, okay?"

"If you say so."

"I say so." The words left a disagreeable feeling in the pit of her stomach. Maggie snatched a bobby pin holding a pin curl in place and scratched her scalp. "What I'm worried about is my aunt. Why in the world would Uncle James fight her over this stupid house?"

"Your uncle obviously doesn't think it's so stupid."

Maggie shook her head, her freed curls bouncing violently. "He can't understand why Granddaddy left Merrilee the family homestead instead of him."

"But he did leave it to your aunt." Donna traced the outline of her lips with her little finger.

"With a stipulation." Maggie explained the moral clause attached to Grandfather Daniels's will.

"You've got to be kidding. Who thinks up that kind of stuff anymore?"

"Granddaddy was very set in his ways."

"You mean, men are men and women should be out in the kitchen, talking about having babies." Donna dipped a cottony puff into the perfumed dusting powder. "Are the rest of the people here as behind

164

the times?"

"No," Maggie said, then clarified herself. "At least most of them aren't."

"And the ones who are?"

"Cause as much trouble as they possibly can."

Donna eyed her warily. "What kind of trouble?"

Thinking about the note, Maggie yanked at another curler, but the thick teeth caught her hair in a tight tangle like vines in a briar patch. She hadn't wanted anyone to know about the threat. After all, loose lips sink ships, and this particular vessel might be the entire WASP program. But Donna had a right to know what kind of danger she was flying into.

Glancing toward the closed door, Maggie met her friend's gaze in the mirror. "Someone at the plant threatened me."

Donna's eyebrow arched. "Someone is always threatening to do something to us. What makes this time any different?"

"They left me a note," Maggie answered, opening the dresser drawer and retrieving the note. She noticed Donna's fingers shook as she took it.

"Someone wants me dead."

Wesley bounded up the front stairs of

Merrilee's, dodging the last of the raindrops. Above, the gray clouds played peek-a-boo with blue skies. But if the weather reports could be trusted, another storm system was on its way. Usually, that meant a quiet day around the airfield.

He needed some peace after today.

He closed his eyes and let out a long sigh. Another Super Fortress down. No cause yet, but an investigation had been launched. The news had left him stunned; he had spent the rest of the afternoon pushing stacks of paper around his desk and wondering what had gone wrong.

Taking a deep breath, Wesley opened the door and stepped inside, the screen door slapping shut behind him. He took his hat off. The dampness of his clothes chilled him, and he had to resist the urge to shake like a soaked dog. He hated being wet, despised it. Reminded him too much of the airfield outside of York, waiting to fly into the Blitz over London.

"You're soaked to the gills."

Wesley looked up. Claire stood on the stairs, her arms loaded down with several towels. "You wouldn't want to give me one of those, would you?"

Claire grabbed one from the top of the

pile and handed it to him. "This one's clean."

"Thank you." Wrapping it around his shoulders, he pointed to the rest of her stash that she'd dropped at the puddles around his feet. "How did you manage to get the rest of those dirty?"

"Don't blame me." Claire leaned back to glare at him. "I'm not upstairs, primping."

"You mean Maggie and Donna?"

"And Ms. Edie." Her head bobbed up and down as she wiped up the water on the floor. "It sure does take a lot of work to get ready to go to Atlanta."

So Maggie was hitting the town with Donna and Edie. They'd probably catch a movie at the Fox before heading down the street to the Varsity. Good. She'd been working so hard here lately. It just seemed fair for her to get out and have a little fun.

A door at the back of the house slammed shut. Within seconds, Merrilee came up the hall, the warm scent of starch radiating from the cloud of clothing piled high in her outstretched arms. She stopped in front of him.

"My word, you're drenched to the skin. Get upstairs and out of those wet clothes before you catch pneumonia."

Wesley smiled. The woman gave orders

better than most generals he knew. He scrubbed the towel through his hair. "Let me dry off some so I don't puddle up the rest of your house."

"All right, but don't take too long. It wouldn't be very patriotic to start an epidemic at the Bell." Merrilee glanced down at her daughter. "Claire Bear, would you go out to the kitchen and make sure I turned off the iron?"

"Aw, Momma."

Even the matted curls framing Merrilee's face couldn't soften her stern look. "Right now, young lady."

"Yes, ma'am." Gathering the towels around his feet, Claire trudged down the hallway.

Wesley pulled at his wet tie. "The girls are going to a lot of fuss for a night out."

Merrilee laughed as she started upstairs. "Well, you can't expect them to wear those nasty overalls they work in when they're going to the U.S.O."

A dull ache settled behind his eyes. Maybe he was catching a cold after all. "Why aren't they wearing their uniforms?"

"They're not reporting in to General Eisenhower." Merrilee laughed. "Besides, the boys shipping out want to see the girls in all their feminine finery, not some horrible uniform."

"I guess you've got a point there." Still, the whole idea didn't sit well. Overalls looked swell, particularly on Maggie. Her dark red hair, her feminine curves in her blue uniform would turn enough heads. Why did she have to get all dolled up for a bunch of freckle-faced GIs right off the farm?

"I've got your dinner warming in the stove." Merrilee started up the stairs. "That'll give you time to change."

"No hurry, Ms. Merrilee." Wesley sat down on the bottom step and shut his eyes. It was the crash. It had to be. Nothing else would scramble his emotions concerning Maggie. He wasn't here to fall in love. He didn't have time. If he did, the girl in question certainly wouldn't be a pilot.

A quiet night at home was just what he needed. Time to focus on his priorities. Get his head back into the battle.

"Are you okay?"

Maggie's voice jolted him out of his thoughts. He opened his eyes to catch a glimpse of red-tipped toes peeking out from beneath a skirt the color of the heather that bloomed in the fields outside Pops's house in late summer.

He looked up. Gone was the grease

monkey who could fix a leaky oil line on a P-51 faster than any man on his squad. Instead, a beautiful woman stood before him. Her hair had been freed from the confines of her snood, dark red curls tumbling around her shoulders in soft waves, her bangs pinned back from her face with a simple barrette. She wore little makeup, only a faint touch of lipstick.

His heart skipped a beat or two. Wesley stood and stepped back. "Why would you ask that?"

"I don't know. You just seem . . . beaten."

He felt beaten. By the storm. By the crash. By life. He didn't realize she was standing in front of him until her hand slid across his cheek.

"You want to talk about it?"

He studied Maggie's face. He'd love to share this burden with her, listen to her sound advice. Why tell her about the downed B-29 when she bubbled with happiness? There would be plenty of time for discussions tomorrow. "Rough afternoon, that's all."

She nodded and dropped her hand from his face. The warm tingle her touch had provoked lingered.

"Is it still raining?" Maggie swept past him, glanced out the window, then looked back at him. "You're wet."

He'd definitely caught something serious. Maybe scarlet fever or polio. This weak-in-the-knees feeling couldn't have anything to do with the concern he saw in Maggie's eyes. Wesley cleared his throat. "I got caught in the last of the rain on my way home."

"Then what are you doing down here? You should be upstairs changing into some dry clothes."

He felt a smile tug at his lips. He liked when Maggie took charge. To a point. "I can take care of myself, you know."

"That's got a familiar ring to it." Her laughter faded into a husky murmur. "No wonder you're dead on your feet. You've been putting in enough time at the plant to kill a man."

What would it feel like to trace his fingers along the gentle slope of her jaw? To tilt her determined little chin back and . . . He shook his head. "There's a war going on. Everyone's putting in long hours."

"I guess you're right." Her expression softened. "I should be thanking you for giving me the afternoon off. I haven't had this much fun since my first furlough at Sweetwater."

He smiled. The thought of Maggie enjoying herself made him feel lighter, almost

171

happy. "You're welcome."

"Maybe you need some time off to forget your troubles."

His spirits dampened to match the uncomfortable feel of his clothes. A lifetime might not be long enough to forget his troubles. How he had failed his sister. How, if he wasn't careful, he might end up failing Maggie, too.

Footsteps sounded on the stairs and he looked up. Donna and Edie floated down the steps in a sea of blue and white, Merrilee close behind. While her friends looked nice, neither woman could hold a candle to Maggie.

"We'd better get going if we're going to make the train." Edie handed Maggie her purse.

Snapping open her bag, Maggie seemed to study the contents. "We don't want to keep Bill and his friends waiting."

Bill?

"Have you got a nickel in case you need to call home?" Merrilee fussed with the collar of Maggie's dress.

"Yes, ma'am." Wrapping her arm around her aunt, Maggie gave her a quick kiss on her cheek that left a faint imprint. "We won't be too late."

The women were out the door and down

the front walk before Wesley finally recovered from the shock. "Who's Bill?"

Merrilee shut the door and turned around. "He's Donna's beau. His squadron is flying out next week, so they're in town for the next couple of days."

"He's a pilot?"

Merrilee nodded. "Donna trained him herself."

A slight sense of relief flowed through Wesley. A man could do worse than having the company of three lovely ladies. Not exactly the way he'd say goodbye to his sweetheart, but to each his own.

"It was particularly nice of him to bring along two of his friends to keep Maggie and Edie company. Guess he just wanted to be alone with Donna for a while." Merrilee glanced at herself in the hall mirror and stopped. "My word, why didn't you tell me I had lipstick all over my cheek?"

He didn't see it until she leaned into the glass. A bright cherry stain. Maggie's lipstick.

"I swear." Merrilee pulled a handkerchief from her sleeve and blotted at the mark. "That girl ruined her makeup before she even got out the door."

The other ways a girl could mess up her lipstick spurred him toward the stairs. "Ms.

Merrilee, I'm going out for the evening."

"But you just got home. You haven't even had your dinner."

"Could you save it? I'll take it for lunch tomorrow." He took the steps two at a time. Maybe Maggie was right. He needed a couple of hours to unwind after the stresses of his day.

And what better place to relax than the U.S.O.?

CHAPTER TEN

The Forsyth Street U.S.O. was packed tighter than a jar of Aunt Merrilee's homemade pear preserves. Local girls in the finest attire war rations could provide were scattered around the gymnasium-turned-dance-floor. Every branch of the military was represented in the hall, with replacement troops lining the walls, hoping for a chance to find a sweetheart before shipping out.

Maggie smiled. Hitler didn't stand a chance against the good ole U.S.A.

She stole a sideways look at her date. All she could hope was that there wasn't any more back home like Lieutenant Anthony Webber. He was okay in the looks department, even had some of the girls giving him the once-over when he'd walked her to their table. But whatever interest she might have had took a nosedive the minute Anthony started complaining about the fueling system on the B-29.

Hadn't he even read the briefings? Wesley would have chewed out any of his pilots for not keeping updated, and with good reason.

Wesley. He'd looked so tired tonight, as if he had the weight of the United States Army resting on his shoulders. If she hadn't promised Donna she'd keep Anthony company, she would have begged off and spent a quiet evening at home.

Who was she kidding? Spending time with Wesley wasn't something she could afford to do, not when just being around him evoked a tenderness she'd never experienced in all her twenty-one years. No, she would not put her dreams at risk.

Then why was she looking at every man who walked by and comparing them to Wesley?

"The army's training me to fly B-29s. You know, the flying coffin." Anthony leaned toward her, and the wolfish gleam in his eyes caused a slight shudder to race down her spine. He must have mistook her repulsion for a chill and draped his arm along the back of her chair.

She leaned forward, glancing across the table at Donna and Bill. Poor things, they looked so uncomfortable. The matchmaking had struck out on both fronts. Edie's date seemed to be a nice guy; it was too bad Jeff was almost engaged. Maggie gave them a slight smile. Not exactly the romantic evening they'd probably pictured for their last night together. Well, she'd dealt with worse situations. If spending a couple of hours with the lieutenant gave Donna and Bill time alone, it was worth the sacrifice.

"Are you listening to me?"

"I'm sorry, it's been a long day." Maggie took a deep breath to clear her head and smiled. "Please go on."

The lieutenant eyed her warily. "Like I said, those guys in Washington are willing to risk good pilots on that piece of junk."

"Come on, Tony," Bill interjected, a smile dancing on his lips as he rose and held his hand out to Donna. "Why talk about planes when you could be out there on the dance floor with a beautiful woman?"

"It's okay. I'm not much of a dancer." Maggie rested her chin in the palm of her hand, watching Donna take her fiancé's hand and lean into him. "I'm very interested in what Anthony has to say."

"Are you sure?" Donna asked, her brow wrinkled in disbelief.

Maggie nodded. "Go on. Have a good time."

The couple drifted toward the dance floor, Donna turning around once to mouth a quick apology. The muffled sound of the trombone announced the beginning of a Glenn Miller song. Couples swayed to the slow rhythm of "Moonlight Serenade."

Maggie reached for her lemonade and took a sip. The cool drink did nothing to sweeten her sour mood. "So, what do you really think about the Super Fortress?"

"Are you sure you want to hear this? It could get pretty technical." The man curled his hand around Maggie's shoulder and pulled her back against him, the overwhelming smell of hair balm and diesel fuel burning her nose. Obviously, not many people asked for his opinion.

She peeled his fingers from her shoulder. "Yes."

"Well, the thing's a huge mess, a design flaw. But do those guys in Washington care?" Webber shook his head, his lips drawn up in a tight smirk. "Those suits just want us up there, bombing the crud out of the Japs."

"Isn't that your job?" Had the sour lemonade turned her voice so tart? Or the company she was keeping?

"Well, sure it is, honey, but within reason. This country can't afford to lose our best up there, hoping on a wing and a prayer. And the test pilots have counted the bodies; they're wising up. So guess what the boys in Washington are going to do now?" He began to laugh, as if ready to let her in on the punch line. "They're giving the okay to train those girl flyers on the B-29. Isn't that a hoot?"

Wonder where I can find those "boys" and thank them. "Maybe having a girl fly the thing would prove to the other pilots it's safe." Maggie balled her fist into the skirt of her dress.

"Everybody knows the mechanics of flying are too hard for the female mind to grasp." He lifted the soda bottle to his lips and took a sip. "Yeah, there are a few that manage it but they're oddballs. Throw in all those feminine emotions and you've got a real recipe for disaster."

Lord, You promise I can do all things through You, but I'm not sure how much longer I can hold on to my temper with this guy.

Maggie worked to keep her voice even. "But didn't Eleanor Roosevelt say that women are the untapped resource with the capacity to free up more men for the front?"

"She's as odd as those girl flyers. What would she know about fighting a war? But that's enough about that." Webber took one last slug of his soda before shifting to face her. "I'd rather spend what time I've got left getting to know a pretty girl like you, Margaret."

Maggie flinched when his fingers made contact with her bare arm. "You sound like you've been handed a death sentence, Lieutenant."

"Maybe I have." Before Maggie could move out of his reach, the man grasped her arm and dragged her to him. She squeezed her hands between their bodies and pushed gently, but he tightened his grip around her.

"I'm shipping out on Monday, baby." His mouth scraped against her cheek, making her skin crawl. "Then what? What if all I have left is this moment with you?"

Bile rose up in her throat, robbing her of her voice. She planted her palms against his chest and shoved him as hard as she could, but to no avail. "Let me go."

"You heard the lady, Lieutenant. Let her go."

Wesley?

The shock of his command loosened Anthony's grip on her, and she retreated back into her chair. Wesley had come to the rescue, just in the nick of time. She'd never been so relieved to see the man in her life.

The sound of chair legs scraping against

the floor made her turn. Anthony stood, his body rigid with tension. "With all due respect, Captain, this is a private conversation between me and Margaret."

"Then we'll ask the lady," Wesley answered, crouching down beside her, the worry creasing his brow causing something deep inside her to melt. His warm hands rested on top of hers. "Are you okay?"

She lifted her head, her eyes traveling over the wide expanse of his uniformed chest, his clean-cut chin, and a glimmer of blond hair, darkened and slicked back by a recent shower. Pressing her backbone into her chair, she took a deep breath. Anthony Webber might have unnerved her, but Wesley's effect on her had alarm sirens sounding in her heart.

"I'm fine, Captain," she answered, more breathless than she would have liked.

Wesley stepped around her, his eyes never leaving hers. "May I join you?"

"Please." Maggie motioned to the vacant chair beside her. "The more the merrier."

"Thank you." Wesley grabbed the seat and pushed it in between her and the lieutenant. He looked around the empty table. "Where are Donna and Edie?"

Maggie nodded toward the dance floor, vaguely amused by the stark look of confusion on Webber's face. "I'm not much of a dancer."

"Maybe you just need the right partner." He threw her a brief smile before glancing over at Anthony. "What were you two talking about before I interrupted?"

The thought of exactly what had been on the lieutenant's mind when Wesley had suddenly showed up sent a shudder through her. She leaned closer to Wesley. "Anthony was explaining to me why he doesn't think much of the Super Fortress, sir."

"Really," Wesley said, eyeing the man before shifting his gaze back to her. "A strange topic to be discussing with such a beautiful woman, Lieutenant."

Heat rose in her cheeks, and she didn't dare meet his eyes. Compliments, especially from men, usually made her uncomfortable, but this one caused her heart to flutter wildly in her chest. "Thank you."

He nodded, then turned back to Anthony. "So what's your problem with the B-29?"

The lieutenant glared at the two of them. "Anyone with a lick of sense knows that the flying coffin is just an accident waiting to happen. Just look at the crash out in Kansas today."

There'd been another fortress go down? Surely Wesley would have told her. She

182

turned around to face him, finding the truth in the lines softly creasing his brow. His eyes met hers, and she ached for the anguish and defeat she found there. How she longed to help him, bring some relief to the pain he felt.

But his voice sounded strong and sure when he spoke. "The Super Fortress is still our best hope for winning the war in the Pacific."

"Spoken like a man who won't be at her helm, Captain," Anthony snapped.

How dare the man! Talking to Wesley, a war hero for goodness sake, as though he didn't understand the dangers of combat. Her palm itched to leave its print on the lieutenant's smug face.

"Then why don't we get the opinion of someone who will be piloting the Fortress?" Laying his arm against the back of her chair, Wesley leaned toward her. "What do you think, Ace?"

The faint scent of lime aftershave and soap filled her lungs, scattering her thoughts like leaves on the wind. Her voice caught, and she wasn't sure if it was that Wesley had asked her opinion or the delicious feel of his arm brushing protectively against her shoulder. Maggie swallowed. No man, not even her dad, had asked her what she thought about an important issue, certainly not in public.

She'd expected to see a glint of humor in his expression, but instead found he honestly wanted her thoughts on the matter. For the first time in her life, Maggie felt her work had value to someone else other than herself.

Anthony chuckled from beside her. "Begging your pardon, sir, but what would a doll like Margaret know about planes?"

Heat gnarled in the pit of her stomach. She jerked her head around to glare at the man. Had the lights taken on a fiery haze or was she actually seeing red? "Did you just call me a doll?"

Anthony reached across the table for her free hand and she cringed. "It's just a sweet nothing, honey."

"Let's get something straight." She snatched her hand away. "I am not your honey or your baby, and I'm certainly not a doll. And if you'd taken the time to read the updated information on the B-29, you would have figured out that the glitches with engine burnout have been resolved, as well as the refueling problem."

"Sounds like she knows quite a bit." Wesley added, his fingers tenderly clasped around her shoulders as if to remind her he was there. As if she would forget.

Webber sat slack-jawed, his focus bouncing between them before finally settling on her. "Who are you? Tokyo Rose or something?"

She lifted her chin a notch. "I'm one of those oddball girl-pilots you appear to have such a problem with, Lieutenant."

"She's kidding, right?" Webber directed the question at Wesley.

"No." Wesley looked at her then, a smile playing around the corners of his mouth. "She's one of the best pilots in my Air Transport squad at the Bell."

Her temper fled at Wesley's statement. Did he really believe she was as good as he had made her out to the lieutenant, or was he simply protecting the reputation of the Flying 83rd?

"She's your best, huh?" Anthony sat back, his arms crossed over his chest, his arrogant smile tugging at his lips. "That's easy to say when there's no way of ever proving it."

Good gracious, the man didn't have enough sense to get out of a paper sack. But he was wrong. There was a way, a little practice maneuver the girls at Sweetwater had done from time to time to get in flight time. "I can prove it."

Wesley leaned toward her, his eyebrows

knitted together in surprise. "How are you going to do that?"

She chose to ignore him for the moment, although his fingers tightening on her arm made that task difficult. For now, her sights were on the lieutenant. "This afternoon before I left, the mechanics returned a pair of Thunderbolts badly in need of a test flight. What better way to see if those planes are battle ready than a little dog fight?"

"You and me in a mock fire fight?"

"Yes," she answered, finally meeting Wesley's gaze. "That is, if the captain here approves."

Wesley's hand dropped from her shoulder to curl around the back of her chair, leaving her with a faint sense of loss. Well, Anthony Webber had backed her into a corner. What else could she do?

"Major Evans does enjoy a little friendly competition between the posts, and it's been his position in the past to give his okay." Wesley stopped and took a deep breath. "But he's never had a woman pilot under his command before, either."

Please, Wesley. Give me a chance, just this once. Humiliation threatened to crash over her. Facing down the lieutenant would be nothing compared to dealing with Wesley every day, knowing he honestly didn't believe in her skills.

"The major's been chomping at the bit to see you in action, but we've got a problem." Wesley leaned over the table, his hands clenched in front of him. "Maggie's due to deliver a plane first thing tomorrow morning."

Webber relaxed back into his chair. "I thought so."

Maggie wasn't about to back down. Resting her hand on Wesley's arm, she stared at him. "Couldn't someone else take my flight?"

"I've never heard you give up a chance to fly." Maggie looked across the table to see Donna folding her skirts into the chair Bill held out for her.

"She has the opportunity to fly against Lieutenant Webber in a mock fire fight," Wesley answered. "That is, if she can find someone to cover her flight assignment in the morning."

Was Wesley trying to help her? She glanced at him. He might put on a good act for the lieutenant, but she knew better. The tightness around his mouth, the icy-blue stare he gave her were warning shots. She had pushed too hard. He wouldn't call her out here, but she would hear about this, probably sooner rather than later.

"Where are you headed to?" Donna asked Maggie.

Maggie shook her head. She wasn't about to ask her friend to fly out and leave her fiancé, not when the man was two days away from shipping out. Who knew how long they'd be separated? No, she'd have to find someone else to help her out.

"Shaw in South Carolina," Wesley answered.

Both Donna and Bill's faces fell slightly at the news, and Maggie frowned. Why couldn't Wesley ask one of the guys in the squad? Maybe like her, he already knew their answer.

"I'll do it, Captain," Donna spoke up.

Maggie shook her head. "I can't let you do that."

"Why? If it hadn't been for the storm, I would have had to fly out this afternoon." Donna clasped Bill's hand tightly within hers. "I just feel blessed to have seen him before he ships out."

"Me, too." Bill lifted Donna's hand to his mouth and brushed a brief kiss across her knuckles. Maybe her friend had been right. Maybe a girl could have it all if she found the right man to dream alongside her.

Maybe someone like Wesley.

"Well, you've got your replacement, Ace."

Wesley's words broke through her thoughts. "Now let's go over the ground rules."

"Are you people out of your mind? I'm not flying against a woman!"

Wesley grimaced at Webber's statement. He'd already decided he must be a marble short of a set to give Maggie permission to fly against the lieutenant. Not that he worried about Maggie losing. He hadn't lied about her being the top pilot in his squadron. Truth be told, she was the best pilot he'd ever seen, male or female.

But Webber? The man was another story. The thought of Maggie getting hurt because of the lieutenant's inexperience made the area around Wesley's heart tighten. All he could do at this point was pray that the predicted storms for the morning would wash out any possibility of this dare taking place.

"Why? You chicken?" Donna asked, leaning into Bill's shoulder.

"No." Anthony picked at his fingernails. "I just don't see any point in a mock dog fight with a woman."

Good, the man was worried, as well he should be. Maggie would give him a whooping he'd never forget. "Why not? You might be facing a woman when you get to the

189

front, Lieutenant. You know, one of the Nazis' most celebrated combat pilots is a woman. And I know for a fact most of those girls ferrying planes for the Royal Air Force could fly circles around you. I've seen them."

"I've heard about the Russians putting women in the cockpit, but the English?" Bill shook his head. "That's a new one to me."

"I didn't know you worked with the girls in the Royal Air Force," Maggie said, the wonder in her voice filling him with dread.

He'd never meant to let Maggie know that piece of information — couldn't because he wasn't ready for the questions she would no doubt have. What would Maggie say if she knew the truth about his sister? That she had died because of him? Suddenly, he felt unbearably tired.

A soft hand slipped into his, giving him a reassuring squeeze. He turned to find Maggie studying him, her eyes darkened by concern and something akin to empathy. Yes, if anyone could understand his loss, it would be Maggie Daniels. Something in his heart broke free. The pain he had carried around for so long suddenly felt a little lighter. He tightened his fingers around hers, then let go.

"This is crazy." Anthony pushed his chair

back and stood. "I'm not flying against some girl."

"Why not?" Donna asked, one blond eyebrow lifted in annoyance. "Didn't a girl teach you how to fly in the first place, Lieutenant?"

"Fine!" Metal clanged as he slammed the chair against the table. "What time do you want me there?"

Wesley cleared his throat. "Nine hundred hours. I'll have one of my men meet you at the front gate."

"I'll be there." The lieutenant came to attention and snapped off a quick salute in Wesley's direction. The man turned, then just as suddenly turned back. He walked the few steps to where Maggie sat and leaned over, his mouth close to her ear. Wesley bent slightly toward them. "I just wanted to help Bill out. You know, give him some time with his girl, maybe even meet a nice girl for myself. Didn't expect to run into a nut case, that's for sure."

Wesley jumped to his feet, the chair clattering to the floor behind him. All the blood had drained from Maggie's cheeks. The music faded into the background, replaced by an angry buzzing noise. His hands balled up into tight fists. He'd like to knock the lieutenant into tomorrow, but the military police he'd seen at the door as he came through were pushing against the crowd toward their table.

"Is there a problem here?" a tall man asked. He wore the same shade of green as half the men present, except for the wide white band on his right arm.

Wesley shook his head, unfurling the fists at his sides and drawing in a slow breath. "No, sir. Just a simple misunderstanding."

The man didn't seem convinced. "Is that right?"

"You see —" Maggie rose beside him, her voice a bit wobbly but firm "— this gentleman thought we had a date tonight but we don't." Maggie glared at the lieutenant. "It's tomorrow morning at nine."

"That's mighty early in the day for a date," the officer replied, looking at her warily.

She flashed the man what Wesley thought was too flirtatious a smile. "Just doing what I can for the war effort, sir."

"And this guy?" The officer pointed a thumb toward him.

"I'm Ms. Daniels's escort for the evening," Wesley answered, his heart tripping over the statement. He glanced down at Maggie, worried she might blow his cover, but was instead greeted with a shy, almost grateful smile.

The officer looked at her for confirmation. "Well?"

"Yes, I'm here with Captain Hicks." Maggie nodded, her gaze never leaving his. He smiled, the thought of spending more time with her growing on him by the second.

The officer turned to Webber and with his baton, pointed him toward the door. "She'll see you tomorrow morning, lover boy."

"I wouldn't miss it for the world." The lieutenant adjusted his tie. He nodded toward the wall where a line of anxious women waited for a dance partner before giving her a dismissive glance. "Now if you'll excuse me, I see a few real women whom I'd like to strike up a conversation with."

Wesley started to lunge for the man, but Maggie's hand on his chest held him in place. He hadn't been thinking straight, allowing that man on his air field, flying against his best pilot. The thought of the two of them dueling it out sent a fresh wave of anger crashing through him. If Webber came anywhere near Maggie after tomorrow, it would take more than the military police to keep him from beating the man to a pulp.

Wesley risked a glance at Maggie. Her cheeks had turned pale once more, and he thought he caught a glimmer of moisture threaded in her sooty lashes. But the line of her jaw was set in that determined line he was quickly coming to appreciate. She watched the lieutenant disappear into the crowd. Had the man's final dig bothered her? Didn't she know the truth, that she was the kind of woman a man would be lucky to share his life with?

He blinked. Where had that thought come from? He had enough troubles in his life without laying his heart on the line.

"Come on, Maggie." Wesley held out his hand to her. "Let's dance."

She lowered her gaze, her fingers knotted together. "I'm not a very good dancer."

He didn't know why, but the uncertainty in her eyes, the way she nibbled on her lower lip, struck him like a blow to the chest. No, he wouldn't let her off that easy. "Then I'll teach you."

She took a quick look in the direction of the front door. "Maybe one dance. Just to throw the police off."

When Maggie slipped her hand into his, tiny pulses of awareness blazed a trail up his arm, settling in the area around his heart.

"Would you excuse us?"

"Certainly, Captain." Donna nodded.

Wesley nodded at them, noting the coy smile Donna threw his way. Maybe asking Maggie for a dance hadn't been such a good idea after all, not if it set folks to talking.

He walked alongside her to the dance floor in silence, not feeling the need to exchange the usual pleasantries he knew women expected when they were asked to dance. But Maggie seemed not to mind, apparently lost in her own thoughts for the moment.

When they reached the dance floor, Maggie turned to face him, a nervous smile playing at her lips. "You're going to regret this."

"You can't be that bad of a dancer." His hand settled at her waist, vaguely surprised at how delicate she felt beneath his fingers.

"The worst."

Before he could answer, lights went down, and the first notes of an Ella Fitzgerald song — "Dream a Little Dream of Me" — drifted through the gymnasium.

Wesley drew her close until her cheek rested on the green wool of his jacket. "You do know how to sway back and forth, don't you?"

He felt her smile against his shoulder. "I may step on your toes."

He chuckled. "I'll take my chances."

Clasping her hand within his, Wesley rested his chin on the top of her head, her silky waves a soft pillow beneath his skin. Couples around them moved in time. While most kept a polite distance, one couple clung to each other, her head nestled against his cheek, his white-clothed arm firmly wrapped around her waist. The shiny gold band on her left hand caught the light. Probably on their honeymoon.

Well, falling in love wasn't on his list of objectives. He didn't have the time, not with proving the B-29's viability and training a capable crew. But he could enjoy this moment. He closed his eyes, the faint scent of lavender stealing across his senses.

Maggie tilted her head back, leaving him with a sense of loss. "Thanks for bailing me out back there."

"It was the least I could do." Wesley looked down at her, his breath catching in his throat. Gracious, the woman was beautiful! "How did you get stuck with that guy in the first place?"

She lowered her chin. "I was trying to help Donna out. That's all."

Wesley laughed, gently tightening his hold and bringing her close. "The man didn't know what hit him after you got through with him."

"Someone needs to put him in his place before he gets himself killed."

"And you figured you would be the one to do it. What if I had said no?"

"But you didn't, did you?"

No, he hadn't, but he should have — for her sake. "You don't have to prove yourself to anybody, Maggie."

Her chin grazed his shoulder when she nodded. "Oh, yes I do, and you know it."

"That's how people get themselves killed."

"Then worry about that flyboy, not me." Maggie nodded toward the group of men lining the nearby wall.

Wesley glanced over her head, shifting his attention to where Webber stood with a group of men, passing a small flask between them, each taking a sip. The last man handed the silver container back to Webber.

Jimbo.

His jaw tightened. At the rate the men were going, neither would be able to walk, much less fly. That made the situation all the more dangerous.

He slid his fingers beneath her chin and tilted Maggie's head back until her face was his entire focus. "Come on, Ace. Don't risk your life trying to prove yourself to that goon."

"If you feel that way, then why did you

give your permission?"

He sighed. "Because I know we're going to have another front coming through in the morning. No one will be flying out of the Bell until at least tomorrow afternoon. By that time, Webber will be gone."

Her eyes widened. "Then why did you give your permission?"

"You're still a part of my squadron, and nobody bad-mouths the Flying 83rd."

She pushed away from him. "You only backed me up to save face. All that talk about me being the best was just that. Talk."

"I know you can take him, Ace," he whispered into her hair when he pulled her close. "But what about the lieutenant? He's the unknown in all this." He leaned his cheek against her head. "I'm not about to put you at risk with some rookie who doesn't know what he's doing."

She relaxed slightly in his arms. "What if it doesn't rain?"

"We'll cross that bridge when we come to it." Wesley swayed them in time to the music. "Though I've got to question the man's judgment. What guy would talk shop when he could have been dancing with you?"

Maggie tilted her head back, her eyes glowing with laughter. "Maybe he knew what a terrible dance partner I'd make."

"Then he's a nut case," Wesley replied. "Any man worth his weight would want a beautiful woman in his arms."

The faint flush of color flared in her cheeks. "For what it's worth, thank you for backing me up in front of the lieutenant. I really owe you one for that."

"No problem," Wesley whispered, her warm smile making him miss a step. "You do know that Webber's wrong, don't you?"

Maggie stepped back half a step, putting some distance between them. "Sure I do. And if it doesn't rain, I'm going to prove it tomorrow."

"That's not what I meant."

"I don't understand."

Wesley chuckled. Was it possible that Maggie didn't have any idea how appealing she was? "The majority of men like intelligent, beautiful women, Ace."

Her gaze collided with his, the unmistakable doubt in her eyes startling him. "How many girls have you used that line on, Captain?"

She didn't realize that he was being honest? He shook his head. "That's not my style."

"Really? That's a first," she said, snorting softly. "So what is your battle plan for winning a woman's heart?"

"Never really had the chance to implement one. I guess it depends on the girl. But every relationship needs honesty, a shared respect, and faithfulness to God and each other." He paused for a second. "I'd want to protect her, make sure she knows she'll always be safe with me."

Though she remained in his arms, he felt her draw away from him. What could he have said that would have bothered her so much? Most women would be thrilled by a declaration of love, honesty and faithfulness, but Maggie wasn't like any other woman he'd ever known. She'd always made it clear that she could take care of herself. But didn't she understand that men felt the need to protect the women they loved?

Maggie finally tilted her head back to look up at him. "What are you doing here in the first place?"

Wesley smiled. The woman was good at maneuvering out of a tight spot. "Someone I know said I could use a break. So I figured I'd come here and dance with a pretty girl."

She stiffened in his arms. "Then don't let me stop you."

"You haven't," he answered, pulling her close.

When her head dropped softly to his shoulder, Wesley took a shuddered breath, his heart tapping out a thunderous beat beneath his breastbone as they danced in silence. He glanced around the room, catching more than a few appreciative looks being thrown toward his partner. Truth be told, Maggie Daniels could have any man in this room, but she was dancing with him. The knowledge satisfied something uniquely male in him.

"You're quiet all of a sudden."

Was that a slight quaver in her voice? He rested his cheek against her forehead. "Just enjoying the music."

"Me, too," she answered, her cheek resting against his shoulder, her breath sending a warm shiver of awareness down his arm. He tightened his hold, and Maggie relaxed further. He closed his eyes to the crowd pressing against them and enjoyed the feel of Maggie in his arms.

When the last note of the song echoed softly against the walls, they clung for just a moment before Maggie reluctantly moved out of his embrace. "Thank you."

"Maggie?"

"Yes?"

"You don't have anything to prove tomorrow, at least not to anyone at the Bell." The words came out rougher than he had intended, almost as an order.

Maggie turned and, after a moment, walked back to him. He wasn't sure what caused her to reach out and touch the medals pinned to his coat pocket. Maybe she had seen the apprehension he felt at the thought of losing her, just as he'd lost Beth.

"You know I have something to prove," she whispered. "Just like I'm betting that girl you're thinking of right now thought she had something to prove, too."

Wesley swallowed hard, caught completely off guard. Had she heard about his sister's accident around the plant? Or was he that easy for her to read? "You're right. Beth did think she had something to prove."

"You're talking about your sister, aren't you?"

His heart sunk a little, just as it did every time he thought about Beth. "How did you know that?"

"You mentioned her once, back on my first day at the Bell," she replied, watching him, her eyes wide with concern. "Why didn't you tell me she's a pilot?"

"Was, Maggie," Wesley answered in a somber voice. "My sister died."

He took a deep breath, studying her as the realization slowly etched itself on her features. She knew the truth about him, or she soon would, once the shock wore off and she started asking questions. Soon — because he wouldn't be able to keep the truth from her — Maggie would know the whole sordid tale.

That he was to blame for his sister's death.

CHAPTER ELEVEN

"Those hot dogs really hit the spot," Wesley said, his arm resting across the back of the train seat he shared with Maggie. "I'd heard about the Varsity, but I never had the chance to get there."

"I'm still surprised you've been here for months and never been there," Maggie replied, watching Wesley as patches of moonlight shone through the cabin window.

"Now that I know someone who shares my love for fried pies, we'll have to go there more often," Wesley answered, the humor in his voice sending ripples of awareness through her.

She cleared the frog out of her throat. "You should try their ice cream. They're not serving it now because of the shortages, but their lemon cream is out of this world."

"Then we'll have to make it a date. The day after the war ends, you and I will head down to the Varsity for ice cream."

Maggie smiled. She'd had no intention of leaving the U.S.O. with Wesley tonight. Being around him, getting to know more about him was becoming more than her heart could handle. But learning about his sister, seeing the slump in his shoulders, the tight line of guilt slashed across his brow, she realized she couldn't walk away.

After Bill had assured her that he and Jeff would see Donna and Edie home, Maggie and Wesley left the gym. She had automatically turned toward the train station, assuming they would head for home. But Wesley hadn't seemed to be in any hurry, taking her elbow and prompting her down a side street that led them deeper into downtown. They walked the streets for hours, talking as they went, eventually ending up at the Varsity. Over onion rings and orange shakes, they talked about almost everything.

Everything except his sister.

Maggie snuggled into her seat, relishing the warmth of Wesley's arm draped across her shoulders. He hadn't spoken any more about Beth, and she hadn't pushed it. He'd talk when he was ready.

It didn't stop her from wondering exactly how Beth Hicks had died.

The steel wheels whined softly against the rails, the chug-a-chug of the train engine in perfect unison with the gentle rocking of the passenger car. A black inkiness hid the cotton fields and flop houses she knew lined the tracks, same as they had since the Civil War. Maggie leaned her head against the window. Around here, everything changed at a snail's pace.

A few minutes later, the dim glow of lights in the station cast shadows throughout the passenger car. As the train whined to a stop, Wesley tightened his hold on her, folding her into his side as if protecting her from a fierce blow. Maggie wasn't sure why she liked the way it made her feel, as if she was something infinitely precious that needed to be defended at all costs.

But it was what she would have to give up in return that bothered her. Maggie retreated to her side of the bench seat. God had given her a dream, and she wouldn't let Him down. The thought reverberated through her as the train gave a final lurch forward.

"Here you go," Wesley said, handing her the light wrap Merrilee had forced on her at the door.

"Thanks." She unfolded the knit shawl, her fingers trembling against the soft yarn.

"Here, let me help you with that." He took the shawl once again and, spreading it out to its full length, wrapped it around her; his warm and reassuring hands coming to rest on her forearms.

"Thank you," she replied, closing her eyes. She shouldn't savor the rumble of his voice against her back, enjoy the comfort of his arms that enfolded her. The price was too dangerous to her dreams, her heart. God's plan.

He released her and stepped back, allowing her room to pass. For a second she hesitated, wished for another moment in his embrace. Instead she stood, and together, they quietly made their way to the door. When Wesley offered her his hand at the stairs, Maggie considered it for a minute then decided it would be a wiser choice to use the railing.

"Would you like me to get a cab?"

Maggie shook her head. No close confinement with this man. "It's turned into a nice night. And I don't know about you, but I could sure use a walk after those hot dogs."

Leaving the station behind, they turned down a dirt path toward Merrilee's. A full moon lit the grooves and crevices in the well-worn trail, the clouds from earlier in the evening giving way to star-filled skies. Crickets chirped softly in the distance, their song rising and falling in the night air. A light breeze carried the fragrant scent of fresh magnolias. The evening had all the makings of a Frank Capra movie, full of promise and romance.

But not for me. A bit disappointed, Maggie shoved the thought aside. "You've never told me what got you in the cockpit."

"Not exactly the question I was expecting," he answered. The rich timbre of his voice held a hint of surprise.

"What can I say?" She chuckled softly. "I like to keep people on their toes."

"So I've noticed." He lifted his head slightly, the moonlight revealing his soft smile. "I guess I could blame my grandfather. Pops heard the Wright Brothers speak in London when he was a young man. He decided then and there to learn how to fly. To this day, I'm not sure what he said to them to take him on as a student, but they did."

"So you took after him?"

"Oh, no. Pops has a passion for flying. He's owned an airfield near Sheffield since before the Great War," Wesley answered, his voice brimming with respect. "But me? I took up flying because I spent most of my summers with Pops, and the village didn't offer much for a teenager to do."

"You almost sound like you don't enjoy it."

"Flying is okay," he answered with a shrug. "There's just other things I'd rather be doing."

It was her turn to be surprised. "Like what?"

Wesley turned to her, his golden hair shooting off sparks in the moonlight. "Designing planes for Bell."

"Is that why you didn't go back to England?"

He shook his head. "I tried. Bell had listed me as essential personnel."

"Then how can you be a captain in the Air Transport Command?"

"It's part of a deal I made with Bell. I agreed to be stationed in Marietta for the duration of the war so that I can monitor and offer suggestions for alterations on the Fortress when necessary."

Stars and stripes, the man must be an engineering genius for Bell to go to all the trouble! Despite the cool night air, heat invaded her cheeks. "You must have thought I was an idiot, asking you for your résumé that first day."

"No." His voice turned playful. "I actually thought it was kind of cute."

A warm glow flowed through her.

"Really?"

"You just wanted to prove yourself."

She couldn't deny he had a point. "I can't image how someone as talented as you are in the cockpit wouldn't want to fly for a living."

"Not everyone is like you, Ace."

She didn't like that answer, particularly coming from him. "So how did you end up in the Royal Air Force?"

The moon slipped behind a cloud, making the night grow a deeper shade of inky black. In the high limbs of trees, an owl hooted a dismal tune that echoed in the darkness.

Maggie had given up any hope of an answer when Wesley finally spoke. "Pops refused to leave. He'd offered his air field to the government when the bombings first started." Wesley drew in a deep breath before continuing. "When he couldn't find enough mechanics to keep the planes going, I decided I'd go over and help him out. Only way I could do that was to volunteer for the Royal Air Force."

"But you told me you saw some action."

"I did. When we got there, it was worse than what I could have ever imaged. Pilots were getting mowed down by the dozens every single day. We were repairing equipment that would have made better scrap metal than weapons to ward off the Germans," he answered, his voice coarse. "It wasn't too long after I got there that I asked to be reassigned to a flying unit."

"And Beth?"

"She signed up before I did." In what little light there was, she could make out the bleak line of his mouth. "It makes sense, I guess. She went to live with Pops after our mother died, so England had become her home."

Wesley turned to her, his eyes shadowed in the darkness and what she knew to be sorrow. "Beth was a cracker-jack pilot. When the call went out for women to ferry planes, she was one of the first in line to sign up."

The respect with which he spoke of his sister caused a knot to form in Maggie's chest. Tears welled in the corners of her eyes, and she had to blink hard to keep them at bay. "What happened to her?"

Wesley lifted her hand, guiding it into the protective nook of his elbow. "Pops's heart was giving him problems, so Beth and I decided it was time to come home. I wanted to enlist in the Army Air Corp — and Beth," he hesitated, his fingers tightened around hers. "I think she'd seen enough and was ready to come home. She found us three seats on a transport plane to the States, but I couldn't make it." He released a hard humorless chuckle. "We had lost three pilots that morning and were short staffed. I volunteered to refuel and make another run."

Maggie turned and looked up at him. "That was extremely heroic of you."

"Didn't feel heroic, Maggie. So Beth signed on for one last mission," Wesley answered, ducking his head. He drew in a deep breath and sighed. "I was coming out of the debriefing room when I got a call from Beth's commander. She got lost in the fog and had ended up out over the sea." His voice grew distant. "They found the wreckage a few days later."

Maggie bit down on her lower lip to keep the sob in her throat from escaping, her eyelids blinking in rapid succession. Wesley wouldn't appreciate tears. Instead, she anchored herself against his arm and rested her head against his shoulder.

They walked in silence. The moon burst out from behind a low cloud, lighting the milky-white walkway to Merrilee's house. The gravel shifted beneath Maggie, much as her world had shifted in the last few hours.

Letting go of Wesley's arm, she climbed

the first step then turned, unsettled, to find one stair had erased the differences in their heights, leaving her face to face with him. Tiny lines in the corners of his eyes begged to be touched and comforted. She took a breath, willing her fingers to be still.

She lost the battle. Reaching out, she rested her hand against his cheek. His new growth of whiskers scratched the tender skin of her palm, sending a wave of tingles up her arm. "I'm so sorry."

"Yeah, me too." He took a step forward.

Their noses gently bumped, and her breath caught in her throat. She dropped her hand to his shoulder. There had to be a million reasons why she should push him away and run up the stairs and inside to the safety of her room. But for the life of her, she couldn't think of one.

The shift was so slight, she barely caught it. He tucked a strand of hair behind her ear and dropped his hand to his side. "You'd better go inside."

The tender lilt in his voice almost caused her chest to hurt. She grabbed the edge of her wrap, gathering the ends tight across her chest between trembling fingers. "I need to rest up for tomorrow."

He took a step back. "We need you in tip-top shape."

"Right." An awkwardness she wasn't accustomed to threatened to overwhelm her. "Thank you for this evening. I had a great time."

The lopsided smile he gave her did crazy things to her heart. "Me too, Ace."

Maggie turned then and headed up the stairs. The handle of the screen door was in her hand before she realized she had forgotten to ask him one question. "Wesley?"

"Yes?"

"How's your grandfather doing now?"

"I don't know." His expression was unreadable, but there was no mistaking the longing in his voice. "He hasn't talked to me since the day of Beth's funeral."

How's your grandfather doing now?

Wesley stared at the front door, the same one Maggie had disappeared behind just moments ago. Of all the questions she'd asked, the one about Pops had been the toughest.

Turning around, he sat down on the top step and stretched his legs out in front of him. It had been over a year since Beth's funeral — sixteen months to be exact — since that afternoon when he'd walked out of his grandfather's study with strict orders never to return.

Unbuttoning his coat, he slipped his hand inside an interior pocket and pulled out the small folded envelope. He opened it and extracted the coin. Memories flooded through him as he palmed the piece, the moonlight causing the gold finish to sparkle. Pops had given it to him the day he left for college. At the time, Wesley had thought it was silly, carrying a coin from the year of his grandfather's birth around with him, but now, it was the only thing left of his relationship with the man who had raised him after his father had died.

Tightening his fingers around the coin, Wesley leaned back on his elbows. Why on earth had he told Maggie about his grandfather? But he knew the answer, remembering that brief moment when he'd almost kissed her, the awareness he'd felt at her warm breath against his cheek.

He was falling for Maggie Daniels.

But Maggie isn't part of the plan, Lord.

The front yard danced with shadows from the nearby trees as Wesley stared out over it, allowing these new feelings to rain over him. If there was one thing he'd learned over the past sixteen months, it was that life changes when you least expect it. Any other time, he might have given serious consideration to courting Maggie. But not now, not with a war raging on both sides of their world and his work on the B-29 in jeopardy.

And what about Maggie's ambitions to fly professionally? A slight chill ran through him. What if something were to happen to her?

He shook his head. No, a relationship with Maggie wouldn't work. Something inside his heart seemed to flicker, as if the moon had stolen behind a cloud, leaving only the memory of light.

A grunt from the path drew Wesley's attention. In the shadows, he could just make out the lines of a man, his gait unsteady as he stumbled from one side of the walk to the other, the pungent smell of whiskey permeating the warm night air.

Jimbo.

Pushing off the stair, Wesley stood and started toward the inebriated man. No, there were too many things he needed to do.

And falling in love with Maggie Daniels wasn't one of them.

CHAPTER TWELVE

Maggie stared up at the ceiling as soft sunlight peeked around the edges of the blackout drapes. She stretched her muscles. Sleep had not come easily, not when every time she closed her eyes, all she saw was the sadness etched in Wesley's face.

She'd been slightly stunned by the news that he hadn't talked to his grandfather since Beth's funeral. In the blackness of the night, she had replayed their conversation over and over again, looking for some clue, some reason. But for the life of her, she couldn't think of one. Wesley didn't strike her as the type to abandon his family in their time of need. All she had to do was look at his treatment of her own family and Eliza Beth and the tent city for her answer. So what had caused the rift between Wesley and his grandfather?

A dull ache filled her heart as she thought of him, of the loss of not only his sister but his relationship with Pops. She couldn't fathom how she would have ever made it through Jackson's death without her parents' faith and guidance. She still suffered from his loss, probably always would. But Momma and Daddy made the burden of losing him so much easier to bear.

Maggie pushed the covers back and sat up. When Wesley was ready to talk, she'd be there. She glanced at the bedside clock. Stars and stripes, seven o'clock already? She'd have to hurry if she wanted to put her plane through its paces before Lieutenant Webber showed up at the airfield.

Thirty minutes later, Maggie headed for the dining room in search of a strong cup of joe. The familiar sight of her father sitting at the dinner table made her smile. "Daddy? What are you doing here?"

He rose and enveloped her in his strong embrace. "Just thought I'd visit with my favorite daughter while your mother is at the market."

Maggie nestled against his shoulder, the familiar smell of hay and hard work like a balm to her tired soul. She wrapped her arms around his waist. "I'm your only daughter."

"You're still my favorite girl." Her father tucked a curl behind her ear, then tugged her ear lobe just like he had since she was old enough to remember. "Something wrong, Magpie?"

"I'm just glad you're here." She tightened her arms around him. "I love you and Momma; you know that, don't you?"

"Of course we do. And we love you, too, darling girl."

"I know, Daddy," she said, leaning back to look into his lean face. Yes, losing Jackson had been hard on their family, but it had also made them stronger.

"Are you sure there isn't something wrong?"

"No. It just hit me how much I miss you guys. That's all." Maggie extracted herself from her father's arms and headed for the serving table. She poured herself a cup of coffee, then held the pot up. "Can I get you some?"

"No, thank you." Her father took a seat at the head of the table and waited.

Putting the cup and saucer down, she sat beside him. "I'm glad to hear Momma is finally getting out of the house."

"Me, too. I was worried about her there for a spell, but she seems to be through the worst of it," her father replied, studying her.

Maggie lowered her gaze, blowing on her coffee, afraid her father would make out the tremble in her lips through the thin cloud of steam. She'd been worried sick about them both right after they'd learned of Jackson's death, especially when her mother had taken to her bed. The news that Momma was out and about again was a relief.

"How are things going with you, Magpie?"

"Swell, Daddy. Just swell," she answered, quickly taking a sip of her coffee. A trail of fire scorched a path down her throat as if God himself was trying to burn the words she had spoken. Life was far from being swell, but she wasn't going to give her dad something else to fret over. Grabbing the cream, Maggie added a generous amount to her cup.

"I ran into your uncle when I was dropping your mother off this morning."

"How is he doing?" Maggie added a lump of sugar to her coffee.

"His usual cheerful self," her father answered dryly, his arms stretched out in front of him. "Said he was going over to the bomber plant to watch one of the pilots take his niece down a peg or two. He says it's about time, seeing how she's been running around here, stirring up trouble."

"That sounds about like him." Maggie took a sip. "Is that what you think?"

"You know I take his word with a grain of salt. But I would like to hear your side of things."

Setting her cup aside, Maggie told him everything — about Merrilec's tent camp, and how Uncle James had caught her and Wesley coming out of the woods, about her uncle's threats to take Merrilee's house. She finished with Lieutenant Webber and the dare. She couldn't bring herself to tell him about the note, not when he already had so much on his plate.

When she was through, her father sat back, his mouth turning up into a slight grin. "That Webber boy doesn't know what he's gotten himself into."

"That's what Wesley said."

"I see." Her father's smile grew, leaving Maggie with the feeling that he possessed some knowledge she had not quite grasped. "Captain Hicks was with you when this happened last night."

"It wasn't like he was my date or something," she stammered, staring at her cup, the pale blue in the flowery design a perfect match with Wesley's eyes. "He just showed up."

And she had been so glad. As she laid in bed last night, she realized that she was indeed developing feelings for him. Where they would lead, she wasn't sure. But if she was going to follow what she knew was God's plan for her life, she had to give her growing feelings for Wesley to Him.

"Margaret."

Her father's use of her given name pulled her from her ponderings. The look of concern in his expression startled her. "What is it, Daddy?"

"While I understand getting caught up in the moment, I can't help but worry what will happen when you beat this man."

Not if, but when. Her father's confidence warmed her. "What do you mean?"

"In the next few days, this lieutenant is going to be staring down his gun sights at an enemy with his eye on destroying the world as we know it." His Adam's apple bobbled. "What's going to be going through his mind if he's beaten by a girl?"

Maggie wondered if she should mention the women pilots Wesley had talked about last night, but thought better of it. Daddy might be more progressive than most men in Marietta, but even he would draw the line at women pilots in combat. She decided to go with facts.

Maggie stretched her arms out in front of her on the table. "Daddy, this is how the army trains new pilots. We get them up in

222

the air, in a controlled environment where there aren't any ground-to-air missiles coming at them, and we practice maneuvers. If they win, then they build up more confidence for a real fight. But if they lose, they're reevaluated. They get some more practice in, then come back and try again."

"But Magpie, this isn't a training exercise," he reasoned. "This is two obstinate people out to prove their point at the risk of their lives and the lives of others."

Her father's opinion cut her to the bone. "That's not what this is about at all!"

"Isn't it?" Her father leaned forward, blanketing her fingers in the warmth of his calloused hands. "You and I both know that you're fighting to be respected for who you are, and there's nothing wrong with that." He looked at her. "But at what cost? How would you feel knowing that you sent a man off to battle who has doubts about his abilities? That kind of thinking can get a person killed."

"What are you saying, Daddy?"

He squeezed her hand. "Your time is coming, sweetheart. This war is changing how people think about women having a career. But for right now, you need to build these boys up, not tear them down with silliness like this dare."

Maggie couldn't believe what her father was saying. "You want me to forfeit?"

"I was thinking more along the lines of bowing out gracefully."

"But I can't. The guys in my squadron are expecting me to go through with this."

"It's never been that important what people thought of you before."

More important than she'd ever confess to anyone, especially to her worried parent.

"Well, it is now," Maggie said, pulling her hand out of her father's grasp. She stood and pushed the chair in. "I'm finally making headway with some of these guys, Daddy. Do you know how hard that's been? If I back out of this, these guys will have every reason in the world not to trust me when I take the helm of the fortress."

"But there's a man's life at stake."

Maggie cradled her forehead in her hand. "You don't think I know that? Every time I climb into the cockpit of one of those planes, I'm slapped in the face with that knowledge." She glanced up at him. "Have you ever thought I might be doing Lieutenant Webber a favor? Think about it. If he can't handle me, how's he going to handle the German army? And what about his squadron? Don't they have the right to know what kind of pilot he is under pressure?"

"Maggie."

"I understand what you're saying, Dad. Really, I do," she said, feeling as if she'd already gone a couple of rounds with the Nazis. "But I'm not going to let my squadron down."

"Margaret Rose!"

The disappointment in his voice followed her out into the hall as she grabbed her gear and headed for the airfield.

Wesley stared up at the pristine blue sky. The pounding rains that had cancelled flights less than twenty-four-hours before had blown out, leaving a perfect day for flying.

Lord, You broke rank.

He glanced down at the weather report on his clipboard. He would have never agreed to this stunt if he'd been in his right mind last night, but Maggie Daniels had a way of making his brain go to mush lately. And last night had been no exception.

He still couldn't believe he had told her about Beth. A dull pain shot through his chest at the thought of his sister and what the aftermath of her death had done to his grandfather. No, he should have kept his mouth shut about the rift between him and Pops. Though he was mildly surprised when Maggie hadn't asked for more details. But a part of him was glad she knew. Maybe now she'd understand why he was so protective of her.

He stared up at the sky once more. For the moment, all he could do was pray for a cloudburst.

Slapping his clipboard against his thigh, Wesley glanced at a couple of men he recognized from the plant floor walking past. A small group had begun to gather along the chain-link fence, all staring at the woman standing near the P-47 at the end of the runway.

Ignoring the growing crowd, Wesley walked toward her, watching as Maggie knotted one end of thick rope around the plane's landing gear, then took the other end and looped it around the trunk of a nearby water oak. She tugged and pulled on the knotted cord then, seemingly satisfied, marched to the step ladder anchored at the wing of her plane.

Wesley banged his fist against the wing. "Problems?"

"No, I just want to see what she's like full throttle," Maggie answered, tiptoeing along the edge of the wing before shimmying into the cockpit. She twisted around in the tight space as if to get comfortable before clicking the harness into place.

The engine growled into a high-pitched whine, cutting off any further conversation. Wesley stood back, watching Maggie put the plane through its paces. He wished he could teach his men this aspect of her flying, this attention to detail.

But he was still worried. If only he had had the opportunity to talk to her this morning, she might have understood the risks. But it was too late. Word of the dare had spread across the plant floor like kudzu vines in the summer heat. For Maggie to back down now would be a reflection on the Bell plant itself.

Wesley took a step toward the plane when Maggie cut the engines. "She sounds good to go."

"She is," Maggie answered, leaning back in the flight seat. "Now if Webber would show up, we could get this show on the road."

Wesley climbed the rings of the ladder. "Are you sure this is what you want to do, Ace? There's still time to back out of this."

"Did Donna get off okay?" Maggie pushed herself up with her forearms before shifting her legs underneath her.

So she intended to ignore him. "She got off without a hitch about an hour ago. Told me to tell you happy landings always, whatever that means. Now what about this dare?"

"You've never heard the WASP send-off?" Maggie answered shortly, climbing out of the cockpit and onto the wing.

Right now, he didn't give two figs about WASP lingo. Something was bugging Maggie, and as her commanding officer, he had the right to know what it was. "What's wrong?"

Her brows furrowed together in a painful expression. "Nothing."

Wesley didn't buy that answer for a second. "I'd say it's something if the glum look on your face is anything to go by."

"It's just." Her mouth flattened into a grim line. "My father came by to see me this morning."

"And?" Wesley asked impatiently. Whatever had upset her could put her life at risk in the air. "You might as well tell me because I'll scrap this flight if you don't."

If looks could kill, the army would be notifying his next of kin. She lifted her chin up a notch. "Major Evans would be upset if you cancelled."

"He'd be a lot more than disappointed if

the WASP under his command got herself killed." Wesley glared at her, not willing to back down for a second if it meant keeping her safe. "So it's your call, Maggie."

She lowered her gaze to the tarmac. "Daddy thinks I should bow out. He said that my winning this dare could cause Webber to put himself and others who go into combat with him in danger." Her shoulders trembled slightly as she took a breath. "I tried to explain to him that this is how we train the guys, that it's better for them to know what they're getting into before they're in the middle of a skirmish, but he wouldn't listen."

Wesley thought for a moment. No, Mr. Daniels didn't understand, but neither did Maggie. It was one thing for Webber to doubt his ability in the cockpit. Then this challenge would be just the exercise he needed to critique his shortcomings and make corrections. But this dare had been made out of prideful anger, and nothing could get a good pilot killed faster than acting off of some silly emotion. Wesley should cancel this flight.

But he respected Maggie enough to offer her a chance. "You're right. Your dad doesn't understand. Webber is a jerk and he'll get what's coming to him."

Maggie smiled softly, completely unaware of the captivating impression she made on him. "Thank you."

He shook his head. "Don't thank me yet. You let your emotions get out of hand. And that's what gets people hurt."

"I see." Her eyes snapped to attention. "And I suppose we girls are only emotional messes in attractive little packages, right?"

"I don't know about you," Wesley started, offering his hand as she planted her foot on the first step, "but I don't happen to think Webber is all that pretty."

She ducked her head, her mouth trembling, but whether from anger or amusement, he didn't know. Maggie grasped his hand, her grip sturdy in his, the hard pads of her fingertips a reminder of her time behind the controls, flying over fields of green beans and corn, tomatoes and cotton. There was nothing dainty in her touch, yet his heart pounded against his breastbone. When she finally lifted her gaze, the laughter in her pale green eyes reminded him of an English countryside after a late afternoon rain. Maggie was growing on him. What that meant, he wasn't sure.

Maggie carefully tiptoed down the steps, then paused in front of him. "How do you do that?"

"What?"

"Make me laugh when I'm fit to be tied."

"I don't know. Must be a gift." He shrugged, then grew serious. "I don't want to keep harping on this, but it's your job to test the B-29 for flight, not help this boy improve his skills in the cockpit. You'll earn respect by doing just that."

Maggie's mouth quirked to the side, her eyes wide and repentant. "I hate to admit it, but you've got a point." She took a deep breath and sighed. "So what do you think I should do?"

Wesley reached out to tuck a stray curl back from Maggie's face, his fingers tingling as he grazed the soft shell of her ear. He dropped his hand to his side. "Teach Lieutenant Webber a lesson he won't soon forget."

Her face lit up, and she smiled. "Would you pray with me before I take off?"

Wesley nodded as a warmth settled deep in his chest. Faith and courage. Maggie Daniels was becoming more than he could resist.

Wesley wants me to win!

A slight thrill simmered through Maggie as she looked up at Wesley. She hadn't expected him to be in her corner today, not

231

after learning about his sister last night. But there he was, checking her plane, getting her focused on the true objectives of this mission. Being protective, yes, but of both pilots taking to the air today, not just her. He was wrong though; it was part of her job to get the boys ready for combat.

And she would do her job to her utmost today.

A cheer rose up behind them. Maggie turned slightly to see Lieutenant Webber stroll along the fence, waving to the crowds as if he were Charles Lindbergh after just landing in Paris. He took his time making his way across the tarmac. His cronies followed close behind.

"I figured you'd be washing your hair or something, doll," Webber called out, strolling up to them. "Isn't that what you girls do?"

Maggie mashed her lips together. She wasn't going to allow this man to get the best of her.

"The day is young, Webber. Maggie's still got plenty of time once she teaches you a thing or two."

Maggie stole a peek at Wesley. For a man who had spent the morning lecturing her on the ills of emotional flying, he seemed to know how to get on the lieutenant's last nerve, if Webber's flushed face was anything to go by.

The lieutenant sneered at her. "Been cuddling up to your commanding officer, huh? Well, that's not going to win you any points up there."

Wesley stiffened beside her. If she didn't stop this verbal war, a physical one might break out. Maggie took a step toward Webber. "Are you finished? I don't know about you, but I'd like to get on with this."

"Fine with me, but I did have an idea."

The half-cocked smile he threw her way gave her a second's pause. "Really, Anthony? Is that a first for you?"

The man smirked. "Very funny, baby doll. Why don't we make this a little more of a challenge?"

"What did you have in mind?" Wesley asked, his tone leery.

"Nothing a good pilot shouldn't be able to handle," Webber answered, cocking a fist on one hip. "Just a hooded flight."

Maggie would have laughed out loud if the two men standing beside her hadn't looked so serious. Webber had to be kidding. Hooded flight was like flying blind.

And she held the record of a perfect score.

Maggie extended her hand to the lieutenant. "You're on."

"Good," Webber answered, then turned toward the flight tower and spun around. "Oh, for your information, honey, I ranked first in my class in instrument flying."

"Glad to hear it," Maggie called out, her hand cupped around her mouth. "Nice to know I may actually have some competition."

Wesley spun her around to face him. His warm fingers burned through the thin cotton of her long-sleeved shirt, scalding the tender skin of her upper arm. "What do you think you're doing?"

"I'm giving Lieutenant Webber a lesson on instrument flying."

"I don't like this." A muscle convulsed at his jaw. "This guy is bad news."

Lifting her eyes to his, Maggie started to tell him the truth, then stopped short at the anxious glare she found staring back at her. Oh, of course. Beth had been flying blind in a fog when she went down. Why hadn't she thought of that before she took Webber up on his challenge?

Because she shouldn't have to. Flying by instruments was part of her job, and hooded flights would keep her reflexes sharp for real-time flights.

Wesley should be the first to understand that fact.

Lord, let me say the right words to give Wesley peace right now. Maggie laid her hand over his chest, the thumping of his heart beneath her palm soothing. "I know you're worried, but don't be. I've never scored less than perfect on my instrument flying, and I've trained dozens of men in hooded flight. I know what I'm doing."

"But this guy," Wesley started, shifting his eyes to stare at the man preparing his plane across the tarmac. "I get the feeling he'd go to any lengths to get back at you, Maggie."

The thought that came to her was so unlike anything she had ever done in the past, but for some reason, she felt it was the right way to go in this situation. "Then it's up to you, Captain. What do you want me to do?"

His blue eyes darkened as if bruised by the struggle Maggie knew was going on inside him. He turned away from her. Her hand hung awkwardly in the air, robbed of his warmth beneath her fingertips. She watched him pace a short distance from her, noted the muscles of his shoulders coiled in frustration beneath his fitted shirt.

"Is the girl going to fly or what?" a man on the civilian side of the fence called out, followed by others asking the two pilots to take their places.

Driving a hand through his hair, Wesley

235

spun around to face her. Though she could tell the battle was over, Wesley didn't look happy with the outcome. "If I okay this, you'll need another pilot who has visual reference at all times. Is that understood?"

Thank You, Lord! She nodded, mashing her lips together. It wouldn't do for Wesley to see her smile. He might think she wasn't taking this exercise seriously. "Do you have someone in mind?"

"Yes." Wesley didn't seem to have to think twice about it. "Me."

Impossible man! Maggie crossed her arms around her waist. "Webber will think you're playing favorites."

"Let him." Wesley's soft voice held something of a dare. "You're not the one going to the front."

But she was. Every day she, or every other WASP that reported for duty, fought a battle — to prove to men and women alike that anything was possible. Even a girl pilot, as long as God was with them. She eyed Wesley for a moment before her attention turned to the crowd continuing to grow at the fence. How could she expect to make anyone else comprehend what the Women Army Service Pilots were doing when she couldn't convince Wesley after all he had lost?

"We don't have any two-seat trainers on the ground," Wesley continued. "And the closest one is either Warner Robbins or Augusta."

He was stalling for time when there was a very simple solution. "Then we'll have to go back to our original plan."

"I don't think . . ."

But she refused to listen. Ignoring the stubborn set of his jaw, the uncompromising glint in his gaze, she started back toward her plane. She felt for him, really she did. But his overprotectiveness wasn't simply based on Beth's death. No, something else was going on here, and until he decided to come clean with her, she had to stick with her plan.

And that included no attachments.

A vague sense of loss rippled through her. Well, she didn't need anyone. All she'd ever wanted was a backdrop of blue beneath her, the scent of engine oil pungent in her nose. It was her only calling. At least, that's what she kept telling herself.

Maggie had cleared her plane's wing when she heard the shout come from the direction of the tower. The pulsating excitement that had electrified the crowds had shifted into a somber confusion. Maggie searched for Wesley and found him amongst a crowd of officers lining the tarmac near the gate. He stood, listening, seeming to concentrate on the lieutenant in front of him. She couldn't see most of Wesley's face, but knew instinctively that the news wasn't good by the slight tightening of the sinew muscles across his back.

He turned, and she met his gaze. The corners of his eyes turned down in a bleak descent while his mouth carved a remorseful line across his face. He walked toward her at a slow, serious pace that at any other time might have been confused for a funeral march. Something big had happened, something that, by the look on Wesley's face, he didn't want to tell her.

Please, Lord! Whatever has happened, please help us get through it! She kept praying, whispering words from deep within her soul until Wesley finally stood before her.

Locking her knees, Maggie lifted her head and looked him square in the eye. "What's wrong?"

"There's been an accident."

Her world tilted slightly, and her heart knotted in her chest. Maybe it wasn't as bad as it seemed. Maybe, just maybe.

But his next words erased any possibility of a happy landing.

"Donna crashed in a field outside of New Hope this morning."

CHAPTER THIRTEEN

The smell of disinfectant stung the back of Maggie's throat as Wesley held open the elevator door that led to the hospital corridor. The bright lights and cold white walls of Crawford Long's surgical floor caused the tears she'd been holding back for the last hour to gather once more in the corners of her eyes, and she blinked. Wesley's hand came to rest at the curve of her back, gently nudging her forward.

"Are you okay?" he asked.

Maggie glanced up at him and nodded. She wouldn't have made it through the last few hours without Wesley. His calming presence had gotten her through the chaos at the air field, held her up during the agonizing train ride into the city and guided her through the crowded streets of Atlanta to the hospital's front door.

"Donna's in Room 415," she said.

They walked down the corridor in silence,

Maggie closely following the sequence of numbers pasted to each door. She'd never been to a hospital. What with money tight as it was, a body either survived Dr. Miller's superior ministrations or died at home. She didn't know what to expect when she finally saw her friend.

As she rounded the corner with Wesley, Maggie saw Bill, his face in his hands, slumped in his chair. She touched his shoulder as she came to him. "How is she?"

His shoulders slumped, Bill looked up at her. "She's banged up pretty bad, and her right leg is a mess, but she's alive."

"Thank God," Wesley said.

Maggie dropped down into the seat next to Bill. "Has she said anything about what happened?"

Bill shook his head. "Not much. Only that she thought she had made it down safely when she clipped a tree."

A wave of guilt assailed Maggie. If she hadn't been so pigheaded about showing Lieutenant Webber a thing or two, Donna would have been enjoying the day with Bill instead of being busted up and in the hospital.

I'm the one who would have crashed that plane instead.

Wesley's hand settled over her shoulder,

241

the tender strength in his fingers as he gently stroked her tense muscles doing little to chase away the harsh realities of the situation. She glanced up at him, her eyes meeting his, understanding rushing through her. He understood her guilt because he felt the same way.

Maggie nodded her head toward the door. "Can I go in and see her?"

"Sure," Bill answered. "The nurse is in there now giving her something for pain, so I don't know how long you're going to have."

"That's all right. I just want to see for myself that she's okay."

Maggie pushed herself up from the chair. Wesley's hand fell from her shoulder and for one long moment, she wished he would go in with her. She nibbled at her lower lip as she walked the couple of steps to the door. What if Donna didn't want to talk to her? Her hand pressed against the door, she looked back at Wesley, but for what, she wasn't sure. His slight smile and encouraging nod helped her to push open the door and go inside.

The room was oblong, with thick curtains hung from the ceiling dividing it into four separate sections. The first three beds were empty, but the fourth was closed off by a set of heavy white drapes.

Maggie tiptoed softly across the room, but before she could reach her destination, the curtains were thrown back. With a cap circling her head like a halo, an older woman dressed in nursing whites hurried toward Maggie.

"May I help you?"

"I'm here to see Donna Lane." Maggie tried to peek around the curtain. But the woman wouldn't budge, guarding her territory as though she was protecting the gates of heaven above.

"She needs her rest," the woman reprimanded, gathering some kind of contraption that looked like a silver bell dangling from two rubber hoses from the nearby table and draping it around her neck.

"I know, and I'm sorry to intrude." Maggie swallowed hard against the knot of guilt in her chest. "I won't stay long, I promise. I just want to make sure that she's fine."

Her eyebrows furrowed into a tight line, the woman stared at Maggie, as if assessing her request. Maggie thought for a second the woman was going to turn her away — then she nodded. "Five minutes. Do you understand?"

"Yes, ma'am."

The woman pushed the curtain back.

"You've got a visitor, Ms. Lane."

"Who?"

"It's me, Donna." Maggie caught sight of her friend, and she felt the blood drain from her face. Donna's rosy complexion was ghostly pale, the lines of her right jaw and eye marred by uneven blotches of purple and blue. Angry red marks scratched up her arm, and her right leg hung suspended from the mattress with ropes and slings like the pulley her dad used on the farm.

"Five minutes." The nurse warned before pulling the curtain shut behind her.

"The old battle-ax," Donna mumbled quietly. "She's worse than anything we had to deal with at basic training."

Maggie smiled. Donna couldn't be too bad off if she was already griping about the nurses. "That's what you get for getting into a fight with a tree."

"If you think I look bad, you should get a load of that dogwood," Donna said through a yawn.

Maggie sat down in a chair next to the bed. "You scared the daylights out of me today."

"You're not the only one."

Maggie glanced toward where the nurse had stood and, satisfied, plunged ahead. "Got any idea about what happened?"

Donna shrugged, then grimaced. "Not really. The plane had checked out perfect and was running great. The only thing I noticed was that my fuel gauge dropped faster than I thought it should. By the time I figured it out, I was in trouble." Donna's voice drifted off.

"You didn't have enough gas to get back to the plant?"

Donna's hair fanned across the pillow as she shook her head. "One minute, it was full; the next, I was scouting out a field to land in."

This didn't make sense. "Did you see any problems in your preflight check?"

Donna's eyelids hung low. "Your Wesley did it for me."

A slight frisson of delight ran through Maggie. "He's not mine, Donna."

A soft smile graced her friend's sleepy features. "Not yet, but you want him to be."

Maggie grimaced. Leave it to her friend to spout romantic nonsense when she could have lost her life today. Resting her forearms on the edge of Donna's bed, Maggie reached out and carefully took her friend's hand. "I'm so sorry about this."

"It's not your fault." She gave Maggie's fingers a gentle squeeze.

"If I hadn't been trying to put Anthony in

his place, I would have been on that flight, not you."

"Which only means you would have been laid up here instead of me." She gave Maggie a weak smile. "Or are you saying you would have gotten it down in one piece?"

"Are you kidding? No one could have gotten that plane down as well as you did."

"I wish I could have landed it a little bit better." Donna dug her elbows into the mattress and pushed her body up in the bed. A low grunt escaped her lips. "Maybe then I wouldn't be so busted up."

At least she wasn't dead. A sobering thought but true. Donna finally seemed settled, her eyelids fluttering closed. Maggie leaned back and watched as her friend's breathing slowed into a restful pattern.

Was someone at the plant gunning for her or for the WASP in general? The memory of the note slammed through her. Had she been so determined to prove herself that she had ignored the possibility that she was putting other people in harm's way?

"Maggie?"

She leaned forward and rested her elbows on the mattress. "What is it, honey? Is there something you need?"

Donna snuggled into her pillow, pulling the sheet up under her chin. "Would you be my maid of honor?"

Maggie chuckled. What a question! "Of course I will. But you need to get some rest. You can't go traipsing down the aisle just yet. We've got to get you back in the cockpit."

"I'm done. No more flying, at least not for a while. I just want to marry Bill before he ships out." Donna closed her eyes. "If he'll have me now."

What an odd thing for her to say. Maggie patted her hand. "Of course he'll marry you, but what's the rush? There's going to be plenty of time for that later."

"Is there? I'm not so sure anymore."

Maggie blanketed Donna's cold hand between her own. Her friend had been spooked by the crash more than she had let on. "Daddy always says the Lord must still have a purpose for you if He hasn't called you home. You've got to get your hours in so that the airlines will reconsider you for a piloting job."

"I want a family, Maggie. A home," Donna whispered, her voice cracking. "Flying is just one part of who I am. What about all those other parts of our lives? What happens to us when we can't fly planes anymore?"

Maggie wasn't sure what to say. She'd never thought about the day she'd have to give up flying, had truly never thought she would. But Donna had a point. She couldn't expect to fly forever. What would happen then? Loneliness formed inside her, rippling through her until it crashed through every part of her being. As much as she wanted, no, needed to fly, she didn't want to reach her goal alone.

Wesley. His name whispered through her heart. She shook her head. No, it wasn't possible. Falling in love with Wesley Hicks wasn't in her plans.

And Wesley wouldn't fall for a girl pilot, not after what he'd been through. He had his own demons to face. Maybe, one day, he could let go of the past, but she didn't think it would be anytime soon.

Maggie shook her head again. No, loving Wesley just wasn't possible.

The memory of her father's words that day he'd driven her to Merrilee's flowed through her. With God, all things are possible.

"Thanks for coming today, Captain," Bill said, motioning for Wesley to sit down in the chair next to him. "I know how busy you are."

"I always make time for my pilots." Wesley sunk down in the fold-out chair, the sharp scrape of the metal legs an odd sound in such an anesthetic environment. Yes, he always made time for his men, but this situation was different. He had done the preflight check. Donna was Maggie's friend; she had been in a plane that Maggie was scheduled to fly.

And Donna had almost gotten killed in the process.

Thoughts nagged at him. What if Maggie had gone up in that plane? Would she have fared as well as Donna or would it have been worse? How would he have made Merrilee understand her loss if he couldn't understand it himself? Despite the chill in the hallway, a bead of perspiration popped out on his forehead.

He swiped his hand across his brow. "You've got yourself a nice girl there, Bill."

"You've got that right, sir." The man broke into a smile. "A little too stubborn for her own good at times, but I guess that's one of the reasons I love her."

"Sounds serious."

Bill gave him a brief nod. "I've known she was the perfect girl for me since the day I met her. Last week, I asked her to marry me and she said yes."

"Congratulations," Wesley replied, extending his hand.

Bill grasped his hand and shook it. "Thank you, sir."

"So when's the big day?"

"Not for a while yet." Bill leaned back in his chair and stretched. "We both decided to wait until Donna gets her flying hours in so that she can pilot commercial aircraft."

"Sounds like a long wait."

If the man's expression was anything to go by, he didn't seem to mind. "Like I said, Donna is a very stubborn woman. But trust me, she's worth it."

So was Maggie.

"When are you scheduled to ship out?" Wesley asked.

"Monday." Bill took a deep breath. "Don't know where I'm going yet."

Wesley stared out over the deserted nursing station. Poor guy, having to leave his injured fiancée behind while he reported for duty.

He frowned. When had his desire to get back in the war disappeared? Sure, there were battles he had to fight here. Training the squad to take the helm of the Super Fortress. Maggie and her occasional skirmishes with her Uncle James to save Merrilee's home. He'd found a battle field that needed protecting just as much as his grandfather's beloved England.

He'd made a life here.

Wesley froze as the truth settled over him. The thought of settling in Marietta didn't bother him at all. No, that wasn't true. He could see making a life for himself here as long as Maggie was a part of it.

He ground his back teeth together. No, including Maggie in his life wasn't an option, not when the possibility of losing her always hung in the air.

He'd train her to pilot the Super Fortress, and that was it. If he got lucky, maybe Major Evans would transfer her to another base. Much as he'd hate it, he'd ask for a transfer to Kansas City or back to Buffalo before he found himself sitting in a hospital corridor wondering if Maggie was alive. His gut knotted up at the thought.

Wesley cleared his throat. It'd been a while since either of the men had spoken. "Did Donna tell you what happened?"

"I haven't had much of a chance to talk to her," Bill answered, his brow furrowed. "But the crew that brought her in said most of the damage was done by a low-lying tree limb."

"Were there any signs of a fire?"

He shook his head. "No, the guys said she looked like she came in on fumes. Almost like she ran out of gas."

251

But that was impossible. Wesley had checked the fuel levels himself. "Could Donna have dumped the gas when she realized she was going down?"

"I doubt it. She didn't have enough time to empty the entire load."

Wesley nodded. "You're right. And even if she only had a little fuel, the tank would have exploded once she hit the ground."

"Thank God it didn't," Bill answered, his voice cracking.

Wesley blew out a harsh breath. "I'm sorry, Bill. I have a habit of saying things out loud so that I can think them through better."

"I understand, Captain Hicks. I would appreciate it if you would keep me informed about the investigation."

Wesley nodded. The army air force might try to tie Wesley up with a lot of red tape, but he intended to stretch that tape as far as humanly possible. After all, he knew what it was like ramming his head against a brick wall. Trying to find out the truth behind his sister's crash had been an ordeal.

"Your girl did a great job of getting herself down in one piece."

"Nothing less than what I'd expect from Donna. She's the best."

Wesley had his own ideas about the best

female pilot in the vicinity, and it wasn't Donna. He leaned back and glanced at the man, a question suddenly weighing heavy on his mind. "You ever think about her getting hurt before today?"

"All the time." Bill dropped his head slightly. "It kind of put me off dating her at first."

Wesley nodded.

"But I couldn't get her out of my head. It got so bad at one point that I actually talked it over with the chaplain. He said if I loved Donna, I had to accept those things about her that kept me up at night. I realized that I had to give God control over the situation."

Wesley had never thought of it that way. "Did it make things easier?"

"A little." He chuckled softly. "Especially when the chaplain pointed out how dodging bullets and facing the Nazis might make Donna a bit uneasy about having a relationship with me."

"Sounds like a smart man."

"The thing is, I'll always worry about her. I love her," Bill replied, raising his head to look at Wesley.

Wesley cleared his throat. "I heard Donna was your instructor."

A warm smile spread across the man's

face. "Yes, sir. She's the best. Why, just last week, I watched her take this new guy up. I swear I thought that boy was going to get them both killed. But Donna —" his voice filled with unabashed respect and pride "— she talked him through it. It was something to see, sir."

Wesley nodded. He felt the same way every time he saw Maggie take off. "Sounds like she has a gift."

"It was at that moment I realized the problem wasn't with her flying but with my fears. I decided then and there to give my worries concerning her over to the Lord and let Him deal with it."

"And now?"

"I have to admit, I was scared to death when my commanding officer told me about Donna this morning," Bill said, the memory playing painfully across his face. "All the way here, I prayed that someone had made a mistake, and it wasn't Donna in the crash." The man hesitated. "I don't know if you've ever heard about the peace that God can give you in times like this. But on the walk over here from the train station, I knew that whatever happened to Donna, whether she lived or died, God had a plan for us."

Wesley leaned back, resting his head against the wall. Easy for Bill to say. He hadn't lost Donna this morning. Would he have felt the same way if she hadn't survived? Wesley glanced at him. There was a contentment in the man's expression that caused a flash of envy to slice through him. If Bill found peace in his faith, what did his fears for Maggie say about his own?

"So you're not going to worry about Donna as much now?" Wesley asked.

"Oh, I'm not that good, but at least I know the Lord will be there to listen. Truth is I hadn't really worried about Donna flying lately, at least not until we were talking about it last night." The man stared at Wesley. "That threatening note really shook up the both of us."

The hair on Wesley's arm stood at attention. "Donna got threatened at the Bell?"

"No sir," Bill answered, looking at Wesley as if he had a screw loose. "Maggie did."

CHAPTER FOURTEEN

"When did you intend to tell me? Or was
that your plan, to keep me in the dark?"
Wesley asked, his fingers painfully gripping
the tender skin above her elbow as they
walked down the hospital hallway thirty
minutes later.

Maggie wasn't sure what Wesley was talking about, only that she felt as if all the
blackout curtains had been drawn, and she
was fumbling around in the inky shadows.
He was steamed about something and had
been since the moment she had left Donna's
room. At first, she'd thought maybe he'd
learned an important piece of information
about Donna's accident, but with this line
of accusing questions, it wasn't likely.

"Did you think you could keep this from
me?" His voice must have carried because a
nurse stepped out into the hallway and with
a stern look, pressed one finger to her lips.

Wesley's grasp on her arm loosened. "If

Roosevelt would send a battalion of nurses over to the front, they'd stare the Nazis into submission within a week."

Maggie mashed her lips together to keep the chuckle from rumbling through her. The man really could be funny when he wanted to be. She gently pulled her arm out of his grip. "You want to tell me what's bothering you so much?"

Wesley glared at her, his eyes issuing a challenge. "Why didn't you tell me you got a threatening note your first day at Bell?"

Donna had always had a big mouth! Maggie thought as her chin went up a notch. She glared back at him. Wesley might be upset, but what was the point? The note was over a month old. "What about it?"

Wesley stiffened. "Didn't you think that as your commanding officer, I should have been notified?"

Maggie clenched her teeth together and silently counted to ten. Of course she should have told him about the note. And she would now, had she received the note today, since she knew she could trust him. Maybe if he heard her out, knew her reasons for keeping the threat under wraps, he might understand.

A small crowd had gathered, eyeing them as if they were a couple in the middle of a lovers' spat. She looked around and spied a stairwell leading to the lobby.

Threading her hand through Wesley's arm, she tugged him toward the door. He didn't offer much resistance. Probably didn't want an audience any more than she did.

Once the door slammed shut firmly behind them, Maggie let go of Wesley's arm and walked over to the opposite wall. "You're right. I should have told you. But I was terrified that if you knew, you'd ground me."

Wesley crossed his arms in a tight knot over his chest. "You're right. I would have."

"I knew it. You were looking for any excuse to keep me out of the air."

"Have I ever kept you out of the flight rotation since you passed all your preflight testing?"

His question echoed off the cinder block walls. She had to give him that point. Even with all of his misgivings in those early days, Wesley had never scrapped one of her flights, not even today against Lieutenant Webber. "No, you haven't."

"It is my job to see to the security of my command," he bit out, lowering his head, the muscles in his neck pulled tight above his collar. "That note was a viable threat."

"But nothing happened," she answered.

Wesley jerked his head up, his fierce glare piercing into her. "Until now."

Maggie bit into the tender flesh of her lower lip. When had she gotten so self-centered? Guilt snaked through her. She'd never even thought about anyone else's safety; she'd been so set on satisfying her own pride that she'd ignored the dangers to her squad and the girls who served with her in the WASP.

"I should have told you about the note."

If she'd thought she was going to get off easy, she'd been sadly mistaken. "Did Donna tell you anything about the crash?"

Maggie dared to look him in the eye and wished she hadn't taken the chance. His face flushed, his mouth pulled into a controlled line, the expression on Wesley's face was the textbook definition of *spitting mad.*

"I'm waiting, Ms. Daniels."

Maggie straightened. She had been wrong, but she wouldn't let Wesley browbeat her over one miscalculation. "She said that her fuel level dropped faster than it should have. By the time she realized it, it was too late to return to the Bell."

"Someone switched the fuel," he said with quiet certainty.

"I don't understand."

"P-51s burn a 101 high-octane fuel," Wesley replied. "But if someone filled the tank with a lower grade, say a 95 or a 98 octane, the tank would register as filled, but the fuel would burn up more quickly."

Her stomach clenched into a tight ball. "You'd run out of gas."

He nodded. "I need to get out to the crash site and go through the wreckage."

"Do you want me to go back to the plant and check out the fuel logs for that plane?"

"No."

"Then what . . ."

But Wesley didn't let her finish. His eyes glittered with a mixture of anger and something akin to fear. "You are to go back to Merrilee's and stay there until further notice. Until I find out who is behind all of this, you're not going within ten miles of my air field."

He couldn't ground her now, not when she had worked so hard to be on the B-29's maiden flight. Maggie fumed. Yes, Wesley had a right to be angry with her, but how much had the loss of his sister played in this decision? Maybe it was time to take her case to a higher authority.

"I'm going to have to agree with Captain

Hicks on this one, Ms. Daniels," Major Evans said in his office that afternoon. He nodded at Wesley. "We can't take a chance on getting you killed."

Wesley relaxed a bit, pleased at how quickly Evans had answered Maggie's request for a formal meeting. He'd feared the major might reverse his decision to ground Maggie until an investigation was completed, but that feeling had soon fled when he noted the seriousness in the man's expression.

Not that Maggie intended to go down without a fight. "But, sir," she began, sitting at the edge of her seat. "We're at a very crucial point in our training. Wouldn't it be a better option to have me continue under Captain Hicks's immediate command rather than lose valuable time?"

Evans turned to look at him. "Captain?"

Wesley took a quiet breath, an uneasiness settling in his gut. The anger he'd felt upon hearing of the threat against Maggie had been replaced by apprehension. Didn't the woman know that her silence could have gotten her killed? Yes, she had apologized — several times since yesterday afternoon — but her words hadn't made a dent in his concerns. Until Maggie fully understood her life was at stake, he wouldn't back down.

"In light of Ms. Lane's accident and the threat that has surfaced, I don't feel that is a viable option at this time, sir," Wesley answered, staring straight ahead.

Major Evans's gaze shifted between them before nodding. "Then I concede to your opinion, Captain. Ms. Daniels, until we have more information, you are hereby relieved of your duties at the Bell and until it is determined if a threat exists."

"Yes, sir." The words were spoken in a solemn tone, as if a death had occurred.

"Until then, I would ask that you stay in town," Major Evans continued. "Investigations of this nature are generally wrapped up very quickly due to the urgency of our mission. If it becomes possible to reinstate you, I'd like you close by."

"I understand, sir."

But Wesley knew that she didn't. He chanced a glance at her. The long wave of hair that had curled in soft clouds around her shoulders just two nights ago was once again pulled back from her face and secured in a snood. The fragile skin beneath her eyes looked purplish blue, as if bruised by the lack of sleep. How long had she walked the floor after she had crept down the stairs next to his room last night? Had she watched the sunrise after the sleepless night, as he had from his room this morning?

Maggie looked at him, her disappointment clear to him before she abruptly turned away. Deep down in his chest, he began to ache.

"Dismissed!"

Wesley rose alongside Maggie, aware that they moved together as if two parts of a whole. They both snapped off a quick salute then walked toward the door. He opened it, then stepped back, waiting for her. Her slight frame was tense as she passed, her hands clenched firmly into the folds of her work clothes. Well, she'd just have to stew a bit. He wasn't about to let her back up in one of his planes, not until he knew he could keep her safe.

Once they were safely out in the hallway, Maggie turned to him. "I'll go finish up, then go home."

Wesley shook his head. "You're leaving right now."

"But . . ."

"I've already reassigned your duties so there's no reason for you to go back on the plant floor." His voice came out rougher than he had intended, and he took a deep breath before continuing. "Just go home, Maggie."

"What have I got to do to make you

forgive me, Wesley?" The words sounded like a plea. " 'I'm sorry' doesn't seem to mean anything to you."

"You don't get it."

"Sure I do. I should have told you about that stupid note, but I was afraid." Maggie shook her head as if she knew the question running through his mind. "Not of the note. The girls got stuff like that all the time when we were in training camp. I knew if I said anything, you wouldn't give me a chance."

She was right. If he had known about the note, there was a good chance he would have found a way to keep her on the ground. Wesley leaned toward her, his fingers closing in over the delicate curve of her elbow. "Someone was counting on you being in that plane yesterday, someone who intended to hurt you. But I didn't know that. You didn't bother to warn me about any potential dangers."

She gasped. "I didn't think —"

"No, you didn't," he said, his voice taking on a razor sharp edge. "If something had happened to you, how would I explain it to your parents? To Merrilee and Claire? I made a promise to keep you safe. How would I deal with breaking another promise?"

"Another?" She backed away from him.

"Is that why you haven't talked to your grandfather since Beth died? You promised him you'd bring her home safe."

He leaned back, her words a physical blow to him. A soul-crushing fatigue swept through him and he closed his eyes. "Go home, Maggie. Just go home."

She didn't need any more prodding. Without another word, Maggie turned and hurried down the hall.

CHAPTER FIFTEEN

Wesley walked down the gravel path to Merrilee's house, exhaustion seeping into every cell of his body. He'd spent the afternoon occupying himself with the mundane task of writing new flight assignments, but no matter how hard he tried, he couldn't push Maggie out of his thoughts.

He'd been no tougher on her than she deserved. Wesley slapped violently at the tall grass with his cap. Her reasons for keeping the threat from him may have been founded in her own desire to get in the cockpit, but she'd been right about one thing. If he'd known about that note, he would have grounded her until the major ordered him to put her back into the flight rotation.

But the situation had changed with Donna's crash. Now it wasn't just a threat, but a violent action. Maggie didn't seem to realize the danger she was in, but he understood it. The idea of someone threatening Maggie, of her being alone and facing the dangers of the sky, sent a foreboding sense of apprehension through him. He hadn't been there for his sister, but he wouldn't fail Maggie. He couldn't.

Not when he suspected he was falling in love with her.

Wesley stared off toward the house. Love hadn't stopped him from failing Beth. Only he'd encouraged her to sign up for the ferrying squad when Pops had been dead set against it. His assurances had finally calmed his grandfather's concerns, that and his promise that Beth would never come close to the battle zone.

But he had broken that promise.

Wesley was at the bottom of the staircase leading to the front porch before he noticed her. There in the corner of the swing, Maggie leaned her head against the back of her relaxed fist. The chains moaned a sad mournful rhythm as the swing moved slowly back and forth.

He studied her for a second from the shadows of the whitewashed beam. Her generous lips were drawn into a sober line, while her nose glowed a faint pink. Those eyes that always turned him inside out had faded to a mint green, their brilliance washed away by what he could imagine was a river of tears. He hated the thought that he might have caused her those tears.

Wesley climbed the last of the stairs and walked over to her. "Hi."

She stiffened. "Hi."

"Mind if I sit down?"

As her answer, Maggie scooted farther into the corner. The chains squealed in protest as Wesley sat down in the center of the swing.

Several awkward moments passed before he spoke. "I'm sorry I blew up at you."

Maggie shook her head. "You had every right to be angry. I was wrong not to tell you about that dumb note, and now Donna's in the hospital because of me."

"Hey," he replied, taking her cool hand and sandwiching it between his. "The crash isn't your fault."

"Yes, it is," she answered, her lip quivering slightly. She dropped her chin to her chest. "By not telling you about that note, I put every person flying out of the Bell at risk. It's like I gassed up that plane myself."

He couldn't stand seeing her like this. Leaning close to her, he reached out and, with his fingers, traced the silky soft skin of her jaw upward until her chin rested in the palm of his hand. "Don't keep beating yourself up over this, sweetheart."

"But I messed up. Big time."

Wesley reluctantly dropped his hand and leaned back in the swing, his face raised to the ceiling. "Yeah, well, I make promises I can't seem to keep."

A few moments lapsed before Maggie spoke again. "Who asked you to watch out for me?"

"Your aunt Merrilee."

"I should have known," she said, the hint of a smile back in her voice. "I thought maybe it was my dad." She paused. "And who made you promise to take care of Beth?"

He should have guessed Maggie wouldn't let it go. Like a dog to a bone, that girl was. But how would she feel after learning the truth? "Pops wasn't altogether sold on the idea of Beth joining the ferrying squadron so she asked me if I'd talk to him, convince him that it wasn't nearly as dangerous as he seemed to believe. It wasn't like she was going to be dodging the Germans." He swallowed hard against the memories bombarding him. "He felt I should have done more to keep her out of the war."

"So he blamed you when she died."

That she had stated it as fact instead of a question surprised him, though he wasn't sure why. Maggie always had a knack for cutting to the chase. Wesley lifted his head, surprised to find her turned toward him, her hand a warm comfort against his arm. Had he been so lost in the past that he hadn't noticed her, sitting so close he could smell the sweet fragrance of lavender that clung to her like perfume. For a moment, he thought of pulling her into his arms and soothing his battered soul in her warmth, brushing his lips across hers and tasting her sweetness. Only Maggie had her lips mashed together in that way he had come to recognize meant she had something on her mind.

"What is it?" he asked, realizing how much he'd like to hear her opinion of his situation.

But she simply shook her head. "Nothing."

Her answer baffled him. She'd never been one to be shy about her feelings, least of all with him. What was she holding back? Was it that she agreed with his grandfather, that he should have done more to stop Beth?

"If you've got something to say," he prodded, "say it."

Maggie hesitated. "What did Beth think about all of this?"

Wesley snapped his head back. "What?"

"It's just that I've listened to what you've

270

said, and I've got some idea of what your grandfather wanted," Maggie answered, her fingers resting against his forearm as if grasping for answers of her own. "What about Beth? What did she want?"

Wesley stared at her hand on his forearm. His sister had always talked about making a difference. "But she was a . . ."

"A woman," Maggie finished for him, her voice reassuring. "That doesn't mean she didn't have an opinion, Wesley."

Wesley's gut tightened. Had he ever really listened to Beth, ever heard what she was saying? He couldn't say yes for sure. "I don't think Beth understood what flying in the war involved, that there was always the possibility she could get killed."

"Beth was an ace pilot. You said so yourself. Of course she knew the possibilities." She leaned closer to him, her shoulder brushing his. "Being a woman had nothing to do with it."

"She shouldn't have died."

"No, she shouldn't have. And Jackson shouldn't have had to die, either." Maggie's thumb grazed the top of his knuckles in reassuring strokes. "But they both believed in a cause greater than themselves and were willing to lay down their lives for it. We should respect their choices and be thankful for what they did."

He didn't know if he'd ever reach the point Maggie described. Wesley stole a look at her. "Is that what you do? With Jackson, I mean."

Maggie leaned back slightly, but didn't break her hold on his arm. "Not all the time. At first, it seemed like I was going to the Lord about it every minute of the day. Now it's a little easier."

Wesley shoved a hand through his hair. Maybe prayer would work for Maggie, but he wasn't so sure it would help him with his situation.

Warm fingers traced his jaw then turned him to face her. He shifted his gaze to meet hers, only to find himself staring into eyes filled with concern and understanding.

"You have to stop blaming yourself, Wesley. It's the enemy that took Beth and Jackson away from us. We had no control over it."

He still wasn't convinced. Beth could have been reasoned with if he could have explained the danger of the situation in a way she would have understood, and he hadn't done that. But Maggie had given him something to think about, just not at the moment — later, when he was in his room, away from everyone.

Wesley drew in a deep breath. "What are you going to do until Major Evans reinstates you?"

If Maggie was caught off guard by his quick retreat, she didn't show it. She shrugged. "I'm not sure. More than likely help Merrilee out around here. Maybe visit Eliza Beth and the kids in the afternoon when it's too hot to be out in the garden." She leaned her head against the wooden slats of the swing. "If Major Evans hadn't asked me to stick around, I'd probably head home for a few days. Momma's finally getting out a little bit, and I could see if Dad needed any help with the business. It is his busy season with crops coming in."

In other words, flying. The woman had the determination of Churchill in the dark days during the Blitz. "Old Blue isn't the same as a P-51."

"No, but at least I'll be keeping myself sharp."

Wesley felt his spirits elevate as if caught up in a light breeze. Maggie Daniels would never, ever give up — on her country or her dreams.

What would it feel like if she never gave up on him?

He pushed that thought to the side. Well, he'd talked Major Evans into grounding her. The least he could do was give her the opportunity to keep up her skills. And, he reminded himself, it would make it easier when she was called back into service.

The swing jolted forward as he stood up. "Come on. I want to show you something."

She inclined her head, the mischief that sparkled in her eyes sending a flash of warmth throughout his chest. Yes, he might enjoy being the focus of Maggie's single-minded determination very much.

"What are we doing here?" Maggie asked as they pulled up in front of the run-down Ellerbee farmhouse.

Wesley shoved the gears into park and pulled on the door handle. "Stay here for just a minute. I'll be right back."

Maggie sat looking over the dashboard of her aunt's old pickup. Abner Ellerbee might run with Uncle James's crowd, but his father, Clyde, had once been one of her father's best customers — owning one of the biggest cotton producers in the state. But the soil and his body had given out about the same time. Now the once-fertile fields lay bare, save a bounty crop of kudzu and weeds.

She watched as Wesley knocked on the front door. The man carried such a burden,

274

bearing the responsibility for his sister's death. Maggie leaned back into the cracked vinyl seat. Being a pilot himself, he had to know, had to understand, that Beth was well aware of the dangers she faced. Surely, glancing over the bloodstained cockpits when she worked at her grandfather's airfield had prepared Beth better than any training film.

Wesley's overprotectiveness was worse than her cousins', and that was saying quite a bit. But it was something else, the fact that he had never considered Beth's opinion on the matter, that stuck in Maggie's craw. She may have always shunned her cousins' protection, but she'd come to the realization that they respected her enough to encourage her rather than hold her back.

The passenger door opened, startling her. "You ready?"

She nodded, taking his hand.

After he shut the truck door, Wesley tucked her hand in his elbow. "When I first was appointed to the Bell, I had to give weekly updates to the War Department," he said, leading her toward the rundown barn at the corner of the lot. "I couldn't see using a military plane when an old mail plane could get me there just as fast and with less fuel. So one weekend, I went home and brought this back." When he pushed open the barn door, Maggie gasped.

There in the middle of the Ellerbees' barn sat a De Havilland Tiger Moth, almost an exact replica of the plane she'd used at Avenger Field. But instead of the drab army green, the body of the plane was painted a bright yellow that matched the color of jonquils in the spring. A large bull's-eye was drawn into the belly of the plane, as if to dare the enemy to take a shot.

"She was in pretty bad shape when Pops got her," Wesley said, running his hand along the fuselage. "We had to drop in a new engine and rebuild the whole right wing section."

Maggie glanced at him. "You and your grandfather did this?"

"Pops took us to an air show while he was visiting, the summer before I headed off to Tech." The corner of his mouth lifted in a crooked smile. "The pilot barely made it down in one piece. Women were fainting, kids were yelling. The whole place went wild. The guy hadn't even made it out of the wreckage before Pops walked up to him. He bought this hunk of junk right then and there. We spent the rest of his time here putting it back together."

"He sounds like a wonderful man."

"He is," Wesley said, the color rising in his cheeks as if such a gift was still too much for him. "He didn't want us to forget what we had learned, which is the main reason why I'm letting you use this plane until you get reinstated."

Maggie blinked in shock. "You want me to fly your plane?"

Wesley nodded. "The last thing I need is for you to lose your edge, not when the choice of who is going to fly the first B-29 out of the plant is between you and Jimbo." He patted the wing, a simple gesture that Maggie found completely charming. "Plus, she always handled better with a woman in the cockpit. So would you take her up, Ace? As a favor to me?"

No words could express how she felt. Maggie nodded, staring up at Wesley, memorizing the lines of his smile, the flecks in his eyes. Maybe there was hope for a future with Wesley. The thought both thrilled and terrified her.

Slow down. It wasn't two hours ago that this man was so angry, he would have thrown her in the stockade if only to keep her safe. She may be on the brink of falling in love, but she couldn't settle for a man who didn't value her opinions, whether in the heavens or here on earth.

But she could hope. For now, she'd enjoy these precious moments with him. She held out her hand. "I'd be happy to."

CHAPTER SIXTEEN

"How's Ms. Daniels holding up?" Major Evans asked, skimming over Wesley's flight schedule for the coming week.

Glancing up from the file he was studying, Wesley looked across the major's desk, battling against the smile tugging on his lips. He found himself grinning a lot these days, especially after spending time with his feisty pilot. "Maggie hasn't said much about it, sir, but I'm sure she'd like to get back to work and finish the job she started."

"That woman is probably antsy after a week on the ground." Chuckling, the major flipped the page.

"I'm sure she'll be glad when the investigation is completed," Wesley answered, returning his gaze to the open file in his hands. No sense telling the major that Maggie was already back in the air, flying the plane built for Beth. He only hoped they found the culprit before he ran out of gasoline rations.

"Then she'll get to fly a real plane, not that two-seater you rebuilt with your grandfather."

Wesley's head jerked up, bracing himself for the coals he was certain he was about to be raked over. Instead, Evans had leaned back in his chair, his fingers threaded at the back of his neck, his head resting in his palms. The corners of his mouth had quirked up in what Wesley could only assume was a fatherly smile.

Might as well come clean. Wesley cleared his throat. "Maggie's not the type to just sit around and wait. She was going to find a way back behind the controls." He shrugged. "I figured it might as well be a plane that I knew was safe."

"That makes sense." The major gave a slight nod of agreement. "I'm a bit surprised she didn't head home even after I told her to stick around."

I didn't give her a chance. A knot formed in Wesley's chest. Wasn't that what he wanted, for Maggie to go back home, to stay safe? A sense of dissatisfaction settled over him. "I'm sorry, sir. I should have informed you of this decision."

"Don't apologize for keeping Ms. Daniels sharp behind the controls while we wrap up our investigation. I just wish I had thought of it." The major cocked his head to one side. "Though I have to say, I would have never thought you'd support putting our girl pilot back in the air. I guess things have changed."

No, things hadn't changed. *He* had, at least the way he felt about Maggie and her desire to fly. Oh, he knew she was a good pilot. The woman proved her abilities every time she took to the skies. But somewhere along the way, the dreams she had shared with him had become part of his own.

And he'd do everything he could to see Maggie reach her dreams safely.

"Well, you can tell Ms. Daniels that she's been cleared to report back on duty." Reaching for a file, Major Evans shoved it across the desk. "General Arnold called this morning and closed the investigation himself."

Wesley edged up to the end of his chair, the news twisting like a knife in his gut. "But we still don't know who sent Maggie that threatening note or if it had anything to do with Donna's crash."

"I know, Wesley." The man's smile had flattened into a straight line. "And I have the same concerns you do. But Arnold feels that any further investigation will cause even more confusion about the flight readiness of the B-29."

"So we're putting Maggie in direct danger?" Wesley asked, scrubbing his damp palms against his pants' legs.

"No more than anyone else in this war." Evans shook his head. "You'll just have to keep an eye on her."

Wesley swallowed hard. That reasoning hadn't worked when he joined the Royal Air Force, thinking he could keep watch over Beth. And it wouldn't work now.

A strong hand settled on Wesley's shoulder, and he looked up to find Major Evans standing beside him. "We'll just have to be diligent, son."

Wesley nodded. Yes, he'd make sure that he inspected every wire, tested even the smallest amount of fuel in any plane Maggie was assigned. And if he found a problem, he wouldn't think twice about grounding her again, hang General Arnold.

And he'd pray. Starting now.

Lord, give me the wisdom to keep Maggie safe.

"You and Wesley got plans for this evening?" Aunt Merrilee asked, glancing up briefly from the pot of peas she was shelling.

"Yes, ma'am." Maggie gave her wet hair a

final pat before huddling closer to the stove and picking up her comb. She'd already changed into her jumper, but would have to hurry if her hair was going to be dry before Wesley got home. He'd promised to take her up before the sun set too low and show her some tricks he'd learned while dog fighting the Germans over the Channel.

"I'm not surprised. You two have been spending quite a bit of time together here lately." Merrilee smiled, picking up another handful of peas and putting them in her pot. "What are you doing? Trying to soften him up so he'll let you go back to work?"

A knot of hair tangled beneath Maggie's fingertips. "Why would I want to do that?"

"I don't know. I just figured you'd be getting tired of being around here all day long." Merrilee rose and went to the sink.

"I'll go back soon enough," Maggie replied, working through the knot, her wet hair against her flushed skin cooling the heat gathered in her cheeks. Truth was, her reinstatement hadn't seemed quite as important in recent days. Between canning vegetables from Merrilee's victory garden, checking on Eliza Beth and the others, and preparing the house for Donna's release from the hospital, Maggie found her days to be incredibly full. But it was the evenings, when she slipped off with Wesley to the Ellerbees' farm, that she looked forward to the most. She didn't get as much air time as she would have liked, not with the afternoons growing shorter, but she didn't care. Sitting beside Wesley, bumbling along the rough roads in the moonlight, lifted the wings of her heart higher than any rocket could.

Not that Wesley had given her any indication that he felt something for her, too. Since their talk on the front porch, he had been his usual kind and attentive self, always ready to accompany her to the hospital downtown for a visit with Donna or carry a load of supplies for her to the tent camp. But he'd kept his distance since she'd learned about his sister. Maggie couldn't help but wonder if his quick retreat had anything to do with protecting his heart.

Maggie freed a strand of hair from the knot. "I knew it was going to take a while to investigate Donna's crash."

"That's what I thought, too, but Evans seems to think we've wasted too much time as it is."

Maggie glanced up through a curtain of damp, stringy hair, and her heart did a flip. In a crisp white shirt tucked into a cuffed pair of blue jeans, Wesley stood just inside the kitchen, his hand still holding the doorknob. His hair was slicked back, its golden hues dampened to the color of field wheat after a sudden downpour. Unlike the precise captain she knew him to be, this man had an air of uncertainty, as if he were truly a stranger in a foreign land.

Maggie flung the damp strands from her face and froze. Wesley's gaze was fastened to her face, his eyes roaming gently over the flow of her hair, from the tendrils rioting around her face to the curls forming along her shoulders. Her mouth went dry.

"What does that mean?" Merrilee asked, wiping her hands on a dishtowel.

"General Arnold has given the okay for Maggie to be put back on the flight schedule," he answered, giving Maggie a grin that caused her heart to stumble against her ribcage. "Starting next week."

"That's great," Maggie said, pushing the comb through her hair one last time, happy to have that particular situation settled. But the excitement she usually had to harness, the sheer joy of fulfilling her dreams, didn't overwhelm her senses as it had always done in the past.

Donna's words suddenly came to her. Dreams grow to include the person you love.

"So you found out who wrote that ugly note to her?" Merrilee asked, interrupting Maggie's thoughts.

"No." Wesley hesitated, scrubbing the back of his neck with his hand. "I haven't caught them yet, but I will."

Dropping the pan in the sink, Merrilee clenched her hands into a worrisome knot. "Then Maggie is still in danger."

"I don't think there's anything to worry about, Merrilee," Maggie laid her comb down. She gave Wesley a quick glance. "General Arnold isn't the type to take any chances."

But her aunt didn't look convinced. "I bet if he had a niece who was a service pilot, he'd think twice about reinstating her."

"General Arnold is a great fan of the women pilots, Merrilee, and he cares about the girls," Wesley answered, walking over to stand beside her aunt. He wrapped his arm around her shoulder. "He's going to do everything in his power to make sure nothing happens to them."

"See, Merrilee. You're worrying for nothing." Maggie glanced up at Wesley to thank him, but instead found concern shadowing his features. Oh, nothing blatant that Merrilee would pick up on, but an underlying uneasiness that Maggie had glimpsed

286

briefly at times when they were in the midst of a difficult project.

Her aunt ignored her, instead focusing all her attention on Wesley. "Will you watch out for her? Make sure she stays safe?"

Her aunt was wrong to ask Wesley to make such a promise. Just like his grandfather had been. But Wesley, being the man that he was, would take ownership of that kind of responsibility. Well, she wouldn't stand for it, not when she was a grown woman who could speak for herself.

Standing, Maggie walked to where her aunt stood. "That's not fair, Merrilee. You know Wesley has no control over what happens when I'm up in the air. Only God does."

Merrilee placed her hand over her mouth, but not before Maggie caught the slight tremor in her lower lip. "It's just that I worry about you so much. What would your momma and daddy do if something were to happen . . . ?" She broke off, tears forming in the corners of her eyes.

Lord, help her. Maggie faced danger every time she'd climbed into the cockpit and had accepted whatever possibilities awaited her in the skies, with the full knowledge that her life was in the hands of the Father. But she had never realized how hard it must be for those on the ground anticipating her return. Merrilee did, holding on to her memories of John from all those years ago. So did Wesley. Yes, he understood better than most the pain of waiting for someone who wasn't coming home.

"You need to stop worrying about that, Merrilee. You've got to know that I'd protect Maggie with my life," Wesley answered in a solemn voice.

The way he said it, so natural, as if the words were a very part of his being, sent a tiny thrill through her. He must feel something for her to make such a statement. Her pulse soared at the thought.

"Thank you, Wesley." Relief softened the worried lines in Merrilee's face. She wiped her hands on her apron then headed for the kitchen door. "I'd better get up to the house and make sure Claire is doing her homework."

The hinge had barely clicked shut when Wesley spoke. "I know you've probably got something to say about my wanting to protect you, but before you blow your lid, could you point me toward the peanut butter and jelly?"

"You didn't eat lunch?"

Wesley shook his head. "I've been in meetings all day."

"Then sit down and rest for a second." Maggie turned toward the sink and, with a few quick pumps, washed her hands. "I'll fix you something."

"You?" Wesley leaned back against the counter top. "I didn't think you were the traditional kind of woman."

"If you mean do I cook, then the answer is yes." Opening the cabinet door, Maggie lifted the jar of peanut butter from its resting place and set it on the counter alongside the bread. "A person's got to eat whether they have a career or not, don't they?"

"I guess so," he answered, his voice filled with a playful kind of awe. He snagged two glasses off the drying board and set them on the table. "Nice kitchen, by the way."

Maggie stopped cutting the loaf of bread mid-slice. "You've never been in Merrilee's kitchen?"

"She always chases me out of here before I can get too comfortable."

"Ah," Maggie answered, slicing through bread before pointing the tip of the knife at Wesley. "That's because she's been taught that the kitchen is a woman's domain. No men allowed."

"Seriously?" Wesley walked over to the icebox and opened the door. "Pops did all the cooking whenever he visited from

England."

Maggie stared at him in surprise as he pulled out an unopened bottle of milk. "That's a bit odd."

"I don't think so," Wesley said, walking to the table then pouring first one, then another glass of milk. "Mom might have been a great business lady but, God bless her, she couldn't boil water without burning it."

"That's an awful thing for you to say." Maggie reached to the center of the table for a jar of Merrilee's apple jelly.

"It's the honest truth." The smile he gave her almost made her drop the knife she'd just retrieved from the utensil drawer. "Pops decided the only way we were going to survive was if he took over kitchen duty whenever he was in town. When he left, he hired us a cook." Wesley found a couple of paper napkins and folded them next to the plates that Merrilee had set out. "What about your family? Did your old man ever venture into the kitchen?"

"Well, nobody knows this." Maggie glanced toward the closed kitchen door. It was so easy, this intimate back-and-forth between them. Something told her she was going to have a hard time giving it up when this assignment was over and they were reassigned. "Daddy's homemade soup won first prize at the county fair the summer before the war started." Maggie grabbed the nearby jar of jelly and opened it. "But then Momma and Daddy are different from most folks around here."

"What do you mean?"

It was an innocent question, one that Maggie had asked herself time and time again. Since she'd been old enough to understand, she'd noticed the keen differences between her parents and most everyone else in town. Maggie spooned a glob of honey-yellow jelly on the slice of bread and spread it evenly across the surface. "Well, my mother was barely twenty-one when she married my daddy, but everyone in the family considered her an old maid."

"And yet your dad took a chance on her. That was very good of him." The lighthearted humor in Wesley's tone melted away any reservations she may have had about discussing the subject with him. "What are they saying around town about you?"

Maggie pieced the two slices of bread together and cut the sandwich in half, aware that Wesley was watching, waiting for an answer. Well, let him wait. She didn't have any intention of telling him that for as far back as she could remember, she had been looked on as a curiosity, as if she belonged in one of those sideshows she'd seen at the fair.

"Why not leave here? Go somewhere that might be more accepting of what you do?"

That he understood didn't surprise her as much as his suggestion that she leave in order to pursue her dreams. Maggie shook her head. "I can't leave my parents. I'm the only kid they've got left."

"So you're going to stand your ground here."

She nodded, picking up each section of the sandwich and putting them on the plate in front of Wesley. "Momma and Daddy have been great about it. They've been a big encouragement even with all the guff they get."

"Your uncle James?" Wesley picked up one wedge of his sandwich.

"And everybody else except for Merrilee. Most people around here are convinced that it's a waste of time to send a girl to college or prepare her for a career or teach her . . ."

The sandwich hovered in front of his mouth. "How to fly?"

"Yeah, that really scrambled their eggs." Maggie wiped a dishrag across the countertop, concentrating on the bread crumbs left behind. "I keep hoping people will get use to the idea, but so far that hasn't happened."

"Why is what these people think so important to you?"

Because they're my kin. If they don't accept me, who will? That's one of the reasons she'd volunteered for this assignment, to prove to everyone in her hometown that she wasn't such an oddity, that God had a definite plan for putting her in the cockpit. But so far, things hadn't worked out the way she'd planned. "They'll come around when I'm piloting the Super Fortress."

But Welsey didn't look convinced. He seemed ready to say so when the kitchen door opened. Edie peeked around the corner of the wooden frame, glancing at Maggie before focusing on Wesley with a look of uncertainty and concern.

"Wes, there's a man in the parlor waiting to see you."

Putting his sandwich down, Wesley wiped his mouth before laying his napkin to the side. "Must be someone from the plant."

But Edie shook her head. "I don't recognize him. And he doesn't talk like anyone I know from around here."

Little warning bells rang inside Maggie's

head. "What do you mean?"

Edie bit her lip as if in thought. "You remember when we went to the movies a couple of weeks ago and saw that news reel on the Royal family?" She glanced over at Wesley. "He sounds a lot like them."

Wesley stopped in the middle of pushing away from the table, his brow furrowed together in a pained expression of recognition. "Is he an older man, kind of looks like a leprechaun if he wasn't so tall?"

Edie's face broke out into a soft smile. "Now that you mention it, he does look like the type who'd be holding a pot of gold at the end of a rainbow. Do you know him?"

Wesley's smile flattened into a somber line. All of the playfulness they had shared moments ago was gone, chased away by a sorrow that seemed to weigh heavy on Wesley's features, a hurt beyond anything Maggie had witnessed. Without thinking, she laid her hands on his shoulders. Each muscle and tendon flexed and tightened beneath her suddenly trembling fingers.

"Yes." Wesley reached up and clasped her hand beneath his, his fingers cold against the tender flesh of her palm. "I'm pretty sure you just met my grandfather."

CHAPTER SEVENTEEN

Her insides shaking, Maggie tightened her grip on Wesley's arm as they took the last step up to the front porch. He hesitated at the door and looked down at her, his blue eyes searching her as if for some kind of comfort. Held in place by the pain in his gaze, she slipped her hand down and threaded her fingers through his. Wesley looked down at their joined hands and, with a tender squeeze, gave her a sad smile then reached for the door knob.

Dear Lord, help him!

If she had any doubts about her feelings for Wesley, they had been answered in those brief moments when the suffering she saw lining his face had become her own. She hurt for him, for the loss he'd felt when Beth died, for the chasm between him and his grandfather. She loved Wesley Hicks with everything that was inside her.

But what about her plans, the gift of flying God had given her?

He knew the plans He had for her, but did they include Wesley?

Maggie stumbled through the screen door that Wesley held open for her, the reality of the situation taking hold. No, she couldn't see how she could reach for her dreams of an aviation career and make a life with Wesley, not when he still felt the burden for his sister's death. Sorrow filled her heart at the thought.

She slowed her pace down the hall to meet Wesley's, forcing her thoughts on the man waiting in Merrilee's parlor. Why had Wesley's grandfather come here? Had he realized that he needed his grandson as much as Wesley needed him? She lifted up a silent prayer. *Please, Lord. Please heal this family.*

A slight movement caught the corner of her eye, and she turned. In the center of the parlor's double doorway stood a man with snowy white hair slicked to the side, his brushy eyebrows arched over bright blue eyes he'd obviously passed on to his grandson. He studied them intensely before the lines in his face softened in what she would describe as approval. He moved then, quite sprightly for a man of his considerable years, not stopping until he stood in front of Wesley.

"My boy!" The man clasped his arms around Wesley's wide shoulders and pulled him into a tight embrace.

"Pops."

"I've missed you," Pops said, the tenderness of the words softening his clipped English accent.

Maggie glanced down at the floor, embarrassed at the emotion clogging her throat. Her family, save Merrilee, didn't much believe in public displays of affection. She wasn't sure why, only knew that the rare occasions when they happened felt awkward and forced. Maybe that's why Maggie often found herself at her aunt's house. Because she knew Merrilee would love her just as Pops loved Wesley.

Unconditionally.

"Where are your manners, boy?" The older man glanced over at her. "Introduce me to your lovely young lady."

Pops's presumption made Maggie's heart thump hard against her rib cage. Wesley stepped out of his grandfather's embrace and turned toward her. "Pops, I'd like you meet Margaret Rose Daniels. Maggie, my grandfather, Donald Rogers."

Maggie held out her hand. "It's a pleasure to meet you, Mr. Rogers."

"Please, call me Pops." The silver-white

head bowed over her hand, the gesture reminding her of Errol Flynn's Robin Hood bowing over Olivia De Haviland's hand. "Margaret Rose," he replied, each syllable rolling off his tongue like a lullaby. "Just like our little princess?"

"Yes, Pops, just like our little princess," Wesley answered, his mouth turned up in a crooked smile.

A hint of Pops's native accent had crept into Wesley's voice, something she'd never noticed before. She tried to dismiss that it added to his charm, but failed miserably.

Maggie waved a hand toward the couch. "Please, have a seat."

"Why, thank you."

Maggie followed Pops to the sofa, with Wesley close behind, his hand gently touching the curve of her waist. Though he'd been welcoming, she sensed Wesley was walking on eggshells, as if he were waiting for the other shoe to drop.

"What are you doing here, Pops?"

Couldn't Wesley let his grandfather get settled before diving in head first? Maggie glanced at the older man. If his grandfather thought Wesley's question was out of line, his expression didn't show it.

"Figured it was time I came and saw you. How have you been?"

"Okay, I guess," Wesley answered. "What about you?"

"Good. I hear you've been taking Old Betsy up quite a bit recently."

Pops knew about their evening flights. Maggie almost asked how he knew, but Wesley beat her to it. "Keeping tabs on me, old man?"

"Clyde Ellerbee is an old friend of mine," Pops answered. "Why do you think he offered to store my plane in his barn?"

Wesley blew out an exasperated breath and relaxed into the cushions. "Why Churchill hasn't enlisted you to be a spy for the Allies, I'll never understand."

"Ah, Mr. Churchill is a fine fellow, but he's not my flesh and blood." The lines of the older man's mouth straightened into a very familiar grimace. "Not like you are, my boy."

Maggie blinked slowly, the love and concern in Pops's words causing the bright yellows and cheery blues of Merrilee's draperies to blur into a watery abstract. Couldn't Wesley hear the love in each note of this man's voice, see the concern as the older man's eyes traveled over his face?

"The truth is, I figured if you were flying Old Betsy, you might be ready to talk," Pops said.

One look at Wesley, and Maggie felt as if the blackout curtains had suddenly been drawn. "So, what did you want to talk about?"

The man shot Maggie a questioning glance, then focused on his grandson.

"I'm being so rude." Maggie chuckled nervously, pushing herself up to the edge of the couch. "Let me go see about some coffee or tea."

But Wesley's hand tightened around her waist. "What is it, Pops?"

Mr. Rogers gave her a slight smile and cleared his throat. "Don't you think it's time we cleared up this misunderstanding between us about your sister?"

"It's pretty straightforward, Pops. Beth is gone. Not much left to talk about."

The older man's face blanched at Wesley's words. "I know. Losing Beth broke my heart. But I don't want to lose you, too."

The cushions shifted beneath her as Wesley stood. "You can't lose someone that you ordered to stay out of your sight."

"I didn't know what I was saying. I had just lost my granddaughter."

"And I'd lost my sister."

Wesley walked across the room, his spine rigid, his hands that had held Maggie's so tenderly moments ago were clenched by his side. A few moments later, he was in the doorway. The mournful slant of his mouth mirrored the expression on his grandfather's face.

"I promised Merrilee I'd do some work out in the garden this afternoon." Wesley glanced at Maggie then dropped his chin to his chest. "If I don't see you before you go, have a safe trip home, Pops."

"Wesley," Maggie said, getting to her feet.

It was too late. A moment later, the front door banged shut, the paned glass rattling in his wake.

An uncomfortable silence enveloped the room. Maggie wasn't sure what to make of the scene that had just unfolded. No sense going after Wesley. He needed some time to cool down. She glanced over at Pops. His silver brows conjoined into one straight line over darkened blue eyes, shining softly with what Maggie suspected were tears. Deep lines slashed his forehead and his mouth, giving her the impression of a weary solider who had seen one battle too many.

Sitting down beside him, Maggie gently touched his arm. "Are you okay?"

After a brief hesitation, Pops nodded. "Nothing less than what I deserve. I'm just sorry you had to be a witness to our mess."

"Please don't worry about it." She patted

his hand. "Everybody hits bumps in the road."

The man crossed his arms and leaned back, as if to study her closer. "So tell me, princess, how did you meet my grandson?"

"He's my commanding officer over at the Bell Bomber Plant."

His eyebrows rose in disbelief. "You're a pilot?"

Maggie nodded. "I'm with the Women's Army Service Pilots."

The older man let out a sharp chuckle. "I bet my boy wasn't too keen about that assignment."

"You can say that again." Maggie laughed, relaxing against the back of the couch. "He spent the first two weeks I knew him trying to figure out ways to keep me on the ground."

"That doesn't surprise me."

Maggie hesitated then thought better of it. "You mean, because of Beth?"

Pops blew out a long sigh. "Wesley has always been overprotective of his sister."

He spoke in the present tense, as if Beth were still alive. The muscles in her chest tightened, ribbons of grief compressing her heart into a painful knot.

Maggie wondered whether to ask the question on the tip of her tongue, then

302

decided that knowing the answer might be the only way to understand what Wesley was going through. "Do you really blame him for Beth's death?"

A spark of something — maybe regret? — flashed in Pops's eyes. "So he told you the whole sorrowful mess."

Maggie shrugged one shoulder weakly, suddenly feeling as if she had walked into an active mine field. "It's been on his mind a lot here lately."

"I'm just surprised. My boy isn't one to be sharing such things." Pops took a deep breath as if to steady himself. "To answer your question, I don't know. Not really. But I can see how he might believe that I blamed him. Both of us were so devastated at the thought of losing Beth the way we did. I didn't realize how much Wesley held himself responsible for Beth's accident until he left to come here. By then, nothing I could say would convince him otherwise."

"But you haven't spoken to him in months."

"Another bad decision on my part." Pops rubbed the tops of his thighs as if the chill of his grandson's reception had sunk deep into his bones. "I thought if Wesley had some time to work through this situation with his sister, he would understand that I

303

reacted out of grief." He looked over at her, his eyes somber. "I could never blame him for what happened."

"I know."

"When I heard he was flying Old Betsy, it gave me hope."

Cocking her elbow on the back of the couch, Maggie rested her head in her hand. "Your plane is a beauty."

Pops glanced back at her, one fuzzy eyebrow raised in interested surprise. "My boy has shown you his sister's plane?"

A sudden awkwardness tangled like a knot in her stomach. Maggie mashed her lips together nervously. Would Pops be upset that Wesley had let her fly his grand-daughter's plane? She sat up straight, waiting for the emotions to unleash. "Wesley thought it would be a good idea if I got some flying time on her, sir."

"I see," Pops replied quietly, scrutinizing her again.

Maggie licked her lips nervously. "It's just that I was grounded for a while, and Wesley thought I needed to be sharp at the controls." The words rushed out before Maggie could stop them. "But I've got to tell you, I've enjoyed every minute of flying Old Betsy. She handles like a dream."

The older man reached out and cupped

her chin in the palm of his hand, his calloused thumb gently scraping the tender skin of her cheek. "I'm glad, my girl. That plane was meant to be flown by someone who would appreciate her, not made into a memorial of what we lost."

"Then you're not mad Wesley let some pilot in his squadron take your Betsy up?"

"Oh no," he answered, his soft gaze resting on her. "But then, you're not just another pilot Wesley is working with, are you?"

Maggie shook her head. No, she wasn't. "We're close friends, sir."

"I see," he answered, the hint of laughter in his voice startling her. "Then as his friend, you need to know that I'm not giving up on my grandson."

She smiled up at him. Well, it was good to hear one of them was willing to act sensibly. "What are you going to do?"

"For one, I'm staying here until I can get through to him. Your aunt has been gracious enough to offer me a room for as long as I need one."

That was a wonderful idea. Wesley hadn't said it in so many words, but she could tell he missed his grandfather terribly. Maybe Pops's presence would help Wesley start to accept Beth's death.

"Can I ask you a favor, princess?"

"What's that?"

"I don't know what your relationship with my grandson is, but I can tell just by looking at the two of you together that you care about each other." The old man swallowed, suddenly looking every one of his advanced years. "Will you help me?"

"I'm not sure that there's anything I can do," she stammered uneasily.

"Oh, I think so. You're already gotten Wesley flying his sister's plane. He never even thought of using it unless he was absolutely forced into it." The man took her hand and patted it. "But I have faith that God will give us the wisdom to know the right thing to do when the time comes."

Most of the uneasiness she felt dissolved. "Me, too, Pops."

"So will you promise to help me?"

Maggie rested her head against the back of the couch. How could she turn away when she loved Wesley as she did, with her whole heart? The burden he carried physically hurt her, more than any words her uncle or anyone else in town had thrown at her. But could she chance the broken heart that might be waiting for her at the end of this particular assignment?

Pops must have taken Maggie's silence for

306

reluctance. "Please help me, Margaret Rose. I've already lost one grandchild. I couldn't bear to lose another."

Maggie rose to her feet and nodded. Wesley needed his grandfather in his life. And she loved him too much not to do everything she could to help. "Let me go talk to him."

"Why did Pops have to show up now?" Wesley muttered to the stand of green beans dangling from thin tangled vines in front of him. Grabbing the pod at the stems, he gave a quick tug, pulling the beans free and dropping them onto a growing pile in a nearby bucket.

"I don't know. Maybe Pops realizes he made a mistake and has come here to make it right."

Wesley glanced over his shoulder to find Maggie walking toward him, the green tendrils slapping softly against her as she drew closer. She looked like a rose among the thorns standing there, her reddish-gold hair, now dry from the warmth of the day, bathed in the soft light of late afternoon. The delicate curls brushing her shoulders seemed to be reaching up, enjoying the last moments of the sun's warmth. Her green eyes shined with an eternal optimism he'd come to appreciate on a daily basis.

But he couldn't deny the cold reality of the situation. "You heard him in there." Wesley yanked another fistful of beans off the vines. "That didn't sound like a man who's ready to admit he was wrong."

She fell in beside him, pushing back the heavy growth of leaves to uncover hidden stashes of beans. "You didn't stay around long enough to listen to him. That man in there is heartbroken."

"Didn't sound like it to me, not when he started up with the same old song."

"He's grieving, Wesley, just like you are."

"I doubt it."

Wesley felt her stiffen beside him and turned to find her glaring at him. "It's hard to admit when you're wrong. I mean, just look at you."

That stopped him in his tracks. The handful of beans he'd held in his hand hit the bottom of the bucket with a sharp thud. "What does that mean?"

Maggie lifted her chin with an intent that told him she was going to have her say. "Pops was wrong, Wesley. He should have never asked you to make a promise that was out of your control. But you were wrong to agree to it."

He crossed his arms over his chest. Heat

flooded his face. "What are you . . . ?"

"You love your grandfather so much," Maggie interrupted, resting her hands on his forearms. "You let him corner you into a promise you couldn't possibly keep."

"You don't have a clue what you're talking about."

"Really?" Maggie jammed her finger into his chest. "Did you or did you not just promise my aunt no more than thirty minutes ago that you would keep me, a test pilot on a questionable aircraft, safe?"

"Stop it," he commanded, grasping her accusing fingers in his hand.

Her fingers relaxed in the warmth of his grip. "Every pilot, male or female, knows the challenges we face when we climb into that cockpit. We can only prepare the best we know how and leave the rest up to God." Her gaze softened. "Your grandfather knows that."

Wesley knew she was speaking the truth. As a pilot, he would be offended if someone else felt responsible for his safety. But it didn't stop the question that had been hounding him since he had stepped inside his commanding officer's tent and learned the news of his sister's death.

"Why Beth?"

Maggie lifted her hand to his face, touching his cheek gently. He leaned into her touch. "I don't know," Maggie whispered. "Why Jackson?"

Wesley stared at her. Had Maggie questioned Jackson's death just as he had Beth's?

"Whenever I think about Jackson, I remind myself that he was no different than the rest of our boys and girls who died for a purpose we all believe in. Jackson is a hero." Maggie's voice cracked. She dropped her hand to her side. "Just like your sister is."

Wesley tilted his head back. The last rays of sunshine couldn't chase the chill from his skin. He hadn't seen Beth's death as anything but a horrible accident, hadn't thought of it as a courageous act for the values she so deeply believed in.

Why did Maggie always have to make him think? Yes, Beth knew what she was doing in the cockpit, probably better than most of the men first drafted into the Royal Air Force. And she had said more than once she would willingly die for the freedoms that Germany and Japan wanted to destroy. As understanding began to sink in, the strands of guilt that had tied him into knots seemed to loosen.

"I'm sorry, Wesley. I'm horrible about giving my two cents even when nobody asks for it." She lowered her chin to her chest and sniffed. "It's just, I can see how bad this is hurting you and your grandfather, and I can't help but want to do something about it."

He wasn't sure he would ever recover from losing his sister. Maybe Maggie was right. Maybe it was as simple as accepting the past and moving into the future. A future he now knew wouldn't be complete without Maggie by his side.

Wesley lifted his hand to Maggie's face, his fingers tracing the soft line of her jaw before tilting her head back. He took a breath, the scent of lavender and fresh earth reminding him of the first time she'd been in his arms, the day James had discovered them coming from the tent camp. Her lips parted slightly, whether in surprise or welcome, he wasn't sure. He bent his head, watching as her eyelids fluttered down before pressing his mouth against hers.

An engine backfired in the distance, and they jumped.

Dazed, Wesley stepped back and glanced at Maggie. He couldn't be sure, but he thought she swayed slightly. "I thought your uncle James might have taken a shot at us."

"You'd better hope not. He wouldn't have missed," Maggie replied, taking a shallow breath before straightening. "Don't you think you've kept your grandfather waiting long enough?"

Wesley glanced at the house. He may have taken his first unsteady steps toward finding peace with Beth's passing, but what about his grandfather? "What am I going to say to him?"

"You won't know until you talk to him." He looked down to find eyes the color of English moss staring up at him. "Just take it a minute at a time."

Ah, that ramrod determination he had grown to admire had kicked in again. He brushed a kiss across her nose. "Will you come with me?"

"Are you kidding?" His heart tightened as she slipped her hand into the bend of his arm, her smile giving him a much-needed boost of confidence. "I'm hoping to get him talking about his time flying under the Wright Brothers. I wouldn't miss that conversation for all the tea in China!"

CHAPTER EIGHTEEN

"Pops really enjoyed listening to the Grand Ole Opry last night." Maggie pushed a tree limb back with one hand while adjusting the canvas bag loaded with groceries on the other shoulder.

Since being rotated back into the flight schedule, she'd been too busy to visit Eliza Beth and the tent families as much as she would have liked. So she was glad when Merrilee had invited her to come along this afternoon. "I guess they don't get that kind of music over there."

"Well, he must have taken a fancy to it. I heard him humming one of the Carter family's songs this morning while we were in the garden. He's got a good voice for a man his age," Merrilee answered, holding on to a sack of freshly picked tomatoes and corn. "And he's such a help. Did you know he's already working on the menu for next week? I'm thinking of asking him to help me with Donna's coming-home party."

"I bet he would like that. Wesley told me Pops is a wiz in the kitchen."

Merrilee nodded. "He's a good man, just like his grandson."

"I like him, too, Merrilee." Maggie held the pine limb until her aunt had cleared it.

"It's easy to see where Wesley gets his looks from. He's the spitting image of his granddaddy."

Maggie had noticed the resemblance, too, especially around the eyes. Donald Hicks had probably broken quite a few female hearts in his heyday.

"I think he's taken a shine to you, too," Merrilee said.

"Who?" Maggie let go of the branch too quickly and got a light swat to her backside.

"Both of them," Merrilee answered, trying her best not to smile. "Anyone with a brain in their head can see that there's something going on between you and Wesley. Pops is just over the moon at the thought that you might be his granddaughter."

"That's just plain silliness," Maggie admonished, the argument sounding weak even to her own ears.

"Uh-huh." Merrilee walked on ahead.

Maggie gathered the canvas bag closer to her side. She didn't blame her aunt for not believing her, not when she couldn't even convince herself. Truth was, she was confused. She'd spent her whole life chasing the dreams God had given her. But recently, dreams of a home and family with Wesley had burst into life within her. Dreams that included little boys with sweet blue eyes, holding their arms out as if taking flight, and a little girl who stubbornly adored her father much like her mother did. Could Wesley be a part of another dream, something bigger than she had even imagined for herself? Only the Lord knew, and right now, He was being quiet on the subject.

But Merrilee wasn't.

"I know you've always talked about flying planes and such, but I've got news for you, sweetie. Love, especially when it's with someone like Wesley, doesn't come along every day."

"I know," Maggie answered, stopping under the shadows of a massive oak to rest. "Things are in an uproar right now. Who knows how long I'll be on the flight schedule before something else spooks Wesley into grounding me? And then there's this whole situation with his grandfather."

"They seem to be getting along okay."

"You're right. I've never seen Wesley so

happy." She dropped the canvas bag to the ground and leaned back against the tree's trunk. "But they've still got a long way to go."

Merrilee rubbed comforting circles on her arm. "Maybe you can help them. I mean, you care so much for both of them."

"I know what you're doing." Maggie shrugged her aunt's hand away. "But you've got to understand. These feelings I have for Wesley, the timing just isn't right."

Merrilee huffed out her disgust. "Nothing in life is perfect. Just think. If I had waited until Daddy got some sense in that stubborn head of his before I married John, I'd still be sitting here, an old maid by now."

"But you ended up divorcing."

The words were out of her mouth before Maggie realized it. Merrilee lowered her head, her hair falling like a curtain over her face. Maggie cringed. She wouldn't hurt her aunt for anything in the world, but she had. "I'm sorry, Aunt Merrilee. I shouldn't have said that."

Lifting her face, Merrilee pushed her hair back behind her ear and gave Maggie a brief smile. "John and I may not have lasted over the long haul, but he still gave me the most precious gift. He gave me Claire Bear."

Maggie draped her arm around her aunt's

shoulders and held her, more convinced now that had Merrilee been given the choice, she would still be Mrs. John Davenport. Is this how it was when you loved a man, this feeling of being connected even when all hope of a life together is lost? Was this longing in store for her after her assignment at the Bell was completed and she moved on?

A faint chill ran through her and she shivered. *She had a job to do.* But even that thought didn't warm her with excitement as it usually did.

Picking up the canvas bag, Maggie slung it over her shoulder; the load was bearable compared to the heaviness saddling her heart. Merrilee fell quietly in step behind her, and they walked in silence until they reached the outskirts of the camp. Several piles of fallen leaves had been brushed along the lines of the camp's perimeter, allowing for the addition of a few more tents since Maggie's last visit. A variety of thread-worn cotton dresses, torn jeans and undergarments dangled stiffly from a clothesline. Nearby, a black cauldron hung over ash remains of what must have once been a small campfire, the smell of lye lightly hanging in the moist air.

Where was everyone?

"Eliza Beth did know we were coming today?" Merrilee asked.

Maggie nodded, studying the vacant landscape. "She mentioned it to me when I saw her at the post office a few days ago."

Her aunt looked at her. "This doesn't make sense."

A tent flap flew open a couple of yards in front of them and they waited. Seconds later, Eliza Beth stood in the doorway, fisting her hands into loose tent material. Her eyes closed, she drew in one breath, then another, as if clearing her head of some poisonous image she'd left in the confines of the tent. No spark of the rosy color Maggie had noticed in recent days could be found in the young woman's cheeks; it was replaced by a chalky paleness like those that flashed across the movie screen at the Strand — footage of prisoners found in what the newsmen called "death camps."

Maggie flung the groceries to the ground and ran toward the woman. "Eliza Beth?"

The younger woman's eyes flew open, her mouth gaped in pained disbelief. Maggie was close enough now to notice the bloated veins making inroads in the whites of her eyes. "Thank God," she whispered, her voice hoarse, barely registering in the silence. "Thank God you're here!"

318

Maggie reached out to Eliza Beth as her knees gave way. Sliding to the ground, she took the brunt of the fall, using her body to cushion the young woman from any further trauma.

Merrilee held a bell jar of water she'd recovered from Maggie's bag to Eliza Beth's lips. "Should we call a doctor?"

Eliza Beth shook her head violently. "No, please don't!"

Maggie pushed back the woman's matted head. "But sweetheart, you're sick."

Eliza Beth continued to shake her head. "I'm just tired from seeing to everyone over the past couple of days."

"You're as weak as a kitten," Merrilee replied. "Maybe the doctor —"

"Please don't." Eliza Beth cut her off. "We don't have enough money to pay him, and my family wouldn't think of taking charity."

"Why didn't you send someone up to the house to get one of us?" Maggie asked.

Eliza Beth shook her head. "Didn't see no point in making your people sick, not after everything you've done for us."

"Next time, you come and get me, you hear? I can't be having folks getting sick under my care." Merrilee admonished gently, silencing Eliza Beth with a sip of water. "Do you have any idea what you may have?"

Eliza Beth shook her head again. "Two of my sister's girls came home from school with a fever a couple of days ago, and by nighttime, they couldn't breathe for the coughing. Then several more in the camp came down with fevers, and the little ones started getting sick to their stomachs. They haven't been able to hold anything down since." She dropped her chin to her chest, her shoulders heaving as a sob tore through her. "I didn't mean to hurt anyone. I promise I didn't."

Merrilee cupped the girl's chin in her hand and lifted her head. "What do you mean, sweetheart?"

Tears pooled in the corners of Eliza Beth's eyes. "We didn't know what the girls had, and none of us have the money for the doctor to come calling. So I mixed up Grandma's cough recipe, and everyone took a dose. After that, everyone got violently sick."

"What does this remedy of yours have in it?" Merrilee asked.

"One part lemon juice, one part honey . . ." Eliza Beth's voice drifted off as she hugged the jar of water close to her and took another sip.

Maggie noticed a dark cloud shroud her aunt's face. "What?"

But Merrilee's focus was on the young woman. "Did you use any spirits in this cough medicine of yours?"

Maggie blinked hard at her aunt's question. Eliza Beth had made do with the few supplies she had, but she'd been thrown into a bad situation. Surely she hadn't fed hard liquor to a bunch of sick kids.

"It wasn't much, Ms. Merrilee. Just a third of the mixture," Eliza Beth blurted out, her eyes lowered as if in shame. "Same as my Grandma Farland's."

If Eliza Beth's answer shocked Maggie, her aunt's question befuddled her. "Did you buy it at the store?"

"Where else would she get it?" Maggie asked.

Both women shot her a look that made Maggie feel as if she had a lot to learn about the ways of the world.

Eliza Beth finally turned back to Merrilee, shaking her head. "No, ma'am, I couldn't afford it."

Maggie glanced at Eliza Beth. "Then where did you get it?"

"I don't think that matters right now," Merrilee answered, patting Eliza Beth's hand gently. "If these folks have been poisoned by a bad batch of corn liquor like I think, they're going to get a lot worse before they get any better. We've got to move all of them up to the house so that we can keep a close eye on them for the next couple of days."

Eliza Beth tugged at Merrilee's sleeve. "Mr. James isn't going to like that, ma'am."

Merrilee leaned toward her, her expression soft with understanding and sadness. "Probably not, but it's my house, and I'm not about to leave your people out here. I'm sure even James will understand that."

Maggie wasn't so certain of that. Apprehension skipped along the nerves down her back. Compassion wasn't Uncle James's strong suit, not even to his own kin. She didn't want to think how the man would take this invasion on the Danielses' family home.

Hopefully, Wesley would be there. She remembered the day he'd stood up to Uncle James when he'd aimed a gun at them in the backyard. Wesley wouldn't put up with any of her uncle's nonsense.

Merrilee grabbed a couple of bell jars filled with water and rose to her feet. "I'm going to check on everyone and see what we're going to need to get them moved up to the house. Maggie, if you could, would you gather all the food and supplies you can get your hands on? We're going to need it to feed this army."

"Yes, ma'am." Maggie smiled at her aunt's retreating figure. Merrilee was as strong a woman as she'd ever met, the kind of woman Maggie hoped to be if she had any hopes of living out all the dreams God had given her. *Please, Lord, please help Merrilee. And please heal these sick ones, Lord.*

"Maggie?" Eliza Beth stirred, pulling her legs under her as if to stand.

Maggie circled the girl's slender waist with her arm and, following Eliza Beth's lead, slowly rose into a standing position. She tried to take a step, but Maggie tightened her hold of her. "Let's give it a second so you can get your balance."

Through the circle of her lips, Eliza Beth drew in a deep breath. Her cheeks, while still pale, now had the faintest shade of pink. "I'm sorry about all this. Y'all have been so good to us, and look how we repay you."

"It's not your fault."

"Yes, it is," Eliza Beth answered, her fingers gripping Maggie's hand painfully as she took a tentative step. "I should have never used that shine Jimbo brought to me."

Maggie stared at the girl. "Jimbo?"

"He was married to my sister, Annie." She

nodded. "He was visiting when our nieces came home sick the other day. I promise I would have used store-bought spirits if I'd had them, but we didn't have enough money. When Jimbo said he knew where he could get a bottle, I told him to get it." Eliza Beth lowered her chin to her chest. "I know I shouldn't have asked him for help, but I was desperate! I thought the children might have diphtheria."

Maggie put her arm around the girl and hugged her close. No telling what she would have done in that situation, so who was she to judge? "Did you see where Jimbo got it from?"

Eliza Beth gave a slight shake of her head. "He headed off into the woods before I could ask him any questions. A while later, he was back with a shoebox in his hands. I'd barely pulled the jar out when he was gone again."

Maggie sighed, letting Eliza Beth go. "So we don't have a clue where he got that poison from."

"Maybe one," Eliza Beth answered. She snaked her free hand into the front pocket of her dress and pulled out a slip of paper. "I thought this was funny at the time, knowing how your aunt is about these things and all. But now . . ." Eliza Beth handed it to her.

Maggie unfolded the paper. It was a receipt for a pair of shoes Merrilee bought the afternoon they had gone shopping. "Where did you get this?"

The pale color in Eliza Beth's cheeks retreated again. "I found it in the shoebox along with the moonshine."

CHAPTER NINETEEN

The next few days consisted of sponge baths and spoon feedings as first the children, then the women fought the ramifications of the poisoned cough remedy. Maggie had requested an immediate temporary leave from her duties, a move that was met with understanding approval by Wesley.

She only wished she could say the same for her uncle James. His sharp words and outright threats to throw Merrilee out on the street could be heard by almost everyone in the house, even Maggie, as she gathered blankets and pillows with Claire from the attic. She'd prayed that Claire hadn't heard any of her uncle's rumblings, but any hopes of that were lost when she saw the taut look stretched on the girl's childish face. Maggie had a good mind to go downstairs and give that uncle of hers what for, but the slamming of the front door as she crested the top of the stairwell told her he had gone.

Good riddance! Maggie sat on the front porch swing, leaning into the solid wooden slants as she retrieved the folded piece of paper from her pocket. The last two children had finally found the strength to escape from their beds this afternoon before Maggie thought about the receipt Eliza Beth had found with the tainted moonshine. Merrilee would be horrified at the thought that such a personal piece of information had found its place alongside the illegal mixture. Why was Jimbo using Merrilee's shoeboxes to transport moonshine? And worse, what would Uncle James do if he ever found out?

Maggie closed her eyes. A bone-weary tiredness weighed down on her, tugging her into a comfortable stillness. She couldn't tell Merrile about the receipt. It would embarrass her too much. And she had to keep Uncle James in the dark, too. No telling what that old grouch would do if he had this kind of information.

She drew in a deep breath, feeling her body relax even as her mind rebelled against the heaviness tugging at her. She didn't have time to be tired, not when there were sheets to be folded and beds to be made. Her eyelids slowly fluttered shut once more.

The scent of sunshine and airplane fuel teased her senses and Maggie smiled, burrowing her head deeper into the softness. Since that kiss they'd shared, Maggie had wondered what it would be like to rest in Wesley's arms, but this, this was better than any dream. She snuggled closer into the solid wall of his chest, her head pillowed against his broad shoulder making her feel safe and secure in a way that only her time in the air had. She stretched her palm against his side, her fingers appreciative of the combination of strength and muscle beneath them.

Maggie sighed.

The soft brush of lips against her hair forced her eyelids open and she tilted her head back. Wesley's face was inches from her, studying her with a soft expression of concern and something else her befuddled mind couldn't quite decipher. She pushed against him and he let her go, stretching his arms along the back of the swing to give her plenty of room to move.

"Sorry about that," Maggie lowered her gaze to her hands clenched together in her lap. Her hair fell forward, thankfully covering the heat rising in her cheeks. "I guess the last couple of days finally caught up with me."

"Don't worry about it." He surprised her by capturing strands of her hair and pushing them behind her ear. "How's everyone doing?"

"Fine."

"And Michael?"

Maggie couldn't help but smile. At five years old, Michael Farland had gotten the brunt of Eliza Beth's cough concoction, so much so that Maggie had quietly feared that the boy might not live through the ordeal. But Wesley wouldn't hear of it.

Maggie glanced at him. The memory of Wesley rocking the tiny boy in Merrilee's dainty rocker, and his comforting whispers as he spun tales of King Arthur and the Knights of the Roundtable while Michael snuggled against his chest, caused her heart to flutter like butterfly wings in a spring tornado. The man was going to make a wonderful father someday.

"Good. We finally let him and Nellie out of bed this afternoon." The dreamy hoarseness in her voice made her clear her throat. "Merrilee wants them to rest a few more days before letting them go back to their camp."

"I'm glad. The thought of sending them back into the woods had me worried. It'll be good to keep an eye on them a little bit longer, just to make sure they're okay." Wesley stretched his long legs out in front of him. "And who knows? We might need their help if we come down with that horrible stuff."

Maggie mashed her lips together. She hadn't had a moment to tell Wesley the real reason behind the camp's sickness since carrying the first batch of kids into the house two days ago. "They don't have the flu. They were poisoned."

Wesley's head snapped forward, his gaze pinning her. "What do you mean, poisoned?"

She took a shuddered breath. "When the kids came in from school the other day with a cough, Eliza Beth made up some of her grandma's cough syrup."

"How do you make cough syrup?" His brows shot up in confusion. "Isn't that something you purchase from the druggist?"

"If you have the money, you do." Maggie pulled her legs up to her chest. "And we both know that Eliza Beth doesn't have a dime. So she used some spirits and made up a batch of her grandma's cough syrup."

"Spirits?"

"Corn liquor she got from Jimbo. Merrilee is pretty sure it poisoned them."

Wesley sat back as if stunned. "Why didn't you tell me this before?"

The hair on the back of her neck stood on

end. She sat up, taking a deep breath to calm herself, but it didn't work. "I don't know if you've noticed it or not, but we've had a houseful of sick people the last few days."

He studied her for a long moment, then pushed the swing into a gentle motion. "You're right. I'm sorry."

Blast, but she couldn't stay mad at the man! Not when he was all agreeable and everything! And she needed to stay angry at him, if only to protect her dream.

But what if God has more than one dream for me?

"There is one other thing." She reached into her pocket for the receipt. "Eliza Beth found this in the shoebox Jimbo gave her."

Wesley glanced over the piece of paper. "So? Merrilee must have forgotten to take it out when she threw the box away."

"That's just it, Wesley," Maggie answered. "She doesn't throw boxes away. She stores her shoes in them."

Resting his arm against the back of the swing, he shifted to face her. "Then how did he get this one?"

"I don't know." Maggie sighed. "What's it going to matter anyway when my uncle hears about this? He's been searching for a reason to invoke that stupid morality clause in my granddaddy's will. If he gets hold of this information, he'll take this house away from Merrilee."

He sat quietly for a moment before one eyebrow arched upward. "That's convenient, isn't it?"

Now that she thought about the situation, it was a bit too convenient. She gasped at the thought. "You think Uncle James is setting Merrilee up?"

"Possibly."

"I don't know, Wesley. My uncle may be as mean as a snake but I don't think even he would hurt a bunch of kids. And I know Jimbo wasn't trying to poison them." Maggie glanced over at him and read the confusion in his expression. "He was married to Eliza Beth's sister, Annie."

"Isn't she the one who died along with her baby?"

Maggie nodded.

"That had to be tough." Wesley leaned his shoulder against the back of the swing. "I still think your uncle is involved. It's like you said — it's killing him that he can't have this house. And what better way to take it from her than to link Merrilee to tainted hooch?"

Maggie suddenly felt sick. "This isn't good."

"Have you talked to Merrilee about this?"

Maggie shook her head. "She's got enough on her plate as it is."

Wesley seemed to think about that for a moment. "What about your dad?"

A sudden heaviness weighed down her chest at the thought of her father. "Last time we spoke, he wasn't too happy with me."

That was an understatement, and from the look on his face, Wesley knew it, too. He paused for a moment, as if switching back to the problem at hand. "So we're the only ones who know about this?"

"And Eliza Beth. Why?"

"If James is behind this, he can't bring a claim against your grandfather's will until news about Merrilee's involvement spreads around town. But if we keep quiet about the receipt, he'll be forced to make another move."

"Maybe we can get enough information to find the still before another batch kills someone," Maggie said, liking the way Wesley included her in this plan instead of the high-handedness she usually got from the male members of her family — most recently her dad. "When should we tell Merrilee what's going on?"

"Not until we have more information. Like you said, she's got a lot on her mind

333

right now." Wesley hesitated, a tiny crease forming between his eyes. "I still think you need to make things right with your dad."

Maybe, but she wasn't ready to back down. Her father hadn't even tried to understand her position or respect the job she'd been trained to do. But she had to admit, even in those instances where they didn't see eye to eye, Daddy had always put aside any hard feelings to talk to her. Just not this time.

She decided to ignore him. "Do you think we should talk to Jimbo? We could feel him out about who gave him the box?"

"Maggie."

"Please don't you start in on me about my father, not when . . ."

His expression grew stony. "Not when I've got my own problems with my grandfather to handle?"

She may have lost her temper but that was no reason to be ugly. Maggie shrugged, despite the miserable knot forming between her shoulder blades.

Wesley caught her chin between his finger and thumb, and lifted her face to meet the sudden storm brewing in his eyes. "Do you always fly off the handle every time someone who cares about you voices their concerns for your safety? What did your dad do, hurt your feelings?"

Maggie opened her mouth to answer, then slammed it shut. Yes, she was hurt. Daddy and Momma had always been there for her, believing in her dreams even when she questioned herself at times.

"He was worried about you, Maggie."

She stared back at him, the anger that had flashed so quickly suddenly tempered. "Well, he shouldn't be."

"From everything I've heard, your mom and dad think you can do anything you set your mind to." Their gazes met and tangled. "So does Merrilee."

What about you, Wesley? Maggie eyed him for a moment, hoping for an answer but not getting one. "Let me think about it."

"Good. While you're doing that, I think I'm going to go hunt Jimbo down. It's time we had a talk."

"But . . ." Maggie stumbled over the words.

"Sorry, Ace, but you're not going anywhere near that guy unless I'm around. You got that?" Wesley stated matter-of-factly, giving her curl a gentle tug before dropping his hand to his lap.

Maggie nodded, her heart breaking into tiny little pieces. If Wesley insisted on grounding her every time danger was involved, he could never be a part of the dreams God had for her.

If the opportunity arose for her to find out what Jimbo was up to, she'd take advantage of it. But she did respect what Wesley was saying. If Jimbo was running moonshine, the man was more dangerous than either of them could have ever thought.

"So you haven't been able to talk to Jimbo yet?" Pops leaned the hedge clippers against his legs while fishing a snowy-white handkerchief out of his pants pocket. "It's been four days now."

Wesley shoved the push mower over a particularly stubborn swatch of tall fescue, the fresh scent of newly cut grass lifting in a slight breeze. He'd hadn't expected to tell his grandfather about the shoebox, but then he hadn't counted on boardinghouse gossip, either. "He had a delivery scheduled in Miami, but got directed to another airfield. I'm expecting him back anytime now."

Pops mopped the back of his neck with the scrape of cloth. "Good! The sooner, the better, if you ask me. How long do you think it will be before Merrilee knows what the rest of us do?"

"She started asking questions when the Nelsons moved out before the end of the

336

month." The metal blades slashed through the grass as he gave the mower a savage push. "Now that Bob Johnson is moving, I don't think we'll be able to keep her in the dark much longer."

"I'm surprised we've kept it from her this long, but something's been preoccupying her mind. Poor girl. Life's cruel like that sometimes." Pops swiped at his forehead in fierce strokes. "But she'll get through this. We'll be there to help her."

Wesley stopped and wiped his sweaty palms against the rough denim of his jeans, dismissing Pops's words. They were making progress in rebuilding their relationship, but there were still times, like now, when he was reminded that Pops had baled on him exactly like Merrilee's renters. "I just wish Eliza Beth had kept her mouth shut."

"Sometimes a person lashes out in anger or in pain and find they regret it later."

Wesley stretched out his arms, the sudden tightness in his muscles threatening to cut off his breathing. Had that been what happened with his grandfather? Had the pain of losing Beth caused his grandfather to rage in anger while he festered in guilt over breaking his word?

Tilting his head back, Wesley closed his eyes. He was so tired of carrying the weight of Beth's death. *Lord, please help Pops forgive me. Help me forgive myself.*

Wesley opened his eyes to a clear-blue sky. The heaviness that had been a constant companion since Beth's death was still there, but, for the moment, the weight shifted, became bearable. What was it Maggie had said? That she had to take her grief to the Lord constantly in those first days. He would stay on his knees then. He lowered his head and glanced over at his grandfather. Pops needed to be included in these prayers, too.

"You're getting a little burnt, Pops. Why don't you take a break over there in the shade?"

Shaking his head, Pops wrapped his weathered hands around the wooden handles and snapped the sharp edges of the clippers together. "We promised to get this lawn cleaned up."

"True, but you're not used to this humidity." Wesley walked over to his grandfather and gently took the blades out of Pops's hands. "Merrilee and Maggie will have my hide if you fall out with a sunstroke."

"Then at least take a break yourself. I could do with the company."

The longing Wesley heard in his grandfather's words were a restful balm to his weary soul. He nodded. "Maybe for just a minute."

They walked over to a nearby oak. A thin cushion of fallen leaves carpeted the area directly under the tree's foliage, which provided a comfortable shade as Wesley and Pops sat down.

"So what do you think will happen to Jimbo?" Pops leaned back on his forearms and stretched out.

Wesley picked up a leaf and tore it in half. Whatever the authorities had in mind would be too good for the man, especially if he had tampered with Donna's plane or sent that threatening note to Maggie. "He deserves to be horsewhipped."

"The sheriff will know how to handle him, I'm sure," Pops answered. Wesley glanced up to find his grandfather staring, studying him as if the old man could almost read his thoughts. It had always been like this between them, which was probably the reason Wesley had never gotten into too many scrapes.

Wesley drew in a deep breath through his nostrils. "I certainly hope so."

A screen door slammed shut, and Wesley looked up to see Edie carrying two quart jars, brimming with chipped ice, slices of lemon and what could only be Merrilee's sweet tea. Claire skipped in her wake.

"Here, Edie. Let me help you with that." Wesley bounded to his feet and met them halfway. The cold glass felt good against his heated skin.

"You taught him well, Mr. Hicks." Edie smiled as both she and Claire joined them under the tree.

"He always was a good boy." A mixture of pride and respect were in the glance Pops gave him. "He hasn't disappointed me as a man, either."

Wesley's heart tightened at the words. Maybe his grandfather had already forgiven him. He gave an awkward chuckle. "Now I'm sure you've had too much sun, old man."

"Well, maybe the tea will help."

"Momma thought you might need it, seeing as how you're cleaning up the yard," Claire said, swinging one leg over the lowest limb and pulling herself up.

"Where is your mother, monkey?" Pops leaned back to look at the little girl who was busy climbing up to the next branch. "I haven't seen her since breakfast this morning."

"She had some business in town with Uncle Jeb. Then she was going to the post office."

Wesley swiped his forehead with the back of his shirt sleeve. Hopefully, Maggie had made peace with her father before her trip. Wesley glanced over at his grandfather as the old man claimed one of the glasses of tea. Building back a broken relationship was proving tougher than outmaneuvering the Germans in a dog fight.

Pops waited until Claire had climbed a bit higher before nodding his head toward Edie in thanks. "Well, I hope you get this thing cleared up before Merrilee hears about what Jimbo has done. I swear, prison is too good for that man."

"Prison?" Edie whispered, her voice shaky.

But his grandfather must not have noticed the woman's distress. "He'll never make it, you know, not with his taste for spirits."

"Everyone deserves a second chance," Edie replied, her face suddenly pale.

With a quick thanks, Wesley lifted the tea to his lips, canvassing the young woman's face for clues as to why she had this unwarranted compassion toward Jimbo. While her voice had steadied, the sadness, a kind of curtained grief in her expression, spoke volumes, as if she herself was searching for another chance to make something right. He didn't have time to dwell on it.

"Well, it would have been nice to clear

this thing up before Maggie got back from Augusta." Wesley lifted the glass to his lips.

"When's our girl coming in?" Pops asked.

Wesley patted his forehead with the back of his shirt sleeve, smiling softly at the endearment. Pops had taken to Maggie like a duck to water, spinning tales of his days with the Wright Brothers, listening to her own flying escapades.

"This afternoon," Wesley finally answered.

"Oh good. Merrilee has missed her terribly this time," Edie replied, casting a quick glance at Claire who had settled on a limb. "But Maggie has been gone longer than usual, hasn't she?"

"The commanding officer in Augusta wanted her to stay for a while, but Major Evans decided that we were too understaffed for us to loan her out." Wesley nodded, setting his glass on the ground beside him. No sense telling them that he had vetoed the idea when Major Evans had presented it to him. With the problems mounting at Merrilee's, along with the threats Maggie had already received, he wasn't comfortable with her being eighty miles away.

And he couldn't deny that he missed the woman like crazy.

"I'd say those tykes missed her, too." Pops threw Wesley a knowing smile before turning back to Edie. "How are our little patients?"

"Reigning terror on the house." Edie laughed. "Michael knotted up poor Claire's jump rope so much, I don't think the Boy Scouts could get out all the knots. When I asked him why, he said something about capturing his horse so that he could track down Sir Lancelot."

Wesley chuckled along with both of them. "That kid's got a wild imagination."

"He's not the only one." Pops winked at him. "It must be hard on Merrilee, with all the children running about."

"I don't think so. If it were, I'm sure she wouldn't have asked them to stay until after Donna's coming-home party."

Wesley turned to his grandfather. "Another girl pilot, Pops, and a friend of Maggie's."

"Why, they're buzzing around here like bees!" The corners of the old man's mouth curled up in laughter. "And to think, old Orville wouldn't stand for a woman entering his flight school."

"*The* Orville Wright?" Edie's eyes grew wide. "The inventor of the airplane?"

"One of the inventors, my dear," Pops answered with a soft chuckle. "I believe his brother had a hand in it, though some think his sister was instrumental in a few of the calculations."

Wesley stood up and stretched, shaking his head as Pops launched into his acquaintance with the infamous Wright brothers. They'd loved Pops's stories, he and Beth, though he had favored the ones about Orville and Wilbur's flying exhibitions while Beth had loved the ones about their younger sister, Katherine.

He smiled. Maggie loved his grandfather's stories, too.

The old man had just started the tale of his meeting with the Wrights while at an airfield for an exhibition when a rustle of leaves caused him to look up. Behind Edie and Pops, Jimbo edged along the fringe of the backyard, a sledgehammer swinging close to his side, his pockets bursting with something Wesley couldn't quite make out at this distance. Jimbo glanced around the yard, not seeing the group tucked under the tree before disappearing into the woods.

Wesley had to follow him, had to find out where the man was going. He glanced over at Edie and Pops, who was deep in the story now. Even Claire had climbed down to a lower limb so that she could hear. An idea formed in Wesley's head.

"Sorry to interrupt," Wesley started,

brushing dirt from his palms. "But has anyone been out to check on the tent camp lately?"

Pops glanced at Edie, then shook his head. "We've been so busy in the last few days, I don't think anyone has thought of it."

"Maybe I should run out there, just to make sure everything is okay."

"That seems like a waste of time, don't you think?" Edie interjected. "Everyone's here at the house."

"You want me to go with you, boy?" The adventure in Pops's voice was suddenly replaced by a thread of concern.

Wesley shook his head as he rolled down his shirt sleeves. Putting his grandfather in harm's way was the last thing he needed. "It won't take that long."

But the apprehension deepening the lines in the old man's forehead and around his eyes told Wesley that Pops wasn't buying it. Wesley clapped a hand over his grandfather's shoulder, steady but not as strong as it used to be. "We promised Merrilee we'd clean up this yard. We can't disappoint her."

Pops studied him for a long moment before giving him a sharp nod. "Alright, boy. But don't dillydally. I'm going to need some help picking up all these clippings."

"I won't be long," Wesley answered, squeezing the man's shoulder lightly before letting go. "If Maggie gets home before I do, tell her to wait here. I'll be right back."

At their affirmative nods, Wesley headed across the yard in the direction he'd seen Jimbo slip into the forest. It didn't take him long to spot the man, scurrying down the dirt-packed trail Maggie had showed him that first day they'd found the tent camp. A light breeze whistled through the leaves, chilling Wesley with a sense of foreboding.

The steadiness of Jimbo's gait told him that the man hadn't been drinking, at least not enough to throw him off balance. To anyone else, it would have looked as though Jimbo was taking a leisurely walk in the woods.

But the sledgehammer gripped in his right hand indicated otherwise.

Jimbo veered away from the ridge leading to the tent camp. Pushing aside low-lying branches, Wesley followed him down a narrow trail that led farther into the woods where he had never been before. Pine thickets crowded together, blocking the sunlight from filtering down, casting the woods in an eerie semidarkness. Briars stuck to his clothing, sometimes plucking the flesh underneath.

Wesley drew in a deep breath, expecting the musty scent of rotting foliage and dead trees, and was surprised by the faint acrid smell of burning logs that seemed to grow stronger with each step. Up ahead, Jimbo sunk out of sight, as if the earth had opened up and swallowed the man whole.

Wesley picked up his pace. Where in blazes had the man gone off to? Thorns pulled at his pants legs as he hurried to the place he'd last seen Jimbo. A sharp clang, much like the multitude of hammers beating against the metal framework he heard every day at the Bell, rose up beneath him, the repetitive pings a radar with its sights set on Jimbo.

A few seconds later, Wesley stared out over the edge of a deep gorge. The side dropped off sharply, vines and overgrown weeds covering the mounds of dirt he knew lay beneath. The waiting hollow could hold an entire squadron of soldiers, as if it had been created for just that purpose. He'd seen this pattern before, in the villages just east of London, but never on American soil.

Dropping down on a rug of pine straw and fallen leaves, Wesley crawled out to the rim of the trench and looked down. Honeysuckle and blackberry vines that were so abundant in this part of the woods had been cut back, revealing a clear patch of land devoid of even a thin carpet of foliage, probably out of fear of fire if the two stoned and blackened rings that stood dead center were any indication. Barrels lay scattered around the area while two lidded pots, moss green from the elements, stood over two fire rings. A short section of pipe stuck out from the top of each pot, then sharply connected to the bottom of a smaller kettle.

Jimbo swung the sledgehammer against one pot, the dented copper winking like a new penny.

Wesley frowned in confusion. Why would a moonshiner destroy his still?

"What do you think you're doing?"

The question drew Wesley's attention back down into the hollow, over the gnarl of twisted coils and broken barrels. Anger flashed through him in a white hot wave as the voice registered. It wasn't any mystery who that voice belonged to.

James Daniels.

The thud of metal against copper rang out again. Jimbo swung the sledgehammer across his body, grasping the head like a shield in front of him. "I'm not doing your bidding anymore."

James leaned against a nearby tree and crossed his arms in front of him. "You mean until you need your next drink."

Jimbo waved an unsteady finger at the contraption of copper and wood. "You almost killed my wife's kin with this stuff!"

"You're the one who gave it to that fool sister-in-law of yours," James bit out. "Looks to me like you're the one with a problem. But then again, problems seem to follow you around like an old coon dog."

Even from this distance, Wesley could see that James's words had hit their mark. "You don't understand."

"Why?" James's voice echoed, his tone sharp as a knife. "Did your wife understand when you left her and your son to die, Jim?"

"What about you?" Jimbo smacked the head of the sledgehammer against the ground. "Trying to scare off your niece with that note?"

Stunned, Wesley flattened himself against the ground, the pain in his chest feeling like a direct blow from Jimbo's sledgehammer. Maggie's own uncle had threatened her. All because she had dreams of flying, a dream God had put into her heart.

James's mouth pulled into an ugly smirk. "You see how much good that did. That fool girl is still trying to prove she's as good as a man."

Wesley clenched his teeth together, his hands clawing into the ground beside him.

Maggie was as good a pilot as any man — better in fact. If James Daniels ever came close to Maggie again, Wesley would beat the living daylights out of him.

"Your niece is a good woman, James. She's kind, even to those who don't deserve it — people like me. And she's a good pilot. You should be proud of her."

"Proud!" James bit out. "Our family is a laughingstock throughout the whole county because of that girl."

Jimbo's face went bloodred. "You're the one everyone's laughing at, trying to steal your sister's house right out from under her. Ms. Merrilee is as good as gold."

"Are you kidding?" James laughed as he stepped away from the tree. "I'm an upstanding member of this community, and my sister —" He paused, his mouth twisting as if he found the idea of Merrilee distasteful. "She's a divorcee who is breaking my daddy's will by running a boardinghouse for men and women. Not to mention housing this still on her property."

"I'll go before the judge as a witness for Merrilee. Tell the court how you ran moonshine on Merrilee's land without her knowledge."

James let out a hard chuckle. "You think anyone's going to believe you? You're a drunk who left his wife and baby to die."

Jimbo let go of the wooden handle, the hammer dropping with a thud to the ground. He crammed his hands into his full pockets.

"It must be hard, knowing that if you'd just stayed in the army a little while longer, you could have gotten them the right medicine. Why, they both might be alive today. But you couldn't stick it out, couldn't you? What did the doctors say — you were unfit to return to duty." James paused for a moment. "It's like you killed them yourself."

Wesley dropped his head down to rest on the top of his hand. The burden Jimbo carried bore down on him like an extended time in the pressure chamber. Did the man know that there was a shortage of medicine everywhere, even on the front? There was nothing he could have done to save his family, no matter how hard he tried.

Just like there was nothing he could have done to save Beth.

Wesley drew in a deep breath, the smell of earth and leaves filling his lungs, the ache around his heart unfurling slightly. It was true; he couldn't have saved Beth any more than Jimbo could have saved his wife and baby. His kid sister had made her own decisions, stubbornly independent choices that

351

were completely out of his control. But then again, if she hadn't made up her own mind, taking the path she had chosen, she wouldn't have been the Beth he knew and loved. He wouldn't have done anything to change the person she had become. Wesley closed his eyes.

I'm such an idiot, Lord.

Something broke loose inside him, leaving in its place a freedom he hadn't felt since before the war. He drew in a deep breath and lifted his head, glancing about as if he were a blind man seeing the world for the first time. When he managed to get back to the house, he'd find Maggie, tell her what he had learned. Spend the rest of his life proving to her he was the man to encourage those God-given dreams of hers.

Tell her how much he loved her.

A shout went up behind him and he lifted his head. Jimbo reached into his pocket and pulled out the contents, a long circular stick.

"Where did you get that TNT?"

"Where do you think, James?" Jimbo pulled out what Wesley figured to be a matchbook. "You're the one who stole it from the plant site when we blasted out the foundation."

"Come on, Jimbo. We're old friends. Surely we can work this problem out,"

James appealed, but he was already backtracking toward the woods. "Maybe make a deal?"

"I'm tired of your deals." A slight scratch preceded a bright flame. "I'm getting rid of this poison before you hurt anyone else!"

The sharp sizzle of the fuse being lit made Wesley push himself up. He had barely gotten his feet under him when the earth lurched beneath him, flinging him on his back. A terrifying rumble grew louder. He flipped over on his stomach and threw his arms over his head as a rush of heat scorched over him.

His last thought was, *Give me the chance to make things right with Maggie, Lord.*

Then the world exploded around him.

CHAPTER TWENTY

"I'm going inside," Merrilee said to her brother and Maggie as she opened the truck door. The hinges squealed in protest as she slid off the bench seat, slamming the door shut behind her. Merrilee leaned into the window, her eyes twinkling with a happiness that had been missing in recent days, a smile playing at her lips. "Dinner isn't going to cook itself, now, is it?"

Maggie watched her aunt walk up the path, the crush of gravel beneath Merrilee's high heels growing more distant with each step, then turned back to her dad. "She's in a good mood."

"She should be." Her dad glanced over at her, the smile he gave her reaching all the way to his eyes. "We found out today that James has been wasting his time threatening to take her to court over Daddy's will. Merrilee owns the house and land outright."

Pulling her knee up onto the seat, Maggie

turned to face him. "How's that?"

Jeb's gaze shifted past Maggie to the front porch. "Seems that John Davenport bought it from Daddy almost ten years ago and put it in Merrilee's name."

"John Davenport? But that doesn't make sense. Why would Granddaddy sell the homestead?"

"It was hard times back then, Magpie. People did what they had to do to put food on the table and keep clothes on their backs." He glanced back at her. "Knowing your grandfather, he wouldn't tell anyone if he was having money problems, not with his pride."

Maggie turned her head, looking out over the dashboard. "Uncle John must have loved Merrilee very much to make sure she had a place to live."

"Yes, I think he did."

Maggie leaned her head back against the headrest and burst into laughter. "I would love to be a fly on the wall when Uncle James finds out."

Her dad's chuckle was warm and homey. "Me too."

Maggie turned her head to look at him. Her parents were such a blessing to her. "Daddy?"

"Yes, baby girl?"

She swallowed. Apologizing had never been her strong suit. "I'm sorry I walked out on you the morning of Donna's plane crash. I know that dare was a silly thing to do."

Her dad stretched his arm across the back of the bench seat and pulled her close. "I know. And I understand why you did it. You felt backed into a corner, just like you used to when your cousins were all over you about something. You think it's the only way you'll ever get their respect."

Maggie buried her face in his chest. "I did, didn't I?"

"Always scares me and your mother to death."

"I'm so sorry," she whispered, her father's scent of peppermint and perspiration calming her jangled soul. "I never mean to worry you."

"We'll always fret about you, sweetheart." He hugged her close. "It's one of the things that keeps us on our knees before the Lord."

Maggie tilted her head back and smiled. "I'll bet."

Her dad returned her smile. "So are we okay now?"

Before she could answer, a low-pitched burst of sound rumbled around them. The truck rocked from side to side, its hinges and springs rattling as if the earth beneath it had shifted.

"What was that?" Pushing her away, her father reached for the door handle.

Maggie scooted across the bench seat and glanced out of the passenger-side window. A white plume of smoke rose and twisted in the breeze above the trees behind her aunt's house. Distant shouts broke the ghostly silence that followed the explosion.

"Call the fire department," her father ordered as he broke into a run. Over the hood of the truck, she saw her father disappear around the corner of the house toward the backyard.

Moving as fast as she could, Maggie headed up the front walkway toward the house. The sickening sweet smell of corn mash faintly clung to the air, causing her clothes to cling and her exposed skin to feel suddenly sticky. A thought hit her with the force of a bomb: a moonshine still, and nearby. She propelled up the stairs two at a time.

Merrilee met her at the door, her face as pale as the whitewash on the walls. "I can't find Claire anywhere."

Alarm knotted in Maggie's chest. "She's probably with Edie."

"I can't find her, either."

"Then they're probably together." Maggie breathed a little easier. "Have you checked the attic? She likes to play up there sometimes."

"I'll go look." Merrilee dashed for the stairs.

"And call the fire department." Not waiting for her aunt's reply, Maggie bounded down the front steps and across the yard.

"You don't think that was our camp, do you?" Maggie glanced up to see Eliza Beth in the corner of the porch, her arms wrapped around the support post as if holding on for dear life. The girl looked down at her, her eyes frantic with worry, her face a sickening shade of gray. "Everything we own in this world is in those tents."

Maggie shook her head as she turned toward the back of the house. Like pollen in the springtime, a murky yellow-gray cloud had settled into the treetops. "No. The smoke didn't come from that direction."

"Then what . . ."

Claire, her braids flying, a stark look of fear pasted on her face, came running around the corner of the house. Tears rained down her dirty cheeks like a sudden cloudburst. When she saw Maggie, she ran straight toward her and flung herself against her legs.

Slipping down to her knees, Maggie wrapped her arms around her tiny cousin and pressed her close to her body, holding on for dear life. She brushed a kiss against the top of Claire's head, inhaling the warring scents of little girl and corn mash. "Are you okay?"

The child didn't answer, but simply nodded, her face pressed against Maggie's shoulder.

"What happened, sweetheart?"

Claire tilted her head and sniffed. "I don't know. Pops was telling Edie and me a story when it happened. It was loud, just like when Mr. Stevens dug up that old cannonball with his back hoe."

"What direction did the noise come from?"

Tears suddenly appeared in the corner of Claire's eyes, and she bit her lip. Her little body shook like a bowl of Merrilee's homemade apple jelly. "Oh, Maggie."

"What is it, baby?"

"It's Pops." Her voice broke. "He's sick."

A ribbon of fear coiled through Maggie. Wesley had mentioned something about Pops's heart. The shock of the explosion must have startled him. Maggie glanced at Eliza Beth. "Could you take Claire Bear to her momma? She's worried sick."

"Sure." Eliza Beth released her grip on the post and turned toward the stairs.

"And call for an ambulance. Tell them to send a couple of them just in case." Turning back to her cousin, she pressed her hand against Claire's soft cheek. "Now darling, I need you to be a brave girl."

Her blue eyes searched Maggie's face. "Is Pops going to be all right?"

A lump rose up in her throat, and she swallowed. "I don't know, but we're going to do everything we can to help him. Now, you go with Eliza Beth here, okay?"

Claire nodded, slipping her hand into the young woman's. "Okay."

Maggie gave her a quick kiss on the cheek. "I love you, Claire Bear."

"Love you, too, Maggie." Eliza Beth tugged the girl gently toward the front of the house.

Turning toward the backyard, Maggie drew in a deep breath; the air was inebriated with the overwhelming smell of spirits. A dense fog cloaked the backyard in a shroud, covering secrets hidden well within the forest.

"Over here, Maggie!"

In the mist, Maggie made out the shadows of three figures crouched down in the doorway of the kitchen and ran toward them. Her father stared up at her, his expression bleak and full of concern. Edie was curled up against him, her head bent to her chest, her shoulders shaking with intermittent sobs.

Fear gripped Maggie by the throat. Huddled against the door, Pops lay stretched out, his eyes closed, his hand fisted into the front of his shirt.

"I told Eliza Beth to call an ambulance," Maggie told her father as she knelt down next to Pops.

"Good idea, my girl."

"Pops." Maggie covered his hand with hers, disturbed by his cold touch. She had to work to keep her voice steady. "What are you doing laid out like this? Taking a little rest?"

"I let worry get the best of me, my girl." His mouth quirked into a soft smile, then tightened into a grimace. "I shouldn't have let him go out there alone."

Anxiety skittered up Maggie's spine before settling in her stomach. She exchanged looks with her father and Edie. "Who is he talking about?"

"Wesley." Edie scrubbed her hand across her cheek to capture a new round of tears.

Maggie couldn't breathe, was unsure if she'd ever draw another lungful of air again, not with this horrific pain centered in the middle of her chest. The cold hardness of the brick wall met her as she stumbled backward. "Are you sure?"

Warm hands covered her shoulders and she glanced up to see her father. "He thought someone should check up on the tent camp."

Why would he do that when everyone from the camp was here? Maggie sat back, wrapping her arms around her legs, cradling her knees to her chest. The answer smacked her in the face.

Jimbo.

Wesley must have seen Jimbo slip into the woods and gone after him. And now Wesley was out there, possibly hurt, possibly . . .

A strangled cry escaped from deep in her gut. The rough surface of the bricks scratched her hands as she scrambled to her feet. "I'm going after him."

A hand at her forearm made Maggie twist around. "No, you can't. The smoke is too thick."

Maggie shook her head frantically, looking out over the opaque cloud that clung to the trees. The haze had lifted slightly, but was still too dense to make out the path again. "Daddy, I know those woods like the back of my hand. You know that."

Her father stood up, his arms going around her, and pulled her into a tight embrace. Daddy must be worried to hold her like this twice in one day. "I know you want to find him, baby girl."

"I do, Daddy. I do," she whispered against his solid shoulder. "I love him so much."

"Then you need to think about what Wesley would want you to do right now."

Maggie nodded. Daddy was right. The last thing Wesley would want for her to do is go traipsing after him, putting them both in danger. She would have to stay here, do what she had to do to get Wesley's grandfather the help he needed.

With a sniff, Maggie nodded. "We need to get Pops up to the house."

"Good idea, sweetheart." He father patted her cheek. "By the time we get him inside and settled, it might be clear enough for me to go in with the fire department and find your young man."

"Thank you, Daddy."

He bent down beside the older man, linking his arm under his shoulder. "Do you think you can walk a bit, Pops?"

"Maybe a little." Pops drew up his knees and sat up slowly. "If I have some help."

The sounds of sirens ebbed and flowed in the distance. Help was on the way. Maggie pressed her hands to the moisture on her cheeks. She couldn't have Pops see her bawling like a baby. "I'm going to get you checked out. We can't have Wesley get back and find you laid out sick, now can we?"

The old man shook his head. "No, we can't."

As she turned to follow her dad and Pops toward the house, she felt a slight touch on her arm. Maggie looked back to find Edie. "Wesley wanted you to wait for him."

"He did?" she whispered, a bit breathless.

Edie gave her a mournful look. "He said he wouldn't be long but that he'd come and find you once he got back."

Maggie closed her eyes. She couldn't find the man of her dreams only to lose him.

I know the plans You have for me are plans for good and not for evil.

She drew in a shaky breath, the words running through her heart. God's plans weren't as small as a simple flying career. No, they included Wesley. She loved him. Her heart never stood a chance against the one man who understood her heart's desire, even while he drove her crazy worrying about her. She would trust him with her dreams all the days of her life, God willing.

The sirens grew louder. A checkerboard of red and white lights lit up the yard beside

Merrilee's. It took everything inside her not to run into the woods in search of the man who had captured her heart, but she held herself in check.

A peace she didn't understand invaded Maggie's heart as she eyed the woods one last time. *Please, Lord, bring Wesley home safe. Give me the chance to tell him I love him.*

Nodding toward the house, she turned to Edie. "Let's get Pops up to his room. The ambulance will be here soon."

The second explosion hit with as much force as the first. Wesley lifted his head slightly, just enough to get a clear shot of the scene below him. Copper and metal pieces lay scattered about like falling leaves in autumn. The sour stench of mash hung in the air like a rain-filled cloud.

Through a veil of smoke, Jimbo carefully positioned another stick of the explosive under his target, the last of the large copper pots embedded in the ground. The sizzle of the fuse was all the warning Wesley had to duck for cover again.

BOOM!

The still fractured apart, raining down on the earth below like mortar fire at the front line. A sharp cry of pain suddenly filled the air around Wesley and he looked up. Beside the shed to the right Jimbo lay bent over, clutching both hands to his knee.

Wesley brought himself up on all fours and rose slowly, testing the ground beneath him. Once sure of his footing, he started down the embankment to where Jimbo lay. Blood had soaked his pants from right above the knee by the time Wesley reached him. Without thinking, he unlatched his belt, whipped it from around his waist and dropped down beside Jimbo.

"Why don't you let me die?" Jimbo gritted out through his teeth.

"I never leave a man behind." Wesley slid the belt under Jimbo's thigh and threaded the buckle, unsure what to say. Condolences were never enough, not when the loss was someone you loved, but they were words to fill the quiet void. "I'm sorry about your wife and baby."

Jimbo's mouth pulled into a pained line. "Yeah. Me too."

Wesley yanked the leather strap tight, eliciting a short groan from the man. He tied off the belt then leaned forward to examine the jagged wound. "Why didn't you tell anyone you were married?"

"It happened before the squadron was formed." Jimbo leaned back against the trunk of a nearby oak. "And those who knew got tired of hearing me talk about them after a while."

"She must have been something," Wesley said, pushing the bloody material up Jimbo's calf to his knee.

"My Annie was something." A faint smile spread across his face. "We were only married a little more than a year, but it was the best year of my life. We were so excited when we found out she was expecting. She was always trying out baby names on me, seeing which name I thought would be best for our boy."

"A boy, huh?"

"That's what Annie said. I didn't tell her this but I sort of wanted a little girl, just like her momma," Jimbo said, his eyes glossing over, whether from the pain or the sorrow, Wesley couldn't be sure. "It doesn't matter. Annie's gone."

Wesley examined the ragged skin around the cut, noting the bleeding had ceased. He couldn't imagine what Jimbo had gone through, couldn't fathom what it would be like if he ever lost Maggie. Glancing around at the evidence of Jimbo's reaction to his family's poisoning, Wesley had no doubts that the man had probably tried everything he could to save his young family.

"That had to be tough," Wesley said quietly.

"It hurt like the devil. The only time I didn't hurt from the pain of losing her was when I was drinking." Jimbo blew out a breath through his nostrils, his eyes glazing over in shame. "I don't want to drink anymore. I just don't."

"If you need help, we'll see about getting it for you, Jimbo."

"You will?"

Wesley gave him a brief nod. "Sure we will. But I do have a few more questions."

Jimbo grimaced as he rubbed his injured leg. "I ain't going nowhere."

"How does James Daniels fit into all this?"

"He found me in the front hall one night just like you and Maggie did. Only he didn't try to sober me up." He shook his head, his forehead creased in pain. "He offered me some of his bootleg hooch if I'd do him certain favors."

Wesley felt his stomach lurch. "What kind of favors?"

Jimbo's gaze dropped to his lap. "He asked me to put that note in Maggie's footlocker her first day at the plant. Said it was a note from Merrilee. But I swear, Captain, I didn't know what he had wrote."

Wesley balled his hands up into tight fists,

the urge to deck James Daniels growing with every passing second, but he needed to know the whole story and Jimbo's part in it before he reacted. "You've never been a big admirer of Maggie's. Why should I believe you?"

"You're right. I don't like the idea of any woman in the cockpit. But Maggie, she's a-okay, Captain. She didn't deserve that note." Jimbo shifted his weight as if trying to find a more comfortable position before finally giving up. "I told James that after the other girl pilot went down."

"I bet James didn't like that."

"He just laughed. Told me it was all a big joke and that I shouldn't worry about it. Then he gave me another shoebox with a bottle in it. That was the last bottle I took from him."

That answered the question of how Merrilee's receipt got in that box. It was a setup. If Merrilee could be linked to the still, even if it was only through circumstantial evidence, it would be enough for a judge to listen to James make his case against his sister.

The muffed sounds of footsteps against the leaf-laden earth rumbled softly, and multiple flickers of light hopscotched through the trees, becoming steady beams as the sounds grew closer. Help would be here soon.

But he had one more question before he turned Jimbo over to the authorities. "Did you have anything to do with Donna's plane being loaded with the wrong fuel?"

Jimbo shook his head. "But there are a few boys at the plant that James has been paying off with hooch. More than likely, they had something to do with the fuel exchange."

"Can you give me their names?"

"Sure." Jimbo nodded sharply. "I owe that to you, and to Maggie and her aunt after all the help you've given Annie's family."

"Good." Wesley breathed a bit easier. The threat to Maggie was finally over.

CHAPTER TWENTY-ONE

The acrid smell of smoke and burnt leaves clung to Wesley and to his clothes, sticking to him from a mixture of perspiration and corn mash. He pulled a handkerchief from his back pocket and scrubbed the square across the nape of his neck, then gave up in defeat.

With Jimbo securely loaded in the back of the ambulance, the driver drove the vehicle slowly across Merrilee's backyard, the red light flickering like the flames that burned the last remains of James's still. The attendant had assured Wesley that Jimbo would only need stitches and a few days of rest. His pilot would be okay.

The questions from the fire department and the police had taken longer. Now he'd grown impatient, scanning the lingering crowd for the two faces he'd longed to see since the first explosion had blasted through his world.

"They're up at the house, son," Maggie's father called out from his post next to Merrilee. The police were still questioning her about the day's events. "In all the excitement this afternoon, your grandfather had a spell."

Wesley's heart tightened. "Is he okay?"

"Oh, yes," Mr. Daniels assured him. "Nothing that a day in bed won't put to rights."

Thank You, Lord! He'd forgotten how a family could truly be a blessing. How he'd missed that shared closeness in the last few years. He would never take his grandfather for granted again. "Thank you, sir. I appreciate you watching out for Pops."

"You need to be thanking my daughter, Captain. She's the one who's been by his side all afternoon."

Wesley's heart sang with joy at the thought of Maggie taking care of his grandfather. "If you'll excuse me then, sir."

The man nodded, the smile he flashed Wesley giving him a hope for a future he hadn't thought possible just a few hours ago. Wesley hopped over sections of water hoses slithering like snakes in the grass as he worked his way through the maze of people and equipment in Merrilee's backyard.

He slipped in the back door and bounded up the steps to his grandfather's room. At the top of the stairs, Edie sat at the window, looking at the activity going on in the backyard.

His footfall on the landing caused her to turn. She stood and hurried toward him. "Thank heavens. We were so worried about you."

Wesley walked toward his grandfather's room. "How's he doing?"

"He's resting right now, but he wants to see you."

"Is Maggie in there with him?" Wesley asked, lifting his fist and knocking lightly on Pops's door.

"Pops sent her outside to get some fresh air." Edie nodded toward the stairwell. "You want me to tell her that you're looking for her?"

Knowing Maggie, he'd find her sitting in her favorite spot on the front porch swing. Wesley grabbed the door handle. "That's okay. I'm just going to check on him real quick."

He opened the door and slipped inside. Two of the three blackout curtains had already been drawn, leaving enough evening light for Wesley to see that Merrilee had left her homey touch in this room, too.

Wesley walked to the bedside. In a single bed pushed against the wall lay the patient. Pops's snowy hair blended into the white pillow until they appeared to be one. His translucent skin stretched over the bony protrusions of his weathered face and hands, displaying a road map of deep purple pathways across his neck and arms. His mouth gaped open, and his respirations came as soft snores that reverberated off the walls.

When had his grandfather gotten so old? But Wesley knew the answer. Losing Beth had done a number on the both of them, but it was time to move forward. He understood that now.

"Wesley?"

He sat down on the edge of the mattress. "Hi, Pops."

His grandfather's frightened gaze traveled over him quickly, looking for what, Wesley wasn't sure. Once the old man was satisfied, he relaxed into his pillow. "Did you catch Jimbo?"

Wesley smiled. Leave it to Pops to cut to the chase. "Yes sir, but he didn't end up being so bad." He explained how James had used the loss of Jimbo's wife and child to blackmail him. "He's going to be in the hospital for the next few days, then after

374

that, we'll see."

Pops drew in a deep breath. "At least everybody's safe now."

"Yes, sir." Wesley picked at a loose thread from the sheet. "Pops?"

"Yes, boy?"

He swallowed against the sudden knot in his throat as he bowed over their joined hands. "I'm sorry for the way I acted when Beth died. I let you down."

"You've never done anything but make me proud, sweet boy." Pops's fingers tenderly plowed a path through his hair. "I'm the one who let you down."

Wesley lifted his head. Pops thought he'd let him down? "Why would you think that? You've always been there for me."

Pops shook his head, his hair sticking out at several different angles. "I knew how stubborn your sister could be when she got an idea in her head. She made her own choices, and there was nothing either of us could have done to change her mind. And yet I blamed you when she died."

"You were hurting. You'd lost your granddaughter."

"And I pushed you away in the process. It felt like I lost you both." The old man tightened his grip on Wesley's hand. "I'm so sorry."

"Me too." Wesley drew in a deep breath, the oppressive weight he'd carried for months slowly slipping from him. Though Beth would always be a part of their lives, he and Pops would be okay. They had each other.

His grandfather's grip on Wesley's hand relaxed. "I'm a bit tired now. Guess all that yard work wore me out."

"Why don't you take a little nap then? Merrilee will have supper on the table in a couple of hours."

"Good idea," Pops whispered, his eyelids drooping shut. He struggled to open his eyes. "Would you tell Maggie she doesn't need to come back up and sit with me?"

Wesley stood and tucked the thin blanket around Pops as the man snuggled deeper into his pillow. "You don't worry, Pops. I'll take care of Maggie."

"I know you will," he answered with a soft smile. "You love her, don't you, boy?"

Wesley nodded, waiting as the old man's breathing became slow and steady in sleep. Pops always had a way of knowing exactly what was in his heart.

Maggie pushed the swing into motion then drew her knee back up to her chest. It had been hours since the last explosion, and while her father had told her Wesley was safe, she wanted to see for herself.

The mournful melody of the swing's chains matched her mood. Shadows of the waning evening fell across the porch, making puzzle patterns of light and darkness. The faint smell of her uncle James's brew hung in the breeze, much like the accusations against him.

It was bad enough her uncle had tried to take Merrilee's house from her, and Maggie wasn't surprised to hear James had been behind that threatening note, not when he'd been bullying people for as far back as she could remember. But to poison innocent children, to have had a possible hand in downing Donna's plane, was even beyond her scope of imagination.

Maggie pressed her face into the palms of her hands. Well, he wasn't her problem anymore. She could only hope that when the police caught him, they would throw him under the jail.

"Maggie?"

She jerked her head up. In the doorway stood Wesley, his shirt dirty and slashed down the sleeves while red clay clung to the knees in his jeans. A sheen of perspiration and dirt covered his face and matted his hair.

He looked absolutely beautiful.

Dropping her feet to the floor, Maggie sat up, her fingers gripping the edge of the seat. "It took you long enough."

His face softened into a cautious smile. The floorboards moaned beneath him as he moved to stand in front of her. "I'm sorry, sweetheart. I never meant to scare you."

Maggie stared up at him, determined to memorize everything about him — the laugh lines around his mouth, the way the area around his eyes crinkled when he had something on his mind — before realizing it would take an entire lifetime. "I know."

She took the hand Wesley held out to her and stood, letting him pull her into his embrace. She linked her arms around his neck and held him tight, resting her cheek against his shoulder. Here, in Wesley's arms, she'd discovered a new dream, one filled with love and children and a life shared with this wonderful man.

"Are you okay?"

Maggie tilted her head back, the mixture of love and concern sparkling in his blue eyes causing her heart to beat out of control. She cleared her throat. "I wasn't the one caught in the explosion. Are you okay?"

"Never better."

"Are you sure?" Her words were a whisper

on an unsteady breath.

As if to prove it, he bent his head to hers. His face blurred as he gently brushed a kiss on the tip of her nose, his breath fanning out across her cheek. She tilted her head back, her eyelids fluttering shut as he pressed his lips to hers.

Maggie felt as if she were soaring through the stratosphere, stars bursting into light behind her closed eyelids. She tightened her arms around his neck and held on for dear life, sure that Wesley would keep her safe.

He lifted his head, but held her close, resting his cheek against hers. "There are going to be times I'll drive you crazy worrying about you, sweetheart. But I promise that whatever dreams God puts in your heart, I will do everything in my power to make them come true."

Maggie hesitated for one brief moment. "Dreams change, you know."

"They do?" His breath ruffled her hair, sending a light shiver down her spine.

She leaned back, her heart ready to burst at the look of love and respect shining on Wesley's face. God had taken her pitiful dreams and made them so much more than she ever thought possible. A godly man who loved her, dreams and all. "When you were out there and I didn't know if you were okay, I realized you're a part of my dreams now."

Wesley lightly pressed his forehead to hers. "I love you, Maggie."

"I love you, too." She gave him a watery smile.

"Will you marry me, Margaret Rose?"

The tenderness in his voice caused her to tighten her arms around him. Maggie nodded, never more sure of anything. "I'd love to be your wife."

As he pulled her close and lowered his mouth to hers, a bubble of happiness popped inside of her, flowing through every cell of her being.

Her dreams had come true.

EPILOGUE

"We're going to make ice cream at thirty thousand feet?"

Maggie glanced out over the hood of the old truck. When he had told her they were going to provide the dessert for Donna's welcome-home party, she'd thought he'd meant to drive all the way to Atlanta for ingredients, but instead he had brought her here, to the airfield.

Wesley held the door while she got out. "I did it for my commander in England a couple of times, you know, to cheer the guys up after a particularly bad day."

Maggie leaned against the frame of the truck. "And did Major Evans give us the okay to do this?"

He smiled, holding out his hand to her. "He was the one who suggested it."

A sense of adventure filled Maggie as she slipped her hand into his, enjoying the warmth of his fingers tight around her own.

Off in the distance, the plant hummed with activity. Only one concern put a damper on her joy in this day.

"Something on your mind, sweetheart?"

The man could already read her like a flight plan, and they weren't even married yet. "Uncle James is in court today. I know I shouldn't but I can't help feeling sorry for him."

"The man brought it on himself."

"But he's all alone, and his sons are overseas. Daddy won't have anything to do with him right now, and James refuses to even talk to Merrilee."

The area between Wesley's eyes crinkled. "Don't you think it's odd, Merrilee wanting to see him after everything he's done to her?"

Maggie shook her head. "She's always had a forgiving heart. And I don't know about you, but she seems happier since finding out that John bought the house for her. Like it confirms the love they had for each other."

Wesley stroked her cheek with his thumb. "Do you think she's still in love with him?"

"Maybe, but they've been divorced for years now. I don't think she has a clue where he might be."

"Then we'll just have to pray on it." He leaned his forehead against hers. "And while we're at it, let's pray for Jimbo. Major Evans is supposed to decide in the next few days what his punishment will be."

"I hope he goes easy on Jim," Maggie said, squeezing Wesley's fingers. "He's been through enough as it is."

"I agree. I'd like to see Jimbo get the help he needs. James is another story." He palmed her cheek in his hand. "That man threatened to hurt you."

Maggie stared into his eyes. "But he didn't."

"Lucky for him." Wesley snorted. "I would have killed him if he had."

Maggie might have chafed at her cousins' overprotectiveness, but the idea of Wesley in the role of her champion had grown on her in recent days — thrilling her right down to her toes. She smiled. "You're too good of a man to do that. Why don't we add Uncle James to the prayer list?"

"You're quite a woman, Maggie." The hard angles of his face softened, then blurred as he narrowed the space between them until he finally claimed her kiss.

"Um . . . excuse me. Wes?"

Wesley lifted his head and turned, though not releasing her. Instead, he wrapped his arm securely around her waist, which was a good thing since she fully intended to bury her heated face in his shoulder. "Yes?"

"The plane is all ready for you." A man Maggie recognized as one of the new flight crew smiled back at her when she stole a glance at him. "The tank's full and your packages are locked and loaded."

"Thanks." Wesley glanced down at her. "Sweetheart, have you met Glenn?"

"I've seen him around in the last few days, but we've never been formally introduced."

Wesley glanced over at the man. "Glenn, this is my fiancée, Margaret Daniels. Maggie, this is Glenn Hancock, one of the best flight mechanics in the Army Air Corp."

The man held out his hand. "Nice to finally meet you. I've heard you're a great pilot."

"Nice to meet you, too." Maggie smiled at the man as she slipped her hand into his firm grasp.

"You've got a beautiful bride, Wes," he said, releasing her hand. "I bet your grandfather is over the moon."

"He's crazy about her." Wesley drew her close to his side, watching her all the while. "Not that I blame him."

Pops hadn't just taken to her, but to her whole family so much so that her father had asked the older man to help him run the crop-dusting business until the war was over.

Glenn nodded toward the pile of leather and flannel heaped at the base of the fuselage. "I brought you a couple of flight jackets like you asked."

"I appreciate it."

As the man walked away, Wesley picked up a coat and handed it to Maggie. "I figured you wouldn't complain if you got some time in the air. You're going to need it."

"Why on earth would you say that?"

"You're going to be in the simulators until the second Super Fortress comes off the line." He smiled at her as he shoved first one, then the other arm in the coat. "Major Evans okayed you for assignment to a B-29 flight crew this afternoon."

"Really!" Maggie threw her arms around his shoulders and hugged him close. "I can't believe it!"

"Are you kidding?" Wesley whispered, wrapping his arms around her waist. "I knew you could do it."

They held each other for a brief moment before Maggie leaned back, nodding her head toward the plane. "So how does this thing churn ice cream?"

"There's not much to it." Dropping his

arms, Wesley stepped back and zipped up his jacket. "We just need to get up there where it's good and cold, rock around a bit to mix up the ingredients, and let nature do the rest."

"I'll believe that when I see it," she answered, fixing the fur-lined collar of her jacket. "Where do you want to go?"

"I figured we'd take a little trip up around the North Georgia Mountains, maybe check out the leaves turning." Wesley gently tugged on the leather straps of her flight cap. "If that's okay with you."

The love she saw in his expression made her stomach flutter. No matter what might come their way, life with Wesley Hicks would never be dull. "I would never turn down a chance to be with you."

"Then we'd better get going. The party starts in a couple of hours and we don't want to keep everyone waiting."

They worked together to do a quick preflight check before climbing into the cockpit. Maggie took the second seat behind Wesley, slipping her oxygen mask and headset on, her anticipation building. Was it just the excitement of soaring through the sky once again or being in the air with this man whom she loved so much?

"Are you ready, sweetheart?" His strong

voice whispered in her earphones.

Maggie gave him the thumbs-up. Yes, she was ready to start her life with him, to live out the dreams God had given them. Wesley hit the throttle, catapulting them down the runway. As the wind lifted them and carried them into the blue Georgia sky, Maggie smiled and lifted her face toward the heavens.

Lord, thank You for dreaming a bigger dream for me than I could ever have dreamed for myself!

Dear Reader,

Thank you for selecting *Hearts in Flight*. I can't think of a better way to celebrate the birth of our great country than with a story concerning the brave men and women who fought the horrors of World War II to keep us free. I hope you have enjoyed reading Maggie and Wesley's story as much as I loved writing it. Never in my wildest dreams would I have believed that one short paragraph from a book on the women of World War II would change my life!

That's what dreams do, change ordinary lives into something extraordinary, but not without hardships. Unlike the other womens' military organizations of the time, the eleven hundred women service pilots were civilian workers without the benefits that came with military duty. They paid their own way, from the oversized jumpsuits they wore to the bus ticket that took them to Avenger Field in Sweetwater, Texas, where they trained "the Army way."

No gold stars — a respected symbol of military service during the war — hung in their families' living-room windows back home. Thirty-eight women died while performing their duties, but they were not afforded the standard military send-off.

Instead, their families were forced to raise money to bring the remains of their loved ones home for burial. It wasn't until 1975 that these women received recognition as veterans of World War II, and on July 1, 2009, received the Congressional Medal of Honor.

Real life heroines for the women of today!

I look forward to hearing from my readers. Please visit me at my website, www.pattysmithhall.com, or contact me at patty@pattysmithhall.com.

Blessings,

Patty Smith Hall

QUESTIONS FOR DISCUSSION

1. Although Maggie's parents approve of her decision to become a pilot, others in her family and community do not. Have you ever felt called to do something that your loved ones didn't support? How did you handle it?

2. Aunt Merrilee is a wonderful encouragement and mentor to Maggie. Do you have an older woman in your life who took you under her wing and helped you grow into the person you are today? What qualities did she teach that you could use to help young women transition into adulthood?

3. Wesley promises Merrilee that he will keep Maggie safe, even though she is a test pilot on an untried plane. Have you ever broken a promise that wasn't within your control to keep? What did you learn from the experience?

4. During the run to Kennesaw Mountain, one of the men in Wesley's squadron makes a derogatory remark toward the poverty-riddled members of a nearby tent camp. How would you react in a similar situation today?

5. When Wesley asks Maggie to expose the culprit, on the run to Kennesaw Mountain, she remains silent in hopes of earning the trust of the men she will serve with. What would you do if faced with such a decision? Why?

6. While Maggie does not approve of Jimbo's drinking, she treats him with gentleness and respect when he passes out on Merrilee's doorstep. How would you react to this situation? Could you show respect for someone even though you disagree with their choices?

7. Maggie and Wesley supply food for Eliza Beth and her family without wounding their pride. Can you give examples of how you can help someone in need while respecting their dignity?

8. James Daniels is bitter over losing the family homestead to his sister and is

determined to take it from her. Have you ever harbored a bitterness toward something in your life that didn't turn out quite as you had planned? What does the Bible say in regards to holding on to bitterness?

9. After telling Maggie about his sister's death, Wesley asks why Beth had to die. Have you ever asked God why something bad had to happen? What did you learn from the experience?

10. When Donna is injured, and the threatening note Maggie received is exposed, Maggie explains to Wesley that the WASP lived under constant threats and she didn't take the note seriously. Was she being dishonest in not telling Wesley about the threat? How should she have reacted to the threat?

11. While everyone is looking for Jimbo after the tent camp is poisoned with bad liquor, Edie says that everyone deserves a second chance. Do you believe that statement? Why or why not?

12. When Wesley and Maggie declare their love for each other, Maggie realizes that

God had a bigger dream for her than she had for herself. Looking back over your life, do you see where God had a greater dream for you than you ever thought possible?

ABOUT THE AUTHOR

A Georgia girl born and bred, **Patty Smith Hall** loves to incorporate little-known historical facts into her stories. Her writing goal is to create characters who walk the Christian walk despite their human flaws. When she's not writing, Patty enjoys spending time with her husband of twenty-eight years, their two daughters and a vast extended family.

Patty loves hearing from her readers! Please contact her through her website, www.pattysmithhall.com.